REVELATION

REVELATION

DONNA M. YOUNG

Published by Donna M. Young
P O Box 76, Lawton, IA 51030
dmywriting@wiatel.net

Author photo by Elizabeth Rose Kahl
Book Cover and Layout by Christina Hicks Creative
www.christinahickscreative.com

Published in the United States of America
ISBN: 978-1-947143-08-1
Fiction / General
Fiction / Christian General

http://www.donnamyoungwriting.com

"When I saw Him, I fell at His feet as though dead. But He laid His right hand on me, saying, "Fear not, I am the first and the last, and the living one. I died and behold I am alive forever more, and I have the keys of Death and Hades."

Revelation 1:17-18

"So when you see the abomination of desolation spoken of by the prophet Daniel, standing in the holy place, then let those who are in Judea flee to the mountains. Let the one who is on the housetop not go down to take what is in the house, and let the one who is in the field not turn back to take his cloak. And alas for women who are pregnant and for those who are nursing infants in those days! Pray that your flight may not be in the winter or on a Sabbath. For then there will be great tribulation, such as has not been from the beginning of the world until now, no, and never will be. And if those days had not been cut short, no human being would be saved. But for the sake of the elect those days will be cut short. Then if anyone says to you, "Look, here is the Christ!" or "There He is!" do not believe it. For false christs and false prophets will arise and perform great

signs and wonders, so as to lead astray, if possible, even the elect."

Matthew 24:15-24

"The Lord roars from Zion, and utters His voice from Jerusalem, and the heavens and earth quake. But the Lord is a refuge to His people. A stronghold to the people of Israel."

Joel 3:16

"After this I looked, and behold, a door standing open in heaven! And the first voice, which I had heard speaking to me like a trumpet, said, "Come up here, and I will show you what must take place after this."

Revelation 4:1

"Now I watched when the Lamb opened one of the seven seals, and I heard one of the four living creatures say with a voice like thunder, "Come!" And I looked, and behold, a white horse! And its rider had a bow, and a crown was given to him, and he came out conquer-

ing and to conquer. When he opened the second seal, I heard the second living creature say, "Come!" And out came another horse, bright red. Its rider was permitted to take peace from the earth, so that people should slay on another, and he was given a great sword. When he opened the third seal, I heard the third living creature say, "Come!" And I looked, and behold, a black horse! And its rider had a pair of scales in his hand. And I heard what seemed to be a voice in the midst of the four living creatures, saying, "A quart of wheat for a denarius, and three quarts of barley for a denarius, and do not harm the oil and wine!" When he opened the fourth seal, I heard the voice of the fourth living creature say, "Come!" And I looked, and behold, a pale horse! And its riders name was Death, and Hades followed him. And they were given authority over a fourth of the earth, to kill with sword and with famine and with pestilence and by the wild beasts of the earth."

Revelation 6:1-8

CHAPTER 1

ullets, whistling through the blazing inferno and raining down like hot ash, meant Josh didn't dare attempt another advance just yet. Peppering the earth all round where he lay, and piercing every vulnerable surface; the ammo came in bursts so regular he could almost predict when the next volley would begin. He looked back over a hundred feet or so, the distance between his own semi safety and Jana, Scott and Becca in the foxhole behind him, halting them with his eyes. Using hand signals he communicated his latest order. Jana looked ready to disobey and bolt to his side, but his steady gaze conveyed a sternness she couldn't ignore. She'd always had a mind of her own, but she also respected his authority on the field of battle, as it'd certainly saved her life more than once in these recent bloody years. And, as stubborn as she was, she'd never flippantly defy an order from her combat hardened husband. Sadly, in this past decade and a half, the battles had been almost too numerous to count. But she'd learned many things about the art of warfare from their joined experiences, and their small troop of soldiers had become, by far, the best in the resistance movement; in large part due to their very capable commander.

An explosion to his hard right made Josh cover his head with his arms, to keep flying rock and debris from blinding him. As the blast ended, he noted that bits of gravel from the discharge had acted as tiny pieces of shrapnel, and embedded into every piece of his exposed flesh. He'd have to ignore the pain for now, just as he'd done many times in the past, and deal with the consequences later. After all, battle melded into battle after so much time in the thick of it, and injuries were an inevitable part of the game. It was one more thing to add to the stress of battle.

As the air cleared he peered through a lingering cloud of dust, to see the foxhole nearest him on his right was hit. Four of his battle weary resistance soldiers lay dead. Four men he'd talked to this morning and gave instructions to, only moments before the blast, ripped to pieces by the detonation, never to see their families again. The sight tore, like sharpened claws, at his exhaustion heightened emotions and he let out a deep, shaky sigh. It broke his heart to lose any of his men. He'd come to love and trust all of them just as he would family, after serving together for so long.

But this war had taken its toll for sure, and losses over these past few years had been immense.

In his grief, and with the smell of singed hair and burnt flesh still heavy in his nostrils, he dropped his gaze for just a moment to offer a brief prayer for his brothers. Then, lifting his head he sighed deeply again, steadied himself and went on, with an even stronger resolve, to resist the blatant evil attempting to take over the world. Honoring those men would be best accomplished by completing their shared mission.

Just as he'd predicted in an elder's meeting, on a cold winter's day so long ago; they were outnumbered and out armed in every battle they'd endured for the cause. UNGC forces were vast, and easily replenished with a compulsory draft, which was enforced by the government's ability to eliminate dissenters with the mere flick of a switch.

Due to their singular control of the mandatory imbedded chips in the right hands of every human being on earth, they held humanity's very life in their hands. Those chips, which started out as a way to control the populace of America, by a previous evil administration, were universally used on the world's populace now, and no one dared refuse to serve when called upon to do so. If a man didn't fear for his own life, you could bet he had a loved one who'd been threatened with death, by UNGC stooges, if he refused to complete his obligatory service.

Yet, conversely, for all these years, Josh and his band of rebels had been forced to depend only on their wits, their hard fought battle training, and the favor of a good and merciful God to see them through. Their numbers were small, but steady, and their weapons limited, but their hearts were courageous, and their resolve unwavering. So, somehow, they managed to win battle after agonizing battle against impossible odds, as they attempted to take back their world for the good of mankind and the glory of God.

In times of stress the mind can do tricky things and Josh's mind was wandering from exhaustion, pain and hunger. He remembered a time when the summer breeze blew through his hair, as he played sand volleyball with his friends, at a picnic in the park. A beautiful young lady was trying very hard to watch him, without seeming to do so. The moment he caught her eye he knew this was the girl for him. He'd loved Jana from the start, through her anger and unbelief, and all of the things that made her fight his every move. He'd always believed God had something special for her, and that he was to be a part of it.

Another blast, so close and loud, it snapped him out of his reverie and into present. The enemy's aim was getting better.

• • • • •

"General Kakos. I come bearing news. Satan has sent word that we must begin, at once, preparing for the great battle."

"Wonderful! Finally, a chance to show mankind what we are truly capable of on earth. Of course there will be steps we must take first. Does he have someone prepared?"

"Yes Sir. He has been grooming the ideal subject for many years, and he believes his student is finally ready."

"Do we have a false prophet in place? None of this will work without a false prophet."

"Yes Sir, that was even simpler. Man's vanity is easy to manipulate, and he's found the perfect example of ego to work with right there in the church."

"And they never even see it coming, do they? It's all been written down for the world to see for centuries, but they still won't recognize what's going on. At least not until it's too late."

"Yes Sir, but that's the best part, isn't it? For once we will have the upper hand, and all those miserable humans will pay the price."

· · · · ·

It hadn't taken long, after Jana and Josh's triumphant homecoming to the high mountain camp all those years ago; returning from setting up communications on all Resistance bases in the continental US, and then witnessing their friend, Paul's, horrendous execution in the town square of the nation's capitol; for the first of those resistance strongholds to be detected, and attacked, by the combined UN 'peace keeping' forces.

What a laugh, 'peace keeping forces', the term rankled Josh's sensibilities whenever he thought about their evil use of force on their own people.

Josh and Jana barely began to settle back in to a routine at home in their high mountain base, with little Alec and Josh's folks, when they'd gotten the first call to battle in defense of one of their sister bases. And, sadly, the calls had come in steadily since. They'd missed so much at home. So much of their son's childhood and his growing up for one thing. But in times of war regrets are a dime a dozen, and it's a fair bet that everyone misses somebody.

· · · · ·

Looking over his shoulder, Josh saw the look on Jana's face, and realized she'd not been able to tell where the last mortar shell landed; until that very second when their eyes met; due to the clouds of dust and dirt just beginning to dissipate. Her relief was palpable. And, even from this distance he thought he could see her lip quiver slightly, and tears shining in her eyes. He gave her a thumbs up, and she returned a small unsteady smile.

Another shell whistled through the air, and hit the ground just left of his position. The earth shook with its impact, and again, rock and sand flew through the air to ravage everything in sight. He had to escape this location, before the enemy's aim was perfected even further, but that could prove to be quite a challenge. Just then, another blast; so close it slammed his head to the ground, and left him with nothing in his ears but ringing; landed directly behind him. His mouth filled immediately with the coppery taste of blood and he spit out dirt and gravel along with a stream of bloody saliva before wiping his mouth with the back of his hand. His vision, clouded over from the blow to his head, was just beginning to clear up as he got his bearings.

Mark, just behind him in the same foxhole seemed to be okay, though equally shaken; and quickly, while dust still hung heavy in the air; Josh yanked on his sleeve to get his attention. Then, before the flying debris entirely vanished, they left the waning safety of their furrow together to seek better refuge.

Mark had volunteered for deployment overseas out of feelings of desperation and retaliation almost two years ago. In the past sixteen years, his kids had grown up, and they'd served their time in the resistance army back in the states. Sadly, his son was lost protecting one of their sister bases, and his daughter was badly injured, losing a leg and her eyesight in a particularly bloody battle on the plains just a year after her brother was killed. His daughter, Eva, never entirely back to her normal self, lived once again in the high mountain base, and helped in the community kitchen alongside Emma, who was patient and kind to her newest charge. The loss of his son gave Mark a singular resolve which strengthened him far beyond any previous capabilities. He was determined to relieve the earth of the blight that had all but consumed it, and make all things right again. Because of that, Josh watched him carefully, as he tended to go a little kamikaze in his actions and put himself in many dangerous positions.

Again, Jana could no longer see her husband, and when the air finally cleared, his former position was empty. Scott grabbed her arm when she tried to scramble from her place of limited protection. "You know Josh would want you to stay here until you receive further orders, Jana."

"But what if he's hurt, Scott. I have to go to him."

"No, if he was badly hurt, he wouldn't have been able to get free of his foxhole. He'd kill me if I let you advance without his say so. Don't do this to me lady."

"Fine! I'll wait. But only for a little while. If we haven't heard anything soon, I'm going to look for him. He might need me."

Josh's group found better cover behind a concrete wall a little closer to the mount, and there they were planning their strategy. Obviously the enemy hadn't noted their transition, as they continued to bombard the previous location with everything they had.

"We clearly can't approach from the north. That's where the bulk of their defenses are positioned. And the valleys are pretty steep from the east, and south."

"You're right Mark. But we're going to use those steep valleys to our advantage. They would never imagine an attack coming from those directions, due to the geographical logistics. They're going to be focusing all their attention on the only direction that makes sense. The north. But I have a little surprise for them, and clearly they have no idea who they're dealing with."

"I see what you're saying, Josh. Do you want me to go back and get Jana and the others before you finish outlining your plan?"

"If you're up to it. Thanks Mark. We'll wait till you get back."

Josh signaled to the other squad leaders to join him, and they made their way as covertly as possible to his position.

Mark made his way carefully, ducking behind stone facades, and jumping in and out of abandoned foxholes, until he reached Jana's party. "Mark! Is Josh okay? After that explosion I couldn't see anything, and then you were all gone."

"He's fine, Jana. A little shaken up, but what's new? He wanted me to come back and get the three of you, so we can devise a plan of attack. We changed positions and I don't think the other side has caught on yet."

"Lead the way, Mark." Scott said, slapping his friend on the back. "Glad you're okay. I'd swear it seems like they're all trying to kill us, wouldn't you?"

"Oh, it gets worse, Scott, believe me. Follow close. I said they haven't discovered we changed positions yet, so let's stay down and out of sight. I don't want to give them a heads up."

"Just a little game of follow the leader, brother. I can do that! We're right behind you."

"Becca and I are right behind you too, so lead on."

"Yes Ma'am, Jana. This way."

By the time enemy troops started shelling Jana's previous location, they were safely away from those compromised coordinates.

All the years of training, and seemingly never ending battles, had kept their group in better shape than most folks tend to be in their mid and late forties. And, though they all woke with more aches and pains these days than they remembered feeling in the past, their years of experience and precise training made them a force to be reckoned with. Jana's bow had gotten them all out of many messes, and Becca, equally valuable, was a close second in that particular skill. Sometimes the silence of bow and arrow was essential in the quick dispatching of an enemy without being detected. They were powerful women, important to the cause, and respected by every man on the force.

When Jana saw her husband she hunkered down beside him in the dirt of the furrow, and her whole body seemed to relax for his nearness. Even with the sound of mortars exploding all around, the tension on her face was replaced by a quiet calm. Josh looked relieved to see Scott and the girls, and some of the anxiety appeared to drain from his face as well.

"It's good to see you're okay. Things got a little dicey for awhile. I have a plan, but I wanted to discuss it with all of you first."

"Go on, Josh, what's the plan?"

"Well Scott, it's pretty obvious from what we can see of the enemy battle stations, that they've concentrated all their fire power on protecting the north entrance. They aren't even pretending to offer fortification for the other three entrance points, because they're so sure no one can accomplish an attack from any other direction. And, if I didn't know of a certain situation in the past that was very similar to this one I would tend to agree with them, due to the steep valleys behind and to the sides of them. Does that remind you of anything, Jana?"

"It sure does husband. Just like the battle on the mountain plateau. Funny how things have come full circle. Will we all be going, or just Becca and I?"

"I'm depending on you and Becca to do our reconnoitering for us. Mark, Scott and I will stay with the troops to keep the enemy's attention diverted while you do your best to stay out of sight and get us some Intel."

"Sounds good to me husband. You on board, Becca?"

"You betcha! Lead on, Jana. Let's go save the day."

• • • • •

Just ahead was the Temple Mount, far enough away that they would have to defy all reason and pretense of sanity to get there from this present location, especially with so much enemy fire going on; but, close enough to witness the abomination which was prominently displayed in that holy place for all to see.

It was just like Amir Bahram to pull a stunt like the one that started this whole mess in the holy land. He was a snake, and as usual he had only his own best interests at heart. After breaking a seven year treaty, only three and a half years into its life, he'd ridden onto the battlefield in his usual arrogant manner, on a white horse, leading kings and Imams from all the surrounding communist and Muslim nations, in the middle east and on the Asian continent, to attack Israel.

In his blatant attempt to steal the holy land from its rightful inheritors he'd been stabbed and mortally wounded, some said by the Israelis and others said by his own men. He fell that day, and was taken away to a nearby hospital. Reports had been that he died on the operating table. Some were excited by the prospect, and others mourned greatly, thinking him somehow the savior of the world. Then, through magic or enchantment; no one outside of his inner circle knew; he survived that terrible injury. Many thought due to the prayers of Nathan Graham who was the 'One World' church's leader and UNGC's puppet.

Due to some pretty heavy media manipulation, and an even better worldwide marketing plan, the world's population seemed to think Bahrain was now raised from the dead to rule the nations. But, even with all of that, the statue of Bahram set up in the Temple Mount for all to see and bow down to, was the last straw as far as the resistance movement was concerned.

Bahram's one man war on Christianity had gained more momentum after the death of 'Paul'. General Cage had been his best friend, or, at least the closest he'd ever had to one. To look more closely at the circumstances, some might even have surmised that Amir was in love with Cage. And, though he'd always considered himself a lady's man, he would have to admit there were certain feelings there that he couldn't explain.

No relationship he'd ever had with a man in his years growing up in a Muslim cultured childhood had ever felt like anything but depravity. How then could he have ever had a positive connection to any man who used him so despicably, and then tossed him aside, as the men in his father's associations had done. And further, how could he have a relationship with any other man in his adult life now that actually made any sense?

His nightmares had grown worse. He was haunted by pictures of the people he'd tortured and killed, pictures that made him more angry. He was only doing his job as UNGC leader, to crush the resistance movement. Anyone in his position would have done the same, wouldn't they?

Memories of his childhood friend, who'd been accused of homosexuality by the city's head Imam, being tortured and killed; and the part he'd played in that; caused him to wake in the night covered in a cold sweat. He despised his own father, but couldn't confront him now that he was dead also. The degrees of his own brokenness were beyond counting. All he could do these days was be proud of what he'd accomplished in his esteemed life. He wished his father was alive to see all he had come to. Perhaps he would finally be proud of his son.

Amir was very proud of the bronze statue bearing his image. So proud, in fact, that he'd ordered satellite powered jumbo screen televisions to be installed in every city square, every village, and every byway in the world, so that he could gloat publically, and internationally, about the great honor he'd bestowed upon himself. Sadly, much of the world bought in to his lies and willingly followed him, even to death. Satan's hold was strong on those who would go to destruction believing these lies.

Shortly after Bahram's initial attack on the citizens of the holy city, another strange phenomenon began to play out. Two men showed up on the battle ravaged streets of Jerusalem and started to prophesy about coming events.

They told the masses they had come to help them, to convict them of their sin, and to warn them of the coming wrath of God. Their visages were seen on every television screen, installed in every city, all over the world. And, because people don't like to be reminded of their sin, those two men were universally hated by most of those citizens who watched them. Yet, day by day they walked the streets with messages of coming destruction and judgment.

Over past centuries the holy city's housing had encroached upon the temple mount like creeping ivy; and in recent years wars had left a labyrinth of desecrated holy sites, and battle torn, empty buildings, which became nothing more than hidey holes for the terrorists who inhabited the once beautiful city. Judaism's Western Wall was merely a memory now, as barely one stone sat upon another in that devastated spot. The country was ravaged by those who usurped the holiest places, then decided they would see it all destroyed rather than allow any of it back in the hands of its rightful owners.

• • • • •

Dr. Bahram, once he'd been appointed head of the UNGC sixteen long years ago, began to make changes that disturbed many Muslim leaders in the world at that time, most of whom had been appointed by Bahram himself, as they were not privy to the inner workings of his devious mind. He'd certainly taken the Quran's advice; to deceive non-Muslims until he could overtake them; seriously. One of his most unpopular decisions; almost thirteen years into his rule; well, unpopular at least for those who practiced Islam, was the edict allowing Jews in Jerusalem to begin worshipping at the temple mount again, after so many decades of being kept from their holiest site.

Permission, at that time, came in the form of a peace treaty between Muslims and Jews, which had been instituted about six and a half years ago, and was promised to be valid for a minimum of seven years. Joy filled the streets of the city, as its citizens came forth to sacrifice again. Once more the temple's alters were filled with sanctified meat, meant to represent the sins of the people, and those sins being burned away.

But, true to his character, Bahram, knowing he had the Jews in a heavily compromised position, reneged on the treaty only half way into its duration and the temple was lost yet again. It had been back in the hands of Islam now, for a little over three years, and Israeli Defense Forces were just about at the end of their resources, and hope, trying again to regain access to their most holy site on all the earth.

Considering their own country's constant state of war during these past sixteen years, America's resistance soldiers hadn't been able to make much of a difference for Israel in their time of need. But, recent years also brought some changes in Jerusalem that Josh and his base's elders, including his parents, thought needed attention. Things which could make a difference for every citizen on the world stage. So leadership had decided to split their already stretched military forces between the U.S. bases, and the need in Jerusalem. His dad sorely wanted to come along on this battle, "To fight the heathens till his last breath", he'd declared. But advanced years prevented that. So, he and Emma would stay back at base and keep the home fires burning. There was much they could do for the cause, even from their secret camp high in the mountains.

• • • • •

The world was starving. There were no two ways about it. The UNGC's tight fisted hold on warehouses holding humanity's food supplies had increased. And though the world's farms were worked harder than ever, they produced less and less. Certainly, in the minds of the very elite, those in positions of power couldn't be expected to go without sustenance, so hunger became a burden for the people alone to endure. America's resistance bases took care of their own, but they also reached out to those in various communities with much needed supplies whenever they could. Their generosity was appreciated and certainly saved many lives that the government's stinginess would have labeled forfeit.

Paul's (formerly General Cage) ministry grew by leaps and bounds, even after his death. Not only did his followers lead converts to Christ by the dozens, daily, but they also helped distribute food stuffs and remove chips from the hands of government dissenters. This caused the ranks of the resistance movement to grow, though modestly, with newly trained recruits. And Josh was rewarded for his generosity with fresh troops, from those whose lives had been touched by a former enemy turned friend. So many good men and women had lost their lives for this cause in America, but now they were making those sacrifices in Jerusalem as well.

Starvation wasn't rampant only in America, but, equally for that matter, around the world. And hungry people are a breeding ground for disease. Now, another problem was beginning to take center stage. A plague of epic proportions swept the globe. This was a plague occurring on every continent at the same time. One whose impact so devastated its victims, that the Global Health Organization closed its doors to those afflicted with even the slightest evidence of its symptoms.

Those symptoms included sores, and blisters, which when burst open, ran with a yellowish-green, putrid smelling, puss. If a non infected person came in contact with the puss, or any airborne contagion, they would also become infected. Victim's throats swelled greatly, causing their necks to bulge unnaturally to at least twice their normal size, and breathing became almost impossible. High fevers accompanied the disease, usually so high that its sufferers wandered about zombie like searching for water and any other comfort they could find, until they died an agonizing death of suffocating, alone. As bodies were discovered, they were collected and burned, but the disease continued to spread in spite of any and every precaution taken.

For reasons unknown, and completely beyond the comprehension of professionals involved at the Centers for Disease Control, this plague didn't seem to affect members of the various resistance groups, or those belonging to the numerous hidden Christian factions. Many experts believed it had something to do with the absence of an electronic chip in their hands, as if perhaps the electronic impulses made patients more vulnerable to the disease, but Jana believed it had to do with the conditions of hearts more than the conditions of hands; and that, as a people, they were protected against those waves of God's wrath being poured out on the nations, simply because of their status as His children. Josh agreed.

Realizing their immunity, resistance members, globally, soon became the outreach workers of the world, organizing ways to take comfort to those poor souls who were wandering the streets in agony. Often ministering to their needs so kindly that the sick were finally willing to hear a message of Christ for the first time in their lives. This caused many to be brought safely into the kingdom shortly before their tragic deaths. And caused Bahram and his regime to consider all outreach workers as enemies of the state.

From their protection in the mountains, Chuck and Emma arranged shipments of food, aspirin, and other necessities for their suffering brothers and sisters; while also sending their own members out to share the Word of the

Gospel, and to remove chips from the hands of those wishing to be free from the UNGC's hold.

As portions of society disintegrated more each day, the earth suffered from various devastating catastrophes in many diverse places around the world. Many of those natural disasters were happening in places that had never experienced a single sign of seismic activity, or adverse weather in the history of their existence. Storms and floods, wild fires and natural catastrophes of all kinds worried the planet. It was as if she was chastising those living on her surface, with punishments, for the evil she'd endured at their hands over the millennia.

Hurricanes and earthquakes in the island regions, and in many southern regions of the continents, raged and vented. Resulting tsunamis caused floods higher than the tallest buildings in many of those areas. Afterward, whole towns and villages were swept into the seas, and bodies of the dead were found in trees and ditches, or anywhere they might be caught by an article of clothing or a broken bone.

Wildfires in America, and in many other places around the world, were leaving piles of ash, where once thriving homes and communities stood. Families were frightened, but didn't know where to turn, as the government had ignored their needs and requests for years.

• • • • •

Through many years of wars and conflicts Josh's folks had faithfully watched over Alec, their grandson, and Elizabeth, Scott and Becca's daughter; raising them and imparting wisdom to the rapidly growing children, as their moms and dads fought for the rights of humanity against the agents of hell.

The youngsters knew more about their parents from Chuck's and Emma's lovingly recited bedtime stories, than through real life connection. Truthfully, they considered their parental figures to be some sort of super heroes, rather than simple ordinary people. So, when those warriors made it home for rare visits, the kids were in awe of their presence. That wasn't originally how Josh and Jana envisioned their parenting role would play out, but they were a positive influence when they could be and the children grew to be exemplary Christians and wonderful young adults, through the tutelage of Alec's devoted grandparents.

Josh and Jana missed Alec terribly, and they missed Chuck and Emma too. Josh had been close to his parents his whole life and Jana had come to love them in ways she'd never imagined. Their devotion to each other, and lifelong love story inspired Josh's treatment of his own wife.

Jana, for her part, respected the pair more than she could describe, but it wasn't just respect she felt for them. She loved them with a love greater than she'd ever felt for anyone besides Josh and Alec. No other people had so impacted her, or helped her believe in herself, more than this wonderful couple.

Over the years Josh shared a story with her, and pretty much anyone else who would listen. A true love story that had weathered time and life's battles, a tale of how Chuck and Emma came together all those decades ago. The story touched everyone who heard it.

It seemed that growing up Chuck and Emma went to the same small country church, and the same public school. They'd been friends since childhood, and both loved the Lord very much, but had never thought about one another in any way other than that of mere friendship. Many years into their friendship, when it came time to attend their senior prom; Chuck, eighteen, was encouraged to ask Emma, seventeen, to the dance and they agreed to attend together.

Emma was extremely shy, much to the amazement of anyone who knew her now, and Chuck, who worked part time at the local auto mechanic shop, seemed to know so much more about the world at large than she, so she was nervous about the upcoming date. On the night of the prom Chuck came to pick up his dance partner, and sauntered up to the door of her parent's house with an almost devil may care attitude, keys to his new, used car twirling in one hand. Her dad had been watching the approaching teen through the transom, and when the bell rang he answered the door and sat with him in the living room. As Chuck sat, he became more nervous, and wiped the sweat from his palms, on his pants, more than once.

Emma's dad sat watching him intently, and as he watched, he knew this was the young man his daughter would someday marry. The room was filled with pictures of Emma at different stages of growing up. There was one in a bunny costume, for her first Halloween; another in a pink tutu, as she became fluent in the language of dance; and yet another with a patient at the local nursing home, where Emma volunteered her time to help care for the elderly. Chuck found himself examining those pictures, and as he looked at the images he smiled, and his soul was calmed.

There were Christmas pictures; a picture of her with a favorite friend at Bible camp; shots of the family on vacation; and one of a toothless little girl blowing out the candles on her birthday cake when she was just six years old. By the time his date was ready to leave, he felt he knew her better than all their years of friendship had allowed. When Emma descended the stairs his breath caught in his throat and his heart skipped a beat. He was sure she must be the most beautiful creature on earth. How had he never noticed before?

Her strawberry, blond hair was swept up on her head, exposing the porcelain skin of her neck and the single strand of white pearls she wore; her dress was light pink, and accentuated the beauty of her perfect complexion and blushing cheeks. Bright green eyes, which were beautifully framed by dark lashes and needed no makeup, batted shyly; and she wore just a touch of pink lipstick on her full lips. She was tiny and slim, yet shapely; and he'd never really noticed before how delicate her hands were, until she brought one up to her face to tame a flyaway curl. He'd bought a wrist corsage, as she'd told him her dress would be sleeveless, but he simply held the flowers in his hand as he stood dumbfounded in the presence of her profound loveliness.

Before they left for the dance, Emma's dad took Chuck aside. He already knew the young man to be honorable, hard working and godly, so he didn't feel the need to threaten his life unduly, but he did say, "My son, you are about to leave this house with my daughter. My only daughter. I know you to be a good young man, so I will come right to the point. This young woman is mine and my wife's life, and she knows very little about the workings of the world. I will expect you to protect her, and to bring her safely home."

"Yes sir. I swear with my life that I will always protect her, and that I will bring her safely home."

After the dance, the young couple didn't drive to make out point, or sneak off to indulge in drinking games with some of their more daring friends. Instead, Chuck drove Emma home, and inside they shared hot chocolate and popcorn with her parents. Emma's parents loved Chuck, and grew to love him more as time passed. As he rose to go, Emma walked him to the front door. Once there she brushed his cheek with a light kiss, and his insides went wild. He knew then that, just as her father had known earlier, that he would marry this winsome beauty one day.

As soon as Emma graduated that year, with rumors of another war brewing, Chuck dropped to one knee and proposed, right in front of her parents. She said yes, and a small, but lovely ceremony was hastily planned. Chucks heart almost exploded with pride and excitement as he watched his lovely bride walk down the aisle on the arm of her father. Her mother had fashioned a floor length dress of white satin and lace. She carried a bouquet of wildflowers, and a lace veil covered her perfectly coifed hair and innocent face. When he lifted the veil to kiss his bride, tears ran down his cheeks, and he knew he was the most blessed man on all the earth. Within weeks of the wedding Chuck was drafted into service and left for duty on foreign soil. Emma wrote to him every day. She didn't want him to be distracted, so she kept him informed on the progression of her pregnancy, and the imminent birth of their child. Josh was ten months old the first time he met his dad, but his mom had showed him pictures of Chuck every day of his life, so when he saw him for the first time, he went straight into his arms, and they'd been best buddies ever since. Through all of that, Emma's mom and dad were there.

Years later, as his father in law lay on his death bed, Chuck covered the older man's hand with his and said,

"You have always treated me like a son, and you were there for me when my own parents passed away. You took care of Emma for me while I was away at war, and you have always cheered me on. I just wanted to tell you that I love you."

"You are a good man Chuck, and I have been proud to call you my son in law. You are a good husband to my daughter, and a good dad to my grandson. I won't be here to help anymore, so I want to remind you to continue protecting Emma, and to always see that she gets safely home."

"I will Dad. You can count on me." He held Emma as her dad died, and they cried together. Emma's mom moved in with them, but she passed away only a month later. Their own love had been so strong, that she simply wanted to go to Jesus and to see her husband again.

Chuck had made a promise, and he would always keep it. He would protect his wife at all costs.

• • • • •

Jana and Becca used their years of stealth training to circle around the temple mount collecting data for the upcoming surge. The backside of their target was woefully under protected, but that was a very good thing for them. Josh, Scott and Mark were busy holding their ground as bombs burst in the air all around them. Enemy troops had discovered their recent change of position and were pelting them with every manner of ballistics from bullets to rockets and heavy mortar rounds. But the guys were giving as good as they got, and were successfully holding the enemy at bay, at least for the time being.

As evening drew near, and the heavens darkened, Josh looked to the sky and was reminded of a particularly joyous fourth of July celebration he experienced as a boy. He longed to give his son memories like that; knowing, at the same time, that was likely never going to be a possibility. As the sky lit up with rocket's fire, deadly munitions found their targets all around, and the sound of shrapnel colliding with the flesh of mortal men, causing deadly consequences, filled the night.

• • • • •

Summer in Jerusalem is hot, but evenings can occasionally bring a slight reprieve. They'd first arrived in winter to join the fight for freedom of the Temple Mount, and they'd survived the cold and snow. After all, at home they lived in some pretty frigid conditions, so a little snow couldn't deter them. Then they'd made it through the temperate months of spring easily, even with the addition of non-stop battles that good weather tends to breed in times of war. But summer. Summer is always brutal in the holy land, and now they were discovering that fact first hand. Josh thanked God that they were finally seeing the first signs of autumn and the cooler evenings that came along with it.

Getting fresh water and supplies past snipers and hostile barricades usually proved to be difficult, so once again they were conserving those precious commodities, and Josh wondered if the rest of the guys were as thirsty as he was. He knew Scott was hungry. Scott was always hungry. Some things never change. But he also knew Scott well enough to know that most of his immediate thoughts were of his son C.J. out here in the battle now, and his wife Becca, doing reconnaissance with Jana.

C.J. had grown into a wonderful young man, and was one of their finest cadets. Bright, powerful, and with great instincts. His dad took care of arranging the bulk of his training as he came up through the ranks, but he'd also become a first rate archer under Becca's tutelage when the pair made it home for visits. Currently assigned to another platoon, farther back from the fray, he was a little safer from the close bombardment they'd been enduring. But Josh saw the concern etched on his friend's face never-the-less, and he felt for him. Being a parent was hard. He and Jana had the same concerns for their son, Alec, as he came of age to join in the resistance battle.

Scott hadn't wanted C.J. to come on this trip, but common sense won out. It was wise to have their best soldiers present at such a pivotal conflict. He just had to get used to the idea that his son was a man now, and that he could, and would, make his own decisions. As far as Becca was concerned, well, Scott was always watching out for her. She was the love of his life, so why wouldn't he? The crux of the situation was, just like her friend, Jana, she was abundantly able to take care of herself. And, as a matter of fact, was even more talented than her husband in the discipline of archery, so she tended to get upset with him when he hovered and tried to 'handle' her. Josh was so much better at letting Jana be who she needed to be, than he was. After sixteen years of marriage, admittedly, he was still learning.

Tonight the men would wait and see what the girls could discover about their best chances of attack. And they would trust whatever those findings were, because their wives were two of the best soldiers, and certainly the best scouts, in the combined resistance forces.

"When the Lamb opened the seventh seal, there was silence in heaven for about half an hour. Then I saw the seven angels who stand before God, and seven trumpets were given to them. And another angel came and stood at the altar with a golden censer, and he was given much incense to offer with the prayers of all the saints on the golden alter before the throne, and the smoke of the incense, with the prayers of the saints, rose before God from the hand of the angel. Then the angel took the censer and filled it with fire from the altar and threw it on the earth, and there were peals of thunder, rumblings, flashes of lightning and an earthquake."

Revelation 8:1-5

"For nation will rise against nation, and kingdom against kingdom, and there will be famines and earthquakes in various places. All these are but the beginning of the birth pains"

Matthew 24:7

"And the beast was given a mouth uttering haughty and blasphemous words, and it was allowed to exercise authority for forty-two months, and it opened its mouth to utter blasphemies against God, blaspheming His name and His dwelling, that is, those who dwell in heaven. Also it was allowed to make war on the saints and to conquer them. And authority was given it over every tribe and people and language and nation, and all who dwell on earth will worship it, everyone whose name has not been written before the foundation of the world in the book of life of the Lamb who was slain. If anyone has an ear, let him hear: If anyone is to be taken captive, to captivity he goes; if anyone is to be slain with the sword, with the sword must be slain. Here is a call for the endurance and faith of the saints."

Revelation 13:5-10

CHAPTER 2

Crouched in his foxhole hungry, tired and quietly humming favorite, old hymns, Josh smiled faintly. Though shells exploded all round him he wasn't afraid. He knew they served a mighty God, and that He hadn't brought them this far to leave them now. Jana and Becca would return with encouraging news. He was sure of it. He had so much to be grateful for. He was married to the love of his life, they had survived by God's Grace through some pretty astounding situations, and they had an amazing son to be proud of. He could feel the battle turning in their favor, he really could, and somehow they would make a difference for the kingdom.

· · · · ·

Josh felt sometimes like he'd been taking care of the world his whole life. Oh, he didn't really mind, it was more of an observation than anything else. His parents attempted to get him interested in other things like sports and after school activities, once he entered high school, but every venture ended with him saving someone, or something, with too many examples to keep track of.

As a little boy he was homeschooled, so the opportunities to meet and play with others his age were limited. Instead, he befriended farm animals and the cats and dogs who lived in the barn. In winter they slid in the snow together, and once he even tied several dogs to his sled, while he pretended to compete in the Iditarod in Alaska. A trip across a nearby pond, on frozen ice, put him in the right place at the right time, to save a deer who'd gotten caught in the freezing water. Somehow he freed the frightened creature, but just about lost his toes to frostbite in the process.

One tiny cat, who he'd named Petey, got caught high in a tree, and was too frightened to make his way down. He heard the plaintiff cries of the creature, and while climbing up the tree to save him, he fell and broke his arm.

Another time he was walking home from town, and ran across a car in the ditch that ran next to the gravel road near his home. He peered inside and saw a man. The man's face was pasty white, and his eyes rolled back in his head. He managed to pull him from the vehicle and lay him on the ground, where he proceeded to perform CPR. A couple drove by, and when they saw the situation, went for help.

The man's life was saved that day, from a heart attack, by a teen aged boy. The man he saved was the president of a bank in a nearby town, and the man was so grateful that he told the local paper, and a reporter came out and took his picture. For Christmas that year, Josh received a nice used car from the man as a gift. He didn't care that the car was used. Now he had wheels!

There was a stint on the local high school football team, where several young men were continually picking on another student, named Benny, just for his smaller size. Josh intervened and befriended the young man; giving him a ride home each day for the rest of the school year. They spent time together doing homework, and even attended sporting events together. Since Josh was so well liked, just the mere fact that they were friends, kept the others from picking on Benny anymore.

Years later he found out from Benjamin that on the day he'd stepped in to save him from the bullies, he'd been planning to go home and commit suicide. He'd felt so alone, he just didn't think he could take it anymore. He'd prayed that very morning, "God, if you're really out there, please help me. If you don't, then I'll know you aren't there, or you just don't care and I'll figure something out on my own." Josh's gesture not only saved his life, but caused him to realize God was really listening. He became a Christian and remained so his entire life.

His desire to help others is what led him to majoring in social work in college, and would lead him to his first major job at a large church, acting as counselor to teens and young adults. Every chance he got he was helping others. During summer breaks for his freshman, sophomore, junior and senior years, he was involved with his church youth group and spent time in other countries on mission trips. Seeing how others lived, and comparing the poverty of the nations he visited, with the bounty of his own country and life, caused him to want to help even more.

In college he planned mission trips of his own. He held fund raisers and set up locations, transportation, supplies and interested parties. Through this venture he made several friends. These were the very friends he was playing volleyball with, in the park, the day he met Jana. He had to smile when he thought of their meeting, because after they began dating he thought Jana was the most interesting, and beautiful, project God had ever put in his path. As with the other assignments in his life, he thought it was up to him to save her, but God had it all under control and used many other people and circumstances to make himself known to this amazing young woman.

• • • • •

The past sixteen or seventeen years had flown by. He and Jana only made it home for rare visits, and they knew they'd missed much. It was a huge responsibility realizing that humanity depended on the work God gave them to do, so their choices were few. During those visits they saw Mom and Dad getting older and more frail, and witnessed their son growing into a strong, able bodied, Christian young man, almost entirely without them.

Alec was just turning eighteen, and was angry when Scott's son, C.J. was allowed to make this trip and he wasn't. That was the difference five years of age could make. And that deployment date even included Scott intervening for as long as he could in a decision about his son's availability for service. Rightly wanting the young man to be home with Angel and Elizabeth when he and Becca couldn't be, the council had made special dispensations for as long as they were able. But the girls were older now and didn't need their big brother as much as the resistance forces needed another able bodied soldier.

Josh was happy they had Alec's age to use as an excuse this time, as he hadn't actually become eighteen until a week after the last deployment date. Realities of war would become a part of his life soon enough. But, they admired his character, because though he was angry, he was respectful. He was a good boy, and they were proud of his reasonable nature.

Alec's parents didn't know that his willingness to wait until a later round of deployments was actually less about good sense, and more about young love. Being a few months older than Elizabeth, who was not quite as far along in her training as he, kept him from making too big a fuss about the timing of the deployment of that current group of fighters to Jerusalem. He would patiently wait for Elizabeth and the upcoming deployment which would occur in six months. Their plans had always been to prepare together, to marry, and to go into the battle together. Their earnest desire was to be a fierce fighting team like Josh and Jana, or Scott and Becca, and they'd trained very hard to accomplish that lofty goal.

To the young, the idea of fighting together for a united cause can be vastly romantic. Sadly, Alec would find out soon enough, just as his parents had, that there was nothing romantic about the stench of death in your nostrils. Let's face it, days, or weeks, without a shower; lack of food and water, sometimes bordering on starvation; injuries that must go untreated for lack of medics and supplies; and watching loved ones cut down on the field of battle, were hardly the bones of a good romance novel.

Alec would continue to train and hone his many talents. God's promises are sure, and he was definitely the best of his father and the best of his mother combined, on and off the battlefield. He'd been raised up for such a time as this, and the time of his proving would come sooner than he knew. Without doubt he was the most accomplished soldier the resistance ever produced, but he was more than that. Alec had a serious, and strong relationship with the Lord for one so young, and he was very sensitive and kind. He'd grown tall like his dad, over six foot six, and though he was agile like his mom he was growing more muscular, and hardened, each year as he trained with the men.

He'd become battle wizened in the past six years too, simply by picking the brains of old soldiers. He'd learned that real wisdom came from listening to men who'd been there, and lived to tell about it, and then never taking that knowledge and experience for granted. Training with these heroes since he was twelve, he felt truly blessed and ready to march into the conflict.

Handsome and intelligent, with thick auburn hair like his mom, and the green eyes of his father, he presented a striking appearance. And, because he was such a shining star among the cadets, many young ladies in camp tried to catch his eye. But, none of that mattered to Alec. He only had eyes for Elizabeth, and his loyalty and devotion were pure as gold.

Best friends since infancy, they'd remained so until this day, and would be for the rest of their lives. Elizabeth was a fiery beauty. Curly, golden blond hair and hazel eyes that changed color with her mood and surroundings; skin like alabaster; and a petite, slender frame that belied her great strength and ability, made her the envy of most women and the desire of most of the young men who'd grown up around her. Together, they were the next, and without a doubt, the better generation of God's army of resistance soldiers.

• • • • •

Josh looked to the night sky and quietly talked to the Father. "Lord, you have always been by my side, and I know you watch over us even now. Please keep Jana and

Becca safe, as they look for ways to take down the enemy of your chosen people. We stand ready to do Your will Father. Thank you for your protection and love."

"You okay, Josh?"

"Yeah, just checking in with the Father."

"I've been doing quite a bit of praying myself lately. I worry about C.J. What kind of world have we made for our children that all they know is war and training for battle? C.J. has been out here for months, and Angel just arrived with the last wave of recruits, so I have two kids out here now. Next thing we know Alec and Elizabeth will be heading here too. We need to get this wrapped up, if for no other reason than to save our youngest kids from this damnable war."

"I know what you mean, Scott. But this will be finished in God's timing, not ours. I have a feeling the next generation of defenders will be His particular favored ones. I'm afraid that you and I will go to our graves as used up old soldiers my friend. I also have a strong feeling that the return of Christ may be coming faster than we know. Our kids might very well be the ones ushering in the beginning of the end."

"You're probably right old buddy. But I have to say that if I have to go out on the battlefield, there is no one I'd rather fight beside, or die beside than you. I just hate to see our wives subjected to this life year after year, don't you?"

"I know what you mean, Scott. But, honestly, do you really think there is anywhere that these girls would rather be, than right out here in the thick of it?"

"You're right again, and we both know it. Our wives are a couple of warriors, which turned out to be a very good thing for us, and for the resistance. I just wish I could have given Becca a different kind of life. You know, nice dresses, fine restaurants and maybe vacations. She sure does deserve it all."

"She does deserve it buddy. So do you. But, if you asked her, I'll bet she'd tell you that she wouldn't have it any other way. She likes what she does, and as for vacations, she's spending time in the Holy Land. What vacation is better than that?"

"Very funny, Josh. You know what I mean. This battle has gone on for so long, and I'm tired. I know you and the girls must be tired too. Will there ever be a time when we are not in a battle for our lives?"

"I can't promise you anything like that, Scott. I know we stepped up and asked God to use us, He put a calling on our lives, and here we are. I believe everything is happening in the way it was meant to happen, and that we are here because this is where the Lord needs us most. I don't know if we will ever see home again, but I know when all is said and done, we will be home with Jesus. That's all that really matters, isn't it?"

"Yeah, you're right. I just miss my kids, and I feel like we've missed so much of their lives."

"I know what you mean there, but knowing that our kids all know the Lord is a blessing. Someday we will all be together again. That is a comfort to me. And, with these last years on earth proving to be the worst kind of hell, it will make going home to the Lord that much more beautiful."

"You're right there. The eternal rest He promises us will definitely be welcomed. Do you really think we'll ever win this battle?"

"I don't know about this battle, Scott. But, we've read the book, remember? And, no matter how many of these battles we have to wade through, we know who wins in the end."

Another barrage of mortar shells lit up the sky, and blasted the ground around where they took cover. Josh heard screams, and then the distinct sound of moaning to his right. "Stay here. I'm going to see if I can find out who's been hit, and if there's anything I can do to help."

"Not without me you're not."

"Scott, stay here in case the girls get back."

"Mark is here, and he'll know where we are if the girls return before we do. I'm not letting you go out there alone. Jana would have me skinned if I let anything happen to you after all we've been through."

"Fine, come on then."

The guys found two bodies in the foxhole closest to them on their right. They said a prayer for their fallen comrades, and checked around further from the furrow. Without light it was difficult to tell where the soldier, who they could still hear moaning, had gone. But, they didn't dare use a flashlight, or matches, for fear of giving themselves away, and providing a perfect night time target for the enemy.

After a few steps Scott tripped on another of their downed brothers. They checked for signs of life, and upon finding none, they said another prayer. Feeling along the ground they finally found the source of the moaning. Examining the soldier as best they could in the dark, they discovered he was missing a leg above the knee, and an arm above the elbow. The entire area was slippery with blood, and they knew under these circumstances, and in the dark, there wasn't much they could do for the young man. The soldier was shivering uncontrollably, even in the relative warmth of an early autumn night, and mumbling something about his wife and baby girl. Josh couldn't see his face. "Soldier, what is your name?"

"Dan. Dan Semple."

"I'm Josh Conyers, Dan."

"Sir. It's an honor to serve with you Sir."

"No, Dan, It's an honor to serve with you."

"Sir, can you get a message to my wife and baby girl?"

"Yes, Dan. I'll be sure to tell them anything you'd like me to pass on."

"General Conyers. I'm saved. I know where I'll be when I leave this place. I also know there isn't anything you can do for me now, so, would you please tell my wife that I love her and my baby Trinity. And tell her I'll see her again in heaven?"

"Yes Dan. Thank you for your service soldier. You have honored your God, and fought hard for the resistance."

Josh knew young Dan well. Back at home he was one of the music leaders for their weekly worship. He and his wife, Wendy, just had a baby girl a week before they were deployed to Jerusalem. If he closed his eyes now, he could see a regular Sunday service, with Dan playing his guitar, and Wendy swaying to the music with her hands in the air. They were beloved of the entire camp, and Josh would now have to tell that young woman that her daughter would be growing up without a daddy.

Holding the injured soldier in his arms, Josh felt his trembling stop at last, as the young man lost his battle for one last breath. Josh squeezed him tight and tears ran freely down his face, leaving muddy tracks in the weeks of dust and dirt caked on his skin. So many young men who would never hold their babies again. So many who would never dance with their wives again. So much loss and pain. They had to win this battle for the Lord, but also for all the troops who would never go home again.

They said a prayer for Dan, and laid him gently in the foxhole; next to his fallen brothers; that would serve as his final earthly resting place. Josh's heart was so heavy in his chest he could barely breathe. For forty eight hours the men held their position, waiting for the return of the girl's scouting party, and when the women finally scurried into the furrow beside them he had a hard time disguising his pain. "Are you okay, Josh?"

"I'm just getting tired of collecting goodbyes from good men to take to the families they will never see again, Jana. A young man, Dan Semple, died in my arms while you were gone, and he asked me to tell his wife, Wendy, and baby girl, Trinity, that he loved them."

"I know babe. This war has gone on forever, and it's been hard on everyone. I wish I could change things, but we are making a difference in the only way we know how. God will make everything right in the end. We have to believe that."

"And I do. You know I do. I know we're doing what we've been called to do. That's the one thing that keeps me out here. But, it hurts to see young people at the beginning of their lives dying such tragic deaths. They've never gotten to experience all the joys of growing up, and growing old, together. We've had that, and I wish we could share it with them. It makes their sacrifices so much more heartrending.

Pretty soon our boy will be out here, and I don't want this to be the only life he knows."

"His life will be whatever God means it to be, Josh. We've always known God had a calling on Alec's life. I would love to see him have everything, just like you would. But, his everything might look completely different than what we would have chosen for him, and he just might be the tool God uses to take His next step in this conflict."

"I'm just feeling very sad right now, and I could use some good news."

"Then you're really going to love us, because we have brought good news!"

"Hey, guys, gather around. Jana and Becca have information for us!"

When the men gathered around, and hunkered down beside the girls, Jana began to reveal the intelligence they had gathered.

• • • • •

Jana's and Becca's reconnaissance mission was more successful than they'd ever imagined it would be. Heavy weapons had done much to destroy the once beautiful, but ancient, city of Jerusalem and the entire country side around her. But, those same bombardments, much to the delight of the girls, had opened up some very old passages in the hillsides surrounding the town. It was obvious that the Muslim intruders were not aware of the presence of these passages, or their uncovering, as was demonstrated by the lack of guards surrounding those openings.

Their scouting mission began behind the Western wall, or what was left of that once important landmark, and continued at different levels, behind and around the mount and down into the valleys surrounding the city. For two days they searched the landscape. On the eastern slope, above the Kidron Valley, behind the City of David, they found an opening.

The city was built on a hill of hard limestone, in which underground water created karstic caves. The Gihon Spring, which had been the only source of water in the city, at the time of King David, emerges from that eastern slope.

Gihon, which is translated 'To gush forth', was supposed to reflect the flow of the spring, which is not steady, but intermittent. Its frequency varies with the seasons and amount of local precipitation. You see, the spring is a siphon-type karst spring, fed by ground water that accumulates in a subterranean cave. each time the space fills to the brim with water, it empties all at once through cracks in the rock and is siphoned to the surface. This natural feature made it necessary, in those ancient times, to dig a pool in which to accumulate the water. For availability when the spring was not 'gushing forth' during those days of King David, and when this was their only supply of the precious resource.

Due to the current dry season, the tunnel, which would normally contain water flow, was mostly empty. A channel emerges from the spring and extends approximately four hundred meters southward, along the eastern slope of the city, around the city's southern end, and empties into a reservoir in the Tyropoeon Valley. The channel's northern part is still covered, but time, and explosive blasts in close proximity to that tunnel, had opened the southern end. Finally, it becomes a rock cut tunnel toward the end. This would be the perfect place of entry, to create a surprise for their enemy.

The ladies were not aware of the history of the place, which would have told them this particular waterway had been abandoned since the creation of Hezekiah's Tunnel. The passageway made its way up the eastern slope, and out through an opening, which was directly behind the Temple

Mount. There was no need to fear flooding during the dry season, so their travel would be secure, and this conduit would let them out right behind the barricades of the enemy. It was perfect.

Getting a sufficient number of men out of the area, and into the tunnel, would pose the biggest problem. They couldn't leave their current positions unmanned without arousing suspicion, but they would need adequate troops on the attack squad to overtake the enemy's position from the rear. The only solution was to divide their numbers and set up decoy positions facing their adversary's machine gun sites. Those soldiers left behind would have to work twice as hard to cover for their missing comrades, but that was doable. Scott and Mark, along with sufficient troops, could hold down positions here, while Josh and the other half the troops would accompany Jana and Becca to the tunnels for an upcoming surprise attack on the mount. They set about collecting all the explosive ordnances they could get their hands on, and supplying the men who would remain behind with the ammunition they would need for distraction. They would wait for the moonless night coming up soon, to prepare for an ambush.

"But when you see Jerusalem surrounded by armies, then know that its desolation has come near. Then let those who are in Judea flee to the mountains, and let those who are inside the city depart, and let not those who are out in the country enter it, for these are days of vengeance, to fulfill all that is written."

Luke 21:20-22

"And Jesus answered them, "See that no one leads you astray. For many will come in my name, saying, 'I am the Christ, and they will lead many astray. And you will hear of wars and rumors of wars. See that you are not alarmed, for this must take place, but the end is not yet. For nation will rise against nation, and kingdom against kingdom, and there will be famines and earthquakes in various places. All these are but the beginning of the birth pains."

Matthew 24:4-8

CHAPTER 3

s far as the general populace was concerned, it had all begun rather innocuously. Could it really have been less than twenty years since the American government mandated that all citizens receive a chip in their hand? It felt more like centuries to Jana. First of all, God had been banned from schools, public venues, and government buildings, removed from the pledge and the money of the land, and even the term Merry Christmas had become an offence punishable by up to five years in prison. So much had happened since then, society's slow march toward godlessness, and decline, had happened in a predictable pattern and the world was a very different, and much more sinister place.....

Jana sat in silence, remembering how devastated she'd been to hear of the supposed death of her husband; and how physically painful it was to hide behind a panel, in the bottom of a bookcase in Josh's study, as men in black ransacked their home. She'd felt lost, vulnerable and frightened as she fled through forest and grasslands to climb a mountain. All in search of what she believed was the safety of an 'America's Resistance Movement' camp, which was supposed to be somewhere in that vicinity. Her tangle with a mountain lion, and weeks healing from her injuries; only to encounter, and almost kill, their friend Pastor Mike, had been an epic story. Nursing him back to health consumed months, but had also given her opportunity to know and grow closer to the Lord. That fall and winter of wonderful, and horrible circumstances seemed so terribly long ago.

Discovering Josh was still alive, and consequently fighting for her own survival when she was shot on the mountain's plateau, made the deep of winter that year an unforgettable time. Meanwhile, the world, and consequently the American dream, had moved on to an unrecognizable mix of socialist and communist policies in the earth they'd once known. By that time the resistance movement had grown, and citizens from all over the country were rebelling, and escaping, to the movement's secret bases around the map.

America's rogue administration came under scrutiny, and the UN council took over not only America, but other administrations and governments around the globe as well, under the auspices of a more inclusive 'One World' government. Soon, citizens of the world were living through the same nightmare as Americans had endured alone, under the government's ominous rule, for those past few years. Food shortages were rampant (made worse by the fact that warehouses were filled to the brim with supplies which were rotting instead of being distributed). Medical help was almost non-existent, and a "One World' church was fully endorsed by the ruling body, at the behest of UNGC leader, Amir Bahram.

Bahram was Muslim, a Twelver to be exact. He knew the secret to fundamentalist Islam becoming the dominant religion in the world was constant deception and clever lies, and he excelled at both.

After all, every attempt at instituting Islam worldwide over the previous centuries; using violence and torture; had only succeeded in creating martyrs for Christendom.

Amir knew he must eliminate Christianity altogether, in order for his evil plans to have a chance. First by destroying access to other religions, by passing laws outlawing the practice of, and the sharing of, the Christian faith. And further, by making it a crime punishable by death, to own a Bible.

By placing a false 'One World' religion to the forefront; a religion which seemed, at least to the average un churched, or anti church citizen, so effortless and rewarding. Perhaps for some, even an acceptable spiritual replacement for their old form of quasi Christianity. This would be an easy replacement if you were a person who'd never really had a true relationship with Jesus.

By doing this, by claiming to the citizenry at large that Christianity was of no effect, and that any variety of ineffective, non-committal religion was just as good as any other, officials maintained, in essence, that it was acceptable to be wishy-washy, and let's face it, wishy-washy is usually easy to do for those who would rather not expend the effort.

Then, simply by slowly bringing Islam out of the shadows, where it had been waiting to pounce on unsuspecting victims since its inception, to encompass the lives of all people; and using Sharia laws and traditions to control the masses; would be Amir's natural choice of paths. His reasoning was that by bringing this extreme change about slowly, and without excess mass violence if possible, he would give the world's sheep a false sense of having made a choice. And, because humans are all about choices and control, if they truly thought the widespread use and preference of Islam, over any other faith, was their own idea; then no one, not even that damnable group of resistance soldiers would be able to sway them.

He just had to play his cards right. Much of his plan centered around getting the rebel forces of the resistance, and those annoying Christians, under control. If time and newly implemented laws didn't deter them; and covert missions to kill them didn't scare them into submission; then all out war might be his only resort. And, if it came to that, he would gladly remove that damnable Josh Conyers' head from his shoulders and display it on a pike for all to see.

He had lost Cage to the resistance movement. His foolish friend had chosen Christianity and this Jesus character over him, and that angered him more than he could express. He'd felt a special bond with the man who later changed his name to Paul, and he felt especially betrayed by that broken connection. He'd also found out later that Josh Conyers, the leader of the northwest resistance, who was now acting general of all resistance forces worldwide, had been right there in D.C. when Cage was killed for his crime of practicing and spreading Christianity. Additionally, intelligence recently told him that this Josh Conyers and his wife Jana weren't just in D.C., but right there in the square when the execution was carried out. This couple was slick, and the best that the resistance movement offered, and most annoying of all, they seemed to be one step ahead of him at every turn.

• • • • •

Bahram's power grew exponentially. Since his council held the key to mandatory service in their UN military forces, by controlling the chips imbedded in the hands of their troops, he had an unlimited supply of disposable militia. Slowly, over the years, he'd added more of his Muslim brothers to the governing bodies of every country, and community, until all administrations worldwide answered directly to him through the United Nations Global Council.

The crowning achievement, in his diagram to deceive the nations, had been that six and a half years ago he created the aforementioned treaty between Muslims and Jews in Jerusalem. A contract, if you will, allowing the Jews of that country to once again have access to their holy site on the temple mount. Thereby, making them able again to begin offering sacrifices to their God. These Jews had been a constant thorn in his side since he took over the council, almost as resilient and unwavering as the Christians who persistently stood in his way. And he considered this the perfect deception to bring them to their knees. Bringing the 'pigs' and 'dogs' all home again, would put them in one place, where he could easily eradicate them once and for all! It was a perfect plan.

Much to his angst, he had to admit that for a country so small, they had more spunk and fight in them, well, besides those infuriating devout Christians, than just about any group he'd ever had the displeasure of encountering. Sure, he'd made the treaty lightly, and very much for his own benefit, to cause them to lower their physical and emotional defenses. But, lower them they did. They'd fallen for his conniving plan, hook, line and sinker.

When he developed the treaty, he'd initially angered many of his Muslim brethren. At least those who didn't realize he always knew what he was doing, and constantly had a plan. But, they were soon put soundly in their places, the fools, as he reneged on the treaty and left the Jews high and dry. With no more access to the temple mount, and no more ability to sacrifice, the Jews were once again at the mercy of Islam. Only now, and much to his amusement, most of them were exactly where he wanted them, In Israel and right at his fingertips.

It had taken every ounce of his strength to act kind to the Jewish scum while he was deceiving them into his ultimate arrangement. But, at three and a half years into the treaty, by all accounts and the latest calculations, most of the filth of Israel was finally accumulated back in their self acclaimed homeland. Once that was accomplished he was able to move on his plan. Finally the world would be free, once and for all, of Judaism.

As mentioned, Bahrain had ordered the installation of giant satellite driven television screens in town squares, and in intersections in cities all across the land, and in all international countries controlled by the UNGC. His motive was purely driven by vanity. He intended to share his statue, boast about his many accomplishments, and show the world who was in charge. And, when he was duly acclaimed for his marvelous deeds, and miracles, the entire world would be forced to bow down to him.

For the past three years, since Bahram had broken the treaty and led Muslim hordes into Jerusalem riding a white horse, and killing as he went (all caught on camera and relayed around the world to every city, town and byway), the citizens of Jerusalem had been in a state of constant battle and total panic, very much like the resistance bases back home had endured for a decade and a half. But, just as the Israeli Defense Forces seemed to start losing ground,

Josh Conyers and his band of helpful, hopeful, resistance, rabble rousers showed up to lend a hand to the IDF. They'd also showed up, sadly, just in time to see the bronzed statue of Bahram set up in the temple (another global, televised event). This was an abomination that couldn't be ignored. Josh was only glad his parents weren't here to see it.

• • • • •

Bahram, with the help of Nathan Graham, the 'One World' church's chief stooge, was busy setting himself up as a deity. The world needed a leader, and he was already acting leader of the United Nations Global Council, so he considered himself the most likely choice. It was easy for the world to begin accepting him in this role, after years in the limelight. And his charismatic personality and swarthy good looks certainly seemed to help him fit the part.

For the past few years and much to the dismay of leaders of America's Resistance Movement; Bahram, with the assistance of Graham, had employed one magic trick after another to convince the world's citizens that he was perhaps, in fact, an actual god. Even the world's Muslims were growing more convinced that he might actually be the Twelfth Imam for whom they'd long waited. Magic and 'miracles' at Graham's hands had millions following him.

At rallies and meetings around the world, and in sanctuaries from one World Church to another, they watched Graham 'heal' the lame and the blind, (all perfectly healthy individuals planted by Graham's own lackeys of course); and call lightening and fire from the sky, (a clever and very convincing illusion). They had supernatural tricks galore, and used them at every opportunity. This was all in an attempt to give him credence as the world's most powerful holy man. Once people began to flock to his services by numbers never seen before, and those who were influenced began to believe in his prophesy and predictions, he had only to declare Bahram the one true god, and the sheep fell over themselves to do the man's every bidding. It also didn't hurt that the masses believed Amir had been raised from the dead.

As Graham's influence multiplied, and the world grew to esteem Bahram as the chosen one more each day, he decided his next logical step would be to take Josh and Jana Conyers out of the way for good. If he could eliminate the leadership in the persistently annoying resistance camp, he would represent the only logical choice of guidance available for thousands of lost souls.

Nathan Graham, self centered as he was, reveled in his own importance these days, almost as much as Bahram did in his. When he'd been promoted to head of the church, he practically burst with pride; and often strutted around in his new vestments, when ordinary clothing would have been more appropriate. Even alone in the privacy of his own rooms, he dressed to the nines whenever possible, just to gaze at himself in the full length mirror hanging on the door. Obviously, he had no idea his promotion had come on the heels of a meeting of the higher echelon of UNGC ranking members, including Amir Bahram.

It was agreed at the infamous meeting, that he would likely be the most easily manipulated of the candidates considered. And due to his non-committal attitude toward Christianity, in previous so called Christian public ministries, he already had a rather large following of superficial, quasi, so called Christian followers, to bring into the 'New World' church family. His promotion did much to smooth over the transition for all those who, before its ban, liked to call themselves Christians without a sliver of proof to support their claims. The same vast group who were fine with the idea of giving up the name of 'Christian', to belong to the current popular group.

• • • • •

Alec smiled as he watched Elizabeth train. He couldn't remember a time when he hadn't loved her, but over this past couple years he'd experienced other feelings as well, feelings he didn't understand. He'd talked to Grampa about those feelings and urges, and gratefully he walked away from the conversation with a better understanding of life, and of what a man of honor would do. He knew he wanted to wait until they were married, but sometimes his imagination went a bit wild. He was after all a young man in love.

Elizabeth saw him watching, and turned up the skill level for his entertainment. She was proud of her new talents, and loved showing them off. Alec had been her best friend since her earliest memory, but, for the last couple of years things had changed. When he walked into a room her stomach seemed filled with butterflies and her breath quickened. She'd tried talking to Angel about her feelings, but, fortunately, or unfortunately, her sister was as dense as she on the topic of men. After much frustration she'd gone to Alec's grandmother, who honestly seemed as much her own grandma as his.

Emma explained so much, and now she understood and felt confident they would wait to explore those feelings further until they were finally married. Both Chuck and Emma had seen the tensions growing over a period of time, and were glad when the kids came to speak with them.

"Elizabeth came to talk to me today."

"Did she? What about?"

"Oh, you know. About her feelings. She's been noticing new things about Alec for some time now, and she thought she might be going crazy."

"Well, I'm glad she came to you. I had a hard enough time explaining things to Alec, and I sure wouldn't have known how to talk to a girl about any of it. I'm glad they both felt comfortable enough to talk to us, but I wish their parents had been here for this one."

"I'm just glad they both love the Lord, and want to please Him. I'm quite sure they will want to marry before they are deployed."

"Well, Alec is already eighteen and Elizabeth very soon will be, so they can make that decision. I just wish Josh and Jana were here. I'd hate to see them miss this."

"I wonder, Chuck. Do you think we'll ever see them again? Josh and Jana I mean. I miss them so much. It seems the whole world is on fire, and almost everyone we know is off in a battle somewhere. Angel is gone now and when we said goodbye I'm sure she felt the same way we did, as if we may never meet again. Scott was pretty adamant about C.J. staying behind until after Elizabeth was eighteen, but he and Angel are both going to miss their sister's birthday too. I know we voted to keep women out of the ranks if they were needed here, so the fact that Angel has made it to almost twenty one before being called to service has been a blessing. But, now that the resistance is desperate for more reinforcements and are calling on all trained troops, I feel as though we will never be able to save another young person from that hell."

"Do you know when Alec and Elizabeth are due to deploy?"

"Elizabeth's training will be complete at the end of the month, just in time for her eighteenth birthday. Let's be realistic, I believe Alec has only been waiting around for her. Once she's reached her birthday, I doubt we'll be able to keep either one of them out of the fight. I think we'd better start making some plans for a wedding, don't you?"

Chuck and Emma went all out to make the young couple's wedding a day to remember, even without the presence of their parents. Alec and Elizabeth missed their moms and dads, but they also understood the world's freedom rested in the hands of those called of God to fight these battles around the world. They couldn't wait to don uniforms, and strap on weapons, to step into the conflict themselves. They'd been raised by warriors, and they knew that human kind depended on the Grace of God, and what the outcome of this long suffering war would be.

••••••

Elizabeth was lovely in a gown fashioned by Emma. White, floor length satin, cinched in at the waist with a golden sash to match her hair, and boasting small embroidered roses and tiny pearls at the neckline. She carried red and yellow roses, harvested with thorns removed that morning, tied with a white satin ribbon; and wore her golden curls piled on her head, fastened with clips designed with more roses and pearls. She needed no makeup, as her cheeks were blushed with excitement, and her beautiful blue eyes flashed with the passion of a young woman going to meet her love. Her parents and siblings were not present for the ceremony, so Chuck walked her down the aisle and gave her away.

Alec was handsome in a white suit, with a simple rose boutonniere. The service was an intimate one. Most of the young people in camp, who the couple grew up with and considered friends, had been recently called to war.

Alec and Elizabeth would have three days together before they were scheduled to deploy, so they intended to make the best of their time. Chuck and Emma would of course be sad to see the last of their charges leave the protection of their high mountain shelter. They knew in all likelihood they might never see them again.

The young couple loved each other their whole lives, and had always dreamed of becoming one, so the wedding day for them was magical, no matter how many were in attendance. Looking into one another's eyes, as they repeated their hand written vows, was a dream come true.

"Alec, I have waited my whole life to be your wife. You are a gift from God, and the man of my dreams. I will spend my life trusting you, loving you, and doing my best to be there for you whenever you call."

"Elizabeth, I thank God for you. You are my blessing and my reward. Your beauty astounds me, and your friendship keeps me going. I promise to spend my life loving you and protecting you, so help me God."

When it was time to kiss the bride, Alec picked Elizabeth up in his powerful arms and held her. Tears fell from his eyes as he gently kissed her and set her back down on her feet.

Later, at a small reception, they feasted on Emma's roast beef and ham, complete with garlic mashed potatoes, silky gravy, homemade biscuits, fruit salad, peas with tiny pearl onions, and a wedding cake made by the woman who adored them both more than life itself.

The mood after their meal was mixed. Chuck and Emma were happy for the kids, but they knew all too well what they would be facing in only a few short days. For now they tried to keep the atmosphere light.

•••••

Their honeymoon was heaven. For three days they held each other and reveled in the discoveries they made as they shared their bodies in wedded bliss. Everything about these experiences was new. There had never been more than a couple of stolen kisses between them, so they were genuinely surprised at the blessings which were available to them as man and wife. After making love they talked about the future. They didn't dare assume that their future might include a home and children, knowing the situation they would soon be in, but they talked about being there for each other and how important the fight was to the resistance cause. They hoped they might see their parents again, and possibly even Elizabeth's brother and sister, but were abundantly aware that they might conceivably never see any of their families ever again. Now, they would simply be the only family that either of them had, and they meant to protect one another's backs. No one would be able to separate them, not ever.

"I love you, husband."

"I waited a long time to hear you say that, wife. I can't remember a time that I didn't love you."

"Why did you wait so long to tell me? You know I always knew we were friends, but I didn't know you were in love with me."

"Oh, I used to see the way Ralph looked at you, and I couldn't tell if you felt the same way about him or not."

"I never cared about Ralph. I was actually rather annoyed with him, but he was always there underfoot."

"If I'd known, I would have come forward sooner, but there were many times when I was sure you only thought of me as a sort of brother type."

"Well, we were both kind of raised by your grandparents."

"I never once thought of you as a sister. And besides, you lived with your brother and sister in a different house. I think I would have felt differently if we'd been raised in the same house."

"For years now I saw you watching me, and I always wanted to do my best when you were watching. Did I ever tell you that when you walked into a room I got butterflies in my stomach?"

"No, you didn't. So, butterflies huh? Do I still give you butterflies?"

Alec finished his sentence with a long kiss, which led to much more. Later they walked through the orchards and out into the fields. Alec loved the smell of the freshly tilled soil. He was so much like his dad. As they walked he fashioned a wreath of daisies and placed it on his lovely wife's golden hair. When they returned home they found a delicious supper waiting for them, compliments of Chuck and Emma, and complete with candles and flowers.

"I'm going to miss those two. They've been here for me my whole life."

"I know what you mean. They know just about everything either of us has ever done, and they still love us anyway. I'm grateful they've been here for me too, since my parents left."

"It breaks my heart to know that we may never see them again."

"We don't know that, Alec. We will go and do our duty. But, I refuse to believe that we will die. God has just brought us together, and we will watch out for one another, always. I can't think of anyone I'd rather have protecting my back than you."

"I feel the same way. But my grandparents are getting pretty old. I just meant that I don't know how much longer they will be here with us."

"Oh Alec, your grandparents will probably outlive us all."

"I'm sure you're right. They are kind of stubborn."

Three days flew by quickly, and it was time for the next round of recruits to be deployed to hot spots around the globe. Some troops were sent to the east coast to serve under the most recent command and help protect an ARM encampment there. But the bulk of the new group were loaded onto cargo planes headed for Jerusalem. This was the battle field which would predict the direction of our world's future, and the playing field of Bahrain's current obsession. He was ultimately intent on gaining the upper hand with Josh and Jana.

Alec and Elizabeth said their goodbyes, hiked down the mountain to the plateau, and boarded a troop carrier headed for the holy city. The aircraft flew low to avoid detection by U.N. radar. Looking out over sea waves and a golden sunrise, as they made their way to a brand new phase of their lives, the young couple smiled and held hands. As they got closer to their destination, they wondered what new adventures might be awaiting them in this ancient land.

"Then He said to them, "Nation will rise against nation, and kingdom against kingdom. There will be great earthquakes, and in various places famines and pestilences. And there will be terrors and great signs from heaven. But before all this they will lay their hands on you and persecute you, delivering you up to the synagogues and prisons, and you will be brought before kings and governors for My sake."

Luke 21:10-12

"For Zion's sake I will not keep silent, and for Jerusalem's sake I will not be quiet, until her righteousness goes forth as brightness, and her salvation as a burning bush."

Isaiah 62:1

CHAPTER 4

It was his choice to stay, and to see his best friends go off to battle in Jerusalem without him. Someone had to protect those left behind in the high mountain base, and make decisions about deployments of essential troops and supplies out east to sister bases, and overseas to Israel. Sure, there was a part of him that would have loved to face the enemy of God's people in the holy land; but there was important work to be done here too.

Pastor Mike was a valuable asset for many reasons. He'd been the spiritual advisor to thousands in his years with the resistance. He and doctor Rose made a formidable team when it came to making decisions for the good of the camp, and deciding how best to help in the protection of their sister bases. He'd also grown ever closer to Chuck and Emma over the years and was slowly taking over many of their responsibilities as their strength waned in old age. He knew those would be enormous shoes to fill, and didn't, for one moment, think he could do it on his own.

His biggest reason for wanting to stay behind, if he had to be honest, as usual, was Jana. Any opportunity to be away from her was good for his sanity. He'd been in love with her since their time in the cave during the winter of his healing. She'd almost killed him, gutting him like a fish, and proving she was more than accomplished in taking care of herself. Then she'd become an able nurse and caregiver, as she gently took care of him through his long recovery. He'd watched her change into a godly, capable woman before his eyes, and his heart ached for her every single day. He'd never told anyone of his feelings, of course. The closest he came was one night as they were studying scripture in the cavern during his recovery, when they both still believed Josh to be dead. But, thankfully, he hadn't blurted out anything he would later regret, since they soon discovered Josh wasn't dead after all, but very much alive in the prison caves on the mountain plateau.

When she was shot by militia soldiers during the infamous battle on the plateau, and was hanging on to life by a prayer, he felt he would die with her if she left this world. Her emergency surgery, performed by Doc Rose was one of the most stressful times of his life. And he thanked God that Scott had universal donor blood flowing through his veins.

Seeing her come slowly back to herself was a blessing. He remembered her time of pregnancy with Josh's son, the trials with her health during that time, and the joy they shared upon the birth of Alec; and he had a hard time being around the small family at that time, because he knew deep in his soul that he wished the baby was his. There was a place in his mind that knew he was being ridiculous, and, if truth be told, he was even a bit ashamed about his strong feelings for Jana, but the heart loves what the heart loves. And, he reasoned, as long as he never shared his thoughts with anyone, he certainly wasn't hurting anybody else.

Watching her maturity and success in recent years, moving about the camp, training recruits and practicing her beloved art of archery, was pure torture. There'd never been anyone else, not for him anyway. Therefore, when women from the camp tried to flaunt their availability over the years, he ignored their blatant attempts at pursuit and went about his way, alone. Believing he would walk this life without a mate to share his faith and love.

He was painfully aware that, for a time, several years ago, there had even been rumors about him being gay. Embarrassing, and false as that might be, it saved him from unwanted advances from the base's single women for a period of time.

As it happened, Jana's presence was such a particular distraction to him, that he intentionally invented reasons over the years to be apart from her. And, he felt that the time he spent removed from temptation, away from her haunting beauty, and away from the nearness of her was a retreat of sorts, from the mental anguish of being so close and yet so far away.

Needless to say, for these reasons and more, he'd never married. The closest he came to having a family of his own, was interacting with his best friend's families. Chuck and Emma were like parents to him, and now that all their fledglings had left the nest, and their children were off fighting in a war a world away, he was spending lots of time with them. They knew more about him than any other humans on earth. For instance, no one but these surrogate parents knew he'd been left on the doorstep of a small Catholic church as a baby.

He'd endured the swats and knuckle raps of the sisters, as he goofed off in class; and many canings by Father O'Conlan, as he goofed off after class; the other children making fun of his 'orphaned' status the whole while; and survived the feelings of hopelessness and helplessness that go along with never fitting in.

He was adopted by an older couple when he was nine years old, and it was abundantly clear to anyone watching that his adoption by the elderly pair had nothing to do with creating a family and was actually more like the legal purchase of a slave. Due to their ages, and the fact that they had no biological progeny, Mike was expected to do everything for them, from cooking, to household chores and laundry, and of course the weekly yard work. In the evenings he spent several hours massaging his father's shoulders, and rubbing his mother's feet, (a task he found especially repugnant), before going off to his room exhausted, to try finishing his homework. There was quite literally never any time for himself.

They weren't mean people, just old and needy. They didn't beat him, or starve him, but they didn't love him either.

As he grew, Mike spent a couple years sneaking out of his basement room late in the evenings, on Friday and Saturday nights, doing things his conscience would later cause him to regret. When he was almost twelve, he got a job as a neighborhood paper boy. He was hard working, so his route grew quickly, and as it grew he found himself out delivering newspapers from three thirty in the mornings until it was time to leave for school. His adoptive parents didn't mind him having a job, as long as it didn't interfere with his ability to take care of their personal needs. After all, if he earned his own money they didn't have to spend any of theirs on his clothing, or school supplies, which made their slave labor all the more sweet.

Across the street, from the location where he picked up his papers each day, was a local service station. One day he found his way onto the lot, and discovered that cars which had been left for maintenance were parked on the property with their keys inside. He had a wonderful idea. A crazy, wonderful idea. Going forward, he arrived at the designated newspaper pick up site, made his way across the street, found a car with enough gas to complete his route, and 'borrowed' the vehicle for the early morning hours.

Things went on this way without a hitch for a couple of years. Each morning he would 'borrow' a car, complete his paper route, and put the car back where he found it, with no one the wiser. Or so he thought. One morning when he was almost fourteen years old, he arrived at the lot with his papers, looked for a likely mode of transportation, and loaded his papers onto the passenger seat. He started the car, and sirens exploded all around him, as bright lights hit him directly in the face and loud voices told him to, "Get out of the car and get down on the ground with your hands behind your head". He'd been discovered. It seemed the owners of the service station had been suspicious for quite some time, as there seemed to always be a single car on the premises each day with less gasoline in it than was recorded in the maintenance department arrival log. When the owners finally decided to call the local police, a sting operation was concocted to catch the culprit. The culprit being one Mike Anderson, student, orphan, minor, and fairly expert car thief.

The juvenile court judge was much more lenient than he had the right to be under these or similar circumstances, but Mike would still pay consequences for his actions. Judge Cooper said he saw something in this hard working young man that he believed was redeemable; that he might even possess a grain of something honorable in his character. Maybe he only needed to be taught in the right environment, exposed to examples of righteous behavior. They would give it a try, and the rest would be up to him.

Truthfully, to Mike it was as if someone had removed him from a perpetual jail sentence, to a place of rest. He was remanded over to the custody of the state, and placed in a minimum security detention center for boys. At the center he was given ample time to do his school work, and had far fewer chores to do than he had in his previous situation. For the first time in his life he felt like he had a real chance.

He was especially glad never to be forced to rub another smelly foot, or scrape another bunion!

In his new circumstances he stayed out of trouble, got excellent grades, and eventually benefitted from a program which allowed wards of the state to attend college for free. He was a fortunate young man, or so the counselors at his detention center tried over and over again to tell him. None of those counselors had lived his life, and they didn't know the feelings of abandonment that haunted him. The feelings of worthlessness that stemmed from believing himself totally forsaken. After all, who would leave a tiny, defenseless child on the doorstep of a church, if he was worth anything at all? His very soul was steeped in anger so strong that it threatened to explode and undo him during the right circumstances.

In his daytime hours, Mike was a good student and an excellent example to all those around him, studying music and elementary education, while being involved in several community volunteer programs. A classmate even invited him to attend her church on a particular Sunday coming up, and for some reason most unfamiliar to him, after the negative religious experiences he'd endured in his younger years, he accepted the invitation.

During nighttime hours, however, he habitually turned his less than confident self over to lusts of the flesh. Mike never really squared his emotions with the fact that his mother discarded him like so much garbage. Leaving him to the wills of a feckless world. He felt unloved and un-worthy, and sought comfort for the soul in anything that numbed his senses. He became an alcoholic and pothead. And, as his fleshly needs took over more hours of each painful night, he began to oversleep in the mornings, and found himself on a series of academic warnings he feared he might never come back from.

On one especially poignant evening, he found himself in a local club, drinking as usual. He saw a young woman being mauled and grabbed by a man twice her size, and in a drunken stupor, his anger came to the surface. He tried to be the gallant hero and come to her rescue, but instead was beaten quite soundly and left with a bloody lip and a black eye for his trouble.

The next morning his phone rang, and a cheerful voice said, "Are you almost ready? I'll be there to pick you up for church in fifteen minutes."

"I think I've changed my mind. I'm not really feeling up to church this morning."

"Nonsense! I'll be there in fifteen minutes. I'll just honk twice so you know I'm out front. See you soon."

Mike jumped out of bed and showered quickly. Looking in the mirror he felt ashamed of what his anger had wrought. There was nothing he could do about the way his face looked, so he determined within himself that if the people in church looked down on him, he would simply never go back there again.

When his ride arrived, she didn't say a word about his bruises, and off they sped to morning services. He walked in the doors of her church to a completely different type of experience than he was used to in a small Catholic church mass. No one pointed a finger, and no one chastised him for his black eye and swollen lip. He didn't feel looked down upon, or judged. The pastor didn't change his sermon to blast him for fighting, and the music was great. Afterward, his friend offered to pick him up for church again, but, still not completely convinced, and not wanting to obligate himself, he told her he'd call her if he was so inclined.

Next Saturday night, he found himself once again drunk and high, and in another bar fight. This time, in the heat of his anger, he missed the face he was aiming for, hit a wall, and broke his hand in five places. He ending up in a hospital emergency room, with nurses and doctors shaking their heads and warning him about his temper. One of the guys from the dorm came and picked him up, and when he got in the car the young man shook his head and said, "Man, you'd better figure out what you're doing. I don't know how you think you're going to play piano with that hand, and you just might lose your scholarship if you're not careful."

As he lay in bed that night, tossing and turning from the pain of his injury, he heard a deep voice calling his name. He was instantly chilled to the bone and sitting up, he tried to make out a dark figure across the room. The shape stepped away from the far wall, just enough for him to gage the size of the creature's enormous outline. He'd never seen anything like it in his life. The beast was so large that it was noticeably hunched over so as not to hit the ceiling with its huge misshapen head; and its scaly, greenish skin covered biceps three times the size of mike's thighs. Its arms were so long they dragged on the floor and its eyes glowed a malevolent red in the darkness of his dorm room.

Mike sat frozen with fear, as the creature seemed to inch closer by the second to his unprotected soul, but then he noticed a faint light to his right. He turned to see, what he could only assume was, an angel, dressed in the shining, metallic gear of a warrior. Huge wings unfurled to fill the space as he watched the sword wielding protector advance a step. And then, without another word, the beast cowered backward to vanish into the wall. When Mike turned back toward the angel, he was gone. He knew in that instant he was being protected, even though he certainly didn't deserve it, by a loving God. But that if he didn't change the course of his life, he would be going straight to hell. He called the girl who'd picked him up for church the week before, woke her, and asked if she would be willing to do the same in the morning, and come get him for services.

That week he heard a message of Grace and life, so powerful, so unlike anything he'd ever heard before; in a service that changed him somehow; that he asked Jesus into his life. He changed his major and eventually went on to seminary where he studied for the ministry, finally becoming a pastor. And truthfully, he hadn't looked back since.

His life's experiences had been his own secret until he shared them with Chuck and Emma. Of course he didn't tell them about his feelings toward their daughter in law. That was just unnecessary information, which could only cause uncomfortable feelings. He knew that Josh and Jana loved each other more than most people could ever understand, and that they would be, and should be, together until death parted them. Besides, on top of all that he's the one who had married them, and that wedding had been his first so he was sure it would always stick. That knowledge didn't, however, relieve his loneliness, or his longing for the only woman he'd ever cared about.

The whole mountain base longed for news from the front in Israel, but it was difficult to get accurate information. Even in an age of advanced technology, and even with satellite phones abundant among the troops, because functioning towers were necessary for a connection. So, news from home was shared upon the arrival of replacement troops to the holy land, and sent back in the instance of injured soldiers being airlifted to home base for long term medical treatment, or release from duty.

Mike traveled to resistance sister bases as often as he could, and when he went he brought as many supplies as he and his men could transport. Their mountain camp was so much better equipped and provisioned than any of the other encampments. The ability to grow a multitude of crops year round, and the fact that they were so well hidden from enemies, were blessings not entirely shared by their brothers and sisters around the country. Traversing open territory was dangerous, as UN troops made regular sweeps of the areas he had to negotiate in order to connect with each base. The last thing he wanted was to help the enemy uncover any more of his battle weary comrades.

Having already evacuated their extreme northeast encampment, and leaving it for soldiers to pillage after the UN discovered its existence more than a year ago; the combined resistance forces had fought for months to protect their home, but only succeeded in losing valuable troops. Losses of that magnitude seemed ridiculous when assessing the situation. They could never use that location again when its coordinates were on the enemy's radar, so they abandoned the location and moved its remaining residents to the mountain camp. Sadly, the lives lost in the raids perpetuated by the U.N. forces were many. Over two thousand of their comrades and friends had been lost in the cowardly attacks.

The high mountain camp location took in several hundred newcomers, (all that remained of that destroyed camp's population, after months of conflict). His base in the heights was effectively up to capacity now, but that would change quickly as many of the newly trained, and newly come of age left the mountain to fight alongside resistance troops from other parts of the country, and as young recruits left to help with the battle in Israel. Mike knew that decisions he made effected many other people, and if it hadn't been for his great faith in the Lord, he wouldn't have been able to take on the responsibility of those decisions.

Left in charge of U.S. operations when Josh and Jana departed for Israel, Mike's latest trip to examine sister bases in the plains and to the east had been eye opening. Jeff, the base's resident lead mechanic and 'appropriations' officer, had been able to secure a number of abandoned vehicles over the years, from various military dump sites. And, after some expert repairs, a fair amount of duct tape and some TLC he kept them running for the most part, along with their fleet of small aircraft and large troop carriers, which had also been picked up from the same sources. Keeping the vehicles hidden between uses was a challenge, but coming up with gasoline for the vehicles, and fuel for the aircraft, was an even bigger one.

His troops left their mountain with ample supplies for outlying bases, riding in their camouflaged carriers, but they encountered so many destitute, diseased and desperate citizens along the way that they quickly went through the supplies they'd brought with them, and had to travel back to restock. They also encountered many sick and dying, not only of starvation, but of the terrible plague which had swept across the land in these past three years.

Sores, blisters and pustules, burst and running, covered corpses which lay decomposing in the streets. Bodies with necks twice the size they should be, bulging eyes, and purple tongues, due to the slow strangulation of the plague which killed them, filled every ditch, dead vehicle and otherwise empty building. Those bodies were present wherever they traveled: cities, towns, villages, and bumps in the road. Equally hard to stomach, was the fact that where the bodies were most abundant, flies and scavengers of all kinds were thick around the new source of rotting food.

They helped where they could, with provisions, medicine and comfort; some wanted their government chips removed and they obliged, taking those people who were not affected with plague with them on their journey if that was their choice. They shared the Gospel with as many as would listen; but, as was always a sad fact, some refused to hear of the Lord even up until their dying breath. It boggled the mind to imagine the depth of depravity which must exist that wouldn't allow a loving Savior into a situation so dire.

So much death and devastation all around them. Mike had been part of the resistance long enough to know the UNGC was a big problem in this country, and, for that matter, the world at large. But, a bigger problem was the crisis that existed in so many hearts around the globe. And not just hearts who didn't believe in any god at all, but those who followed other, false gods, and religions that would lead them right down a road to total destruction.

• • • • • •

Amir Bahram was an evil man who caused the deaths of many, but he wasn't the only problem. No, humanity couldn't get off that easily. The God of the universe had been trying to give the gift of Grace, FREE Grace, life eternal, to humanity since the death and resurrection of Jesus Christ. So, lack of salvation was a condition entirely and firmly resting on the doorstep of any who would not accept that free gift.

Mike, being a reader of Biblical prophecy, wasn't fooled by the signs and wonders occurring all around the world and around Amir Bahram over these past years, many of which were planned out and performed by Nathan Graham. He knew that neither Bahram, nor Graham were divine in any way. He knew instead that mankind's sovereignty on earth as they all knew it, was close to the end, and that the Lord would come to reign at any moment. That fact didn't frighten him, as he was a true follower of Christ, but he also knew, as a believer, it was incumbent upon him to try to take as many of the lost and lonely, as he could, to the kingdom with him. And, that meant thwarting men like Bahram, and Graham, as often as possible.

The killing of Christians, when they were discovered in any capacity of worship or sharing the Gospel, was still rampant across the country. And, no one could count the numbers of believers who had lost their lives for merely owning a Bible. Mike and his troops encountered many towns and villages where the heads of martyrs, impaled on pikes, were the first thing they witnessed before entering the gates. They had to be careful who they revealed themselves to, as they never knew who was friend and who was foe. Larger cities were a bit safer, as there were usually well established Christian undergrounds to help. But, wherever they went, the signs of the end were everywhere. All they had to do was look around them.

For any who couldn't see the signs of the times, he would fill them in when they would listen. Almost all resistance adherents, at least the ones he'd met, were Christians. And, though there were a few who didn't believe in end time signs, they at least trusted Jesus and would be alright when the time came. But the world was also filled with atheists, and those following other religions, including Islam and the substantially practiced, phony, 'One World' religion. He didn't want to see anyone lost, so he shared the Gospel with no regard to his own safety.

Signs and wonders of coming end times, in the past three years, were obvious to those with knowledge of Biblical truth, and Bahram, though he didn't adhere to the teachings of Christianity, was knowledgeable about the contents of the Bible. He believed in the age old tactic of knowing what your enemy knows, so you can hit him where it hurts. He would gladly have covered up every end time sign going on around the world if it were possible, just to keep his ulterior motives veiled; but those in Josh and Jana's camp were pretty well versed on the subject, so fooling any of them would have been difficult to pull off.

When Bahram unexpectedly broke his manufactured treaty between the Jews and Muslims, a little over three years ago; he was able to lead hordes of enemy soldiers into the city of Jerusalem, without much resistance; due to the fact that the great river Euphrates was now dammed in two places, at the Aswan Dam in Egypt, and the Anatolia Dam in Southeastern Turkey. This had been one of a few remaining Biblical prophesies left to be fulfilled before the end of days.

And because no one expected this newest betrayal from the man who touted himself as savior of the new world order, he was able to amass an army of kings and leaders from most of the Middle East to help in his deception. But, now that he had not succeeded in wiping out the Jewish people on that first attack three years ago, and due to the fact that the scrappy IDF continued to fight against his soldiers with everything they had in order to survive this latest onslaught, he would certainly try again. Perhaps when they were weakened by years of battle.

Now, because of the great dams built on the Euphrates, there were no significant physical obstacles keeping invading armies of the North out of the holy city. This path would become a route of importance during the great battle of Armageddon when that time came.

At about the same time that invading armies flooded into the city, the region began to experience a drought unlike anything ever seen in the area. At last accounting, there had been no rain for over three years. Water was being trucked in for soldiers, and both IDF and resistance forces were forced to conserve wherever possible.

Shortly after that attack on Israel, a volcanic eruption occurred in Turkey. This was an eruption more powerful than any the earth had ever seen. The explosion was so great it sent smoke and fire many miles into the atmosphere, and was followed by a storm of giant hail stones and fire from the sky; that reached for thousands of miles in every direction in the region. Hundreds of thousands were killed. The smoke and dust so thick that they extinguished the light from the sun for over a week, and even the moon was red as blood for many days after that. Residual ash still continued to blanket the region in many areas.

Every continent around the globe was experiencing wild fires to a degree never seen before. And in areas where the world wasn't burning, there were floods and storms destroying everything within their reach. Earthquakes killed hundreds of thousands, tornadoes and hurricanes, along with their following storm surges killed hundreds of thousands more. When waters receded, islands and shorelines were littered with the bloody and beaten bodies of those who simply hadn't escaped in time. It was becoming more dangerous by the day, for Mike and his men to take help and relief to their military counterparts and the suffering people of the country.

Then, shortly after the battle began in Jerusalem, the two prophets appeared on the streets of the holy city and began to speak words of warning to the world. Resistance leaders weren't fooled by the UNGC's lies, trying to convince the earth's inhabitants they were merely crazy men who needed to be controlled. Further proof came when UN forces tried to arrest the two men, and they were destroyed by the prophets who shot fire from their mouths and burned up any and all who got in their way.

Bahram did try to cover up that incident, but, due to his vanity, in the form of big screen televisions that he'd installed in every major city of the world, and the tenacity of certain rebel news outlets around the globe; who refused to be silenced; attempting to get information out there in spite of government overreach, the encounter was visible to millions upon millions of witnesses. Those two men had been wandering the streets of Jerusalem, speaking words of prophecy since that time, and now and then when Mike was in one of the cities that depended on him for supplies, he would catch a glimpse of the prophets on a life sized television screen. Evidencing to him again, that end times were nearer than most people realized.

• • • • •

Back home again, after his latest supply mission, Mike was summoned to the quarters of Chuck and Emma. Emma's health had been failing for some time, and though he was aware of her worsening condition he was still surprised when he walked into their chambers. The stark difference between the strong little woman of action, and this ghost of his friend was something hard for anyone who knew her to witness. She'd always been a stalwart saint, forever taking care of others. And since Mike was very close to these special friends, he was especially shocked to see how much of a drastic decline there'd been in her physical appearance over just these past few weeks.

Chuck sat next to his wife's side and held her hand. The look on his face was one of pure anguish. This sweet woman was his life. He couldn't imagine living in a world without her. They'd been through so many of life's ups and downs together, that he didn't know if he could navigate existence alone. She opened her eyes when Mike walked in. He didn't want to cry, but his eyes welled up with tears anyway.

"Hey there Mother. How are you doing?"

"Hi Pastor Mike. I've been better. I'm glad you made it back in time to say good bye."

"Don't be silly, Emma, you're going to outlive us all. You should just rest now."

"Now, you're the one being silly, Mike. I called you here for a reason. I want you to promise me that you will look out for Chuck when I'm gone. And, as for rest, I'll be getting plenty of that soon enough. I have a feeling we will all be seeing each other very shortly at any rate, what with the way things are going out there in the world. I'm so glad everyone in our family has trusted Jesus with their hearts.

It makes it much easier to go on ahead, knowing that I will see you all again. Chuck was just telling me last night that we would all be together soon. He had a dream, and in the dream we were in a place that could only be described as paradise."

"Well, as to your request. Of course I will keep an eye on Chuck. He's just like a dad to me, just as you are like a mother. I don't want you to leave, but if you have to go on ahead, I know where you will be and I'll see you again. I love you Emma. You are one of the best people I've ever known, and you have always treated me like one of your own."

"Thank you, Mike. You have also treated me with kindness and respect. It has been nice to have you around when our own son is gone. I do love you as one of my own, and I know that we will see each other again very soon. I'm very tired now. I think I'll try to take a nap."

"Good night, Mom. I'll see you soon."

As Mike left he saw Chuck crawl onto the bed with his wife, and wrap her in his arms. As he got to the hall outside Emma's room he wiped his eyes and took a deep breath.

"Doc, maybe you'd better go in to check on Emma now. She didn't appear to be doing very well, but Chuck is with her."

Mike stood for a moment more, wiping tears from his eyes that didn't seem to want to stop, before venturing outside.

"Hey, Mike, you'd better come quick."

"What's going on Doc?" Only a moment had passed since his exchange with the older couple.

"I don't know what to say. When I came in the room I found them like this." Mike looked in and saw the couple wrapped tightly in each other's arms, both wearing radiant smiles. Doc had already checked them, and they were quite dead.

"I can't believe it. I was just talking to them. But, I have to say, you know that story Josh used to tell everyone about how his folks met? In the story he makes a point. Chuck made a promise, and it looks like he wanted to be sure he kept it. He was just making sure she got safely home."

"I wish we could get word to Josh, but it will have to wait till the next wave of troops goes out. I have paper work to fill out, but I need to head out for a walk first. These two have been such a huge part of my life for so long. I just can't believe it."

"A huge part of all our lives, Doc. This is going to be a shock to everyone. All we can do is try to honor their lives by continuing on in the work that has been so important to them. They wanted to be sure everyone heard about the Lord, and I for one will see that happens as far as I am able. I was headed out this afternoon for another supply run to our sister bases, but I can wait if you think it would help."

"No, Mike, I'm sure the council will agree. We can't have a service until Josh and Jana return. I will get word out to all the elders and we'll schedule a meeting."

"Just let me know what you figure out. You know, with the way things have been going on in the world, and the more I think about it, I just can't be too sad about the loss of Chuck and Emma from this time and place. They deserve a rest, and I really believe we will all be together much sooner than many people realize."

"I agree. Be safe out there, and let us know if you need anything."

"I will. God bless you Doc."

"God bless you too my friend."

"The first angel blew his trumpet, and there followed hail and fire, mixed with blood, and these were thrown upon the earth. And a third of the earth was burned up, and a third of the trees were burned up, and all the green grass was burned up."

"The second angel blew his trumpet, and something like a great mountain, burning with fire, was thrown into the sea,"

Revelation 8:7-8a

"And it shall come to pass afterward, that I will pour out my spirit upon all flesh; and your sons and your daughters shall prophesy, your old men shall dream dreams, your young men shall see visions:"

Joel 2:28

CHAPTER 5

Fresh in country, and at their new duty stations, Alec and Elizabeth went about getting ready for battle. They'd hoped to be assigned to Josh's platoon, and still held out hope that they could work their way to the front lines, but Josh didn't like newbie's out front in a skirmish, even if he knew them to be excellent warriors. War was hell, and the shock of it could dull the senses. It was a good way to get young people, and everyone around them, killed quickly.

Josh, Jana and Becca would go about setting up their nighttime ambush, against the enemy soldiers on the temple mount, as soon as the sun set that evening. Scott and Mark would be using their men to divert the attention of the enemy with all the forward fire they could muster. It was a good plan, and he was sure they would succeed with God's help. He was remembering a time when his wife used a similar method of attack, on the mountain plateau militia camp, against Colonel Cage. God gave her the wisdom to follow the battle plan He'd given to Gideon. She used lots of noise to fool her enemy into thinking she was accompanied by a large army, when in fact she was the only attacker.

He was proud of the fact that his wife had learned to tune her ear to the voice of the Lord in such a practical way. She'd come so far from the angry young woman he'd met so long ago. The young woman who refused to accompany him to church, or hear of saving Grace.

Josh knew they, as a generation, were in the last days. He wondered if he would ever see his parents again, before they were all taken home. He was aware of the natural disasters that were taking place, not just here in Israel where they were currently located, but all over the world; famine, disease, plagues of unimaginable horror, earthquakes, floods, wildfires, storms and every other form of destruction; but was also very much aware that his own people, people of the Lord, didn't seem to be struck by the sickness and disease that worried the land. Oh, he wasn't deluded into thinking that they couldn't be killed by an enemy bullet, a sharp sword, or the effects of a storm, but he knew the scriptures well enough to know that the angels who were sent out to bring God's wrath on the earth in the last days, were directed to touch only those who did not have the seal of God in their foreheads. He and his people were sealed by their trust in Christ the Savior, and would not fall into the hands of that enemy by any of those means.

As the trio readied to leave the foxhole on their imminent mission, the night sky was suddenly filled with flashes of light; Jana looked up and stopped for a few seconds trying to determine what exactly she was seeing. Josh yelled, "Down, get down". The sky, in every direction and as far as the eye could see, was filled with meteorites streaming toward the earth. Fireballs were everywhere and began hitting the ground all around them like giant mortar rounds. Josh grabbed Jana, and Scott grabbed Becca.

As general, in charge of all international resistance troops, he yelled orders back to his lieutenants to get the rest of the soldiers down into the bomb shelters in the center of the city, while those troops who were up front with him followed their general. There were many such shelters around the city center, left over from previous wars, which could be most handy in moments like this. But, while they'd been in the holy land they'd not had occasion to use them.

In the midst of chaos he knew at least that Alec and Elizabeth, CJ, and Angel would all be safe and out of the way, but now he had to get those nearest to him out of harm's way too. Mark grabbed his weapons and followed the two couples and the other soldiers who'd occupied the front line trenches, out of their foxholes, and through heavy fire to the edge of the temple mount.

With flaming rocks falling all around, some of which were bigger than a man's head; and the smell of smoke, burning hair and melting flesh filling the air; they had all they could do to make their way down the steep embankments and hills of the Kidron Valley. Dodging flames all the way, they made their way to the tunnels the girls had discovered only days before, without being decimated by the molten projectiles. Hopefully the passageways would offer sufficient shelter from the fireballs raining down from the sky. What Josh and his team didn't know, in fact couldn't know, was that theirs was not the only location in the world being bombarded by virulent meteorite showers. Countries all over the earth were reporting the strange and dangerous phenomenon, and a single blazing meteor the size of a very large mountain was just reported to have landed directly into the middle of the Pacific ocean.

A meteor of that size would cause surges of ocean water deep enough to cover significant stretches of coastland in America, Canada, South America, Russia, China and Australia. And would virtually wipe out the Philippines,

North and South Korea, Japan, Indonesia, Hawaii and many other small island chains. But there was not a thing anyone could do to prepare the people in those areas for what would be coming soon. All they could do was pray for God's Grace and mercy.

This was an event so catastrophic, as to send the entire world into a tailspin of epic proportions. Bahram; who was currently in the Middle East putting together another contingent to wage war on his enemies in the holy land, which also included the use of nuclear weapons aimed at Israel and the American continent; was not sufficiently inconvenienced by the worldwide tragedy, even with flaming rock devastating every city on earth, to bother sending help of any kind to areas touched by the calamity. After all, he had his own cozy bunker for emergencies such as this. And the ocean surges wouldn't do sufficient damage to the Eastern coast of America, Europe, or Arab the countries where his major properties and holdings were located for him to get involved. So, he hunkered down in his underground playground of luxury to outwait the multiple disasters. The earth reeled from this latest blow.

Safely tucked, now, into tunnels below the city, that had thankfully been discovered while Jana and Becca were out on reconnaissance, the rag tag band of resistance soldiers were free to decide what their next steps might be. A number of critters had taken to the tunnels as a way to protect themselves from the loud noise and burning rocks, and the troops decided that as long as they kept to themselves, it was okay with them. They didn't dare try to come above ground to set charges, until the devastation of the current fire storm was finished, so they decided to rest for now. And, from the looks of things above ground, and the fact that enemy troops had been hit especially hard, the surprise they'd planned for that night might not even be necessary after the wreckage and death being caused by meteorites was finished. Josh wrapped his arms around Jana, and even with the pandemonium of destruction going on above them, they slept a sleep of pure exhaustion secure in each other's arms.

In sleep, Jana stood before the Lord. It had been a long time since she was in his presence, after being badly wounded on the mountain plateau so many years ago, but His voice was like music to her ears. "Hello my child."

"Oh, Lord, I've missed your voice. Is it time for me to come home?"

"Not quite, Jana. You know that no man will know, not even the Son, but only the Father, when that last hour will be; but I can tell you it will be much more quickly than many realize. Prepare yourself, your husband, your son and all your people, for what is to come. I will be coming soon."

Meanwhile, while Josh slumbered, his mother came to him in a dream, and when he woke with tears on his cheeks, he knew his parents were gone. She'd told him she loved him, and that she would see him again one day, but his heart felt as if it was being ripped from his chest. "Josh, are you okay?"

"No, Jana. I just talked to my mom."

"What do you mean you talked to your mom?"

"She came to me, Jana. She and my dad are both gone and she came to me in a dream."

"Oh, my love, I'm so sorry." Jana put her arms around her husband and they cried together for all the loved ones in their lives who had gone on before them. But then she shared her own dream. "While I slept I was in the presence of the Lord."

"What did He say?"

"He told me that I should prepare. That we should all be ready, because He would be coming soon."

"Praise God. Then we will all be going home." And again they rested while the skies rained fire.

• • • • •

Alec and Elizabeth were busy planning their next moves. They didn't intend to stay sheltered for long. The moment the meteors stopped falling they would be out on the field of combat, with or without their superiors. They'd come to do battle, and do battle they would. They intended to find their parents for one thing. They hadn't come this far to stay hidden. The city was devastated, and the enemy scattered. Now was the time to strike, to take back for the people of God what was rightfully theirs.

Inside the shelter they found Elizabeth's Brother C.J. and sister Angel, and the four prayed together and talked about what was going on outside. They'd all seen fellow soldiers shot in battle, but that was nothing compared to seeing someone hit by a ball of fire from the sky. Those hit by the meteors seemed to vaporize into a puff of lit ash when hit by the flaming rocks. Deciding to set out as a group, as soon as the fiery rain stopped, they were filling their packs with water, extra ammo and food stuffs. They would find their loved ones and make a difference for the resistance. So far none of their time in Jerusalem had gone as they'd expected, but that would change if they had anything to do with it.

● ● ● ● ●

Waking again in the tunnels beneath the holy city, Jana could still hear the devastation going on outside, and hoped the kids had gotten to safety before all hell broke loose. She was still a mother after all. She also knew they had very little in the way of supplies, and understood she needed to at least find water as soon as possible. A couple of the soldiers with them in the tunnel were injured, so she did what she could to relieve their pain with aspirin and a little of their limited water supply. She'd seen one soldier hit head on by a large fireball, and he seemed to incinerate instantly upon impact, with nothing left to show for a human life but glowing ashes. She'd witnessed many things in her life, but that image would leave a definite impression on her mind for a long time.

Jana knew the tunnels they were hiding in were usually filled with water during rainy periods, and though precipitation had been non-existent for several years in this region, she had a hunch. She took a long stick and a rock, and began pounding the first with the last. Once she'd sunk the stick into the ground to about three or four feet, she wiggled it back and forth and pulled it from the ground. Suddenly water appeared slowly gurgling to the surface, sufficient to fill all the empty canteens and water bottles.

Those in the tunnels and shelters were not aware of the giant meteor that made its destructive landing in the Pacific, and they hadn't seen, in person, the millions of victims around the world, the sick and diseased, the rich and poor, who'd met their creator at the end of a flaming piece of space rock, but they were very aware that the world as they knew it, was falling apart around them.

• • • • •

Mike had made his way out on his regular weekly supply mission with a group of soldiers, taking food, ammunition, and other necessities to sister bases, when the meteors began to fall. His soldiers ran for cover. They took shelter in the subway system, of the mostly deserted city where they'd found themselves at the time of the emergency. One of the men was hit head on, as they ran, by a meteor the size of a basketball; and Mike was dumbfounded by the way he seemed to vaporize into thin air upon impact.

There was simply nothing left of him but glowing ash, and the hardened war veteran could honestly say he'd never seen anything like it. A shiver ran the length of his spine as he dashed for his life to the only cover he could find. The rest of the guys all made it into the tunnels safely, and they sat stunned and confused as flaming projectiles beat down on the earth, sounding for all the world like thousands of bombs exploding, one after another, directly above them.

Slowly, over these past months and years, on their many trips out to other resistance bases with supplies and comfort; and in their efforts to help the country's citizens wherever they were able; they'd seen the population of the country declining. Natural disasters; diseases like the horrendous plague which continued to sweep around the world; deaths of Christians, executed simply for practicing their faith; starvation; and lack of money spent on infrastructure, or the simplest needs of their people, by the UNGC, had killed millions upon millions of their fellow countrymen and women. And, anywhere where there was still anything resembling a neighborhood of citizens, those groups had been reduced to almost nothing while they were drawn upon as militia recruits for battle by the UNGC. Wherever men and women from the high mountain camp went on their scouting and supply missions they saw want and need so severe they couldn't help but desire to be of service. Now with this latest chaos, millions more would be killed and wounded. Frantic, hurting people would need their help.

After what seemed like hours of mind shattering destruction, bombardment stopped as suddenly as it had started, and Mike's rattled soldiers slowly ascended stairs to the surface. What they witnessed was annihilation and devastation so terrible that their minds couldn't properly process what was left around them. Buildings of steel and concrete pulverized; anything made of wood burning, creating a raging inferno in all directions; and even the streets were destroyed, with heaved up and melted asphalt, and large holes, which in some cases opened into portions of the tunnels of the underground subway system below. The group felt blessed that the burning masses hadn't breached the area of tunnels they'd used for protection. Survivors, many diseased, and others so thin they looked like skeletons walking, wandered the streets with vacant eyes stumbling over debris and mumbling to themselves. Mike's soldiers weren't sure where to begin, but begin they would.

Meteors stopped pounding the earth, as suddenly as they had begun, and Jana's group emerged slowly from the tunnels where they'd been hiding. Pictures of destruction meeting them wherever they looked. They made their way up from the Kidron valley, to the city above, and could hardly believe their eyes. Buildings, ancient and modern alike, were completely devastated, in most cases not one brick upon another. Streets were barely recognizable. Anything made of wood or flammable substances was still ablaze. Those soldiers, friend or foe, who'd been hit head on were gone, simply incinerated; but there were many who'd been wounded by flying debris who laid in the streets and byways. Those cried out for help from anyone passing. Jana and Josh decided they could not help them all, but tried to focus on members of the IDF and those few resistance troops who hadn't made it underground in time.

They bound wounds, and concentrated on getting Israeli soldiers to shelters in the center of the city. "You know we have to get out of here, Josh. Everything is destroyed and our forces are terribly diminished. The Lord wants us to be ready, and I don't think we can do that from here."

"I know, Jana. I'm going to have to try to line up troop transport to get everyone back. And, you're right, there isn't going to be much more we can do here anyway. The city is all but wiped out. I can't see, at this point, how it could be of much value to anyone including Bahram. So far I haven't been able to reach anyone state side."

"We need to check the shelters and find the kids."

"We will, Babe. I'm not going to leave our kids behind."

"Thank you, Josh. I agree. There won't be much else we can do here; and Becca and I are ready to scoot as soon as we find our kids."

"You're welcome, Scott. Now let's see how many of these wounded we can round up and get to safety and then I'll focus on trying to get us a ride back home."

After hours of backbreaking labor, most of the wounded had been moved to places of protection. IDF soldiers had systematically dispatched any enemy who was not already killed by the prior devastation, and helped to get their own wounded underground into bomb shelters where there would be medical help, food and water. There were surprisingly few wounded among the resistance fighters, and they would be able to carry those few to transports when that help arrived. No one knew, at this point, how many of their own soldiers had met their end by the meteors. That would take a role call.

Jana, Josh, Scott, Becca and Mark arrived at the shelter with the last batch of wounded.

"Mom, Dad, I'm so glad you're okay."

"Oh, Alec, thank God you're safe. Is Elizabeth alright?"

"Yes, she's fine. She's around here somewhere helping with the wounded. Is Uncle Scott with you?"

"He sure is, somewhere in this mess, and carrying a wounded soldier no doubt. So is Becca."

"Elizabeth will be relieved. She's been worried sick about her folks."

"Well, they've been worried about her too. We, on the other hand, were not worried, because we knew God would be taking care of you."

"Oh, Mom, I can always count on you and Dad to keep things in perspective. But, what are we going to do now? It looks like the meteors took care of the bulk of enemy presence in the area, so there isn't much for us to do except tend to those who were unlucky enough to get caught out in that storm. I for one am not a doctor, or a nurse, but I'll help where I can. Are we headed home?"

"We're going to have to confer with the commander of the IDF forces for Jerusalem, but it looks like that will be a possibility. For now, let's help with the clean up and getting the injured settled in the shelters."

"It's really weird, but while we were here in the shelter during the meteor shower, we could see the two men; you know, the ones who have been wandering the city's streets warning people about God's wrath for the past three years? They were big as life on the television screen here. The meteors didn't seem to be bothering them at all."

"I believe they wouldn't be bothered by anything like that, Alec. Your dad and I have been talking and we believe the two men might actually be the two witnesses spoken of in the book of Revelation. Their story is too similar to those end time scriptures to not take seriously. They've been doing their job, wandering around trying to get people ready for what was coming. Did anyone take them seriously? Who knows. Only God knows for sure. We can hope and pray that their warnings were heeded. And, if the timing is right, then we really do need to get home as soon as possible. I had a dream while we were in the tunnels during the meteor storm. In my dream I was standing before the Lord, and He told me that we need to get ready.

Your dad is trying to line up troop transports to get us all back to the mountain now."

"Do you really think this might be it, Mom?"

"Well, no one will know the exact time, Alec, but it sure feels like this could be it. Dad had a dream, and Grandma came to him. He said that she told him she loved him, and that she and Grandpa have gone on ahead. She said she'd be seeing him soon. And, if I had to guess that anyone would have God's ear, it would be your Grandma."

"Grandma and Grandpa are gone? We just saw them. My gosh, that's so hard to believe. They gave Elizabeth and I the most perfect wedding. I can't even imagine a world without them."

"A wedding? You're married? We didn't know. I can't believe I missed my only son's wedding. What kind of a mom does that make me? Was it wonderful?"

"You know Grandma. She did everything in her power to make it a great day. Elizabeth looked so beautiful that she took my breath away, and, of course, the food was great."

"Well, of course the food would be great! I can't wait to taste Mom's biscuits again...... Oh, I almost forgot. She isn't there. There won't be any more biscuits. I know that probably sounds like such a small thing to you, but she's been like a mother to me since I met your dad, and anything I know about cooking, I learned from her. Her death will be especially hard on your dad. Oh, who am I kidding? It will be hard on all of us. Getting used to a world without Grandpa and Grandma in it is going to just be downright tough. And, wouldn't you know. Even with all the cooking lessons, I never really did get the hang of making Grandma's biscuits."

"I got pretty good at it." Elizabeth walked up behind the pair, with a huge smile on her face, as they spoke. "But I can help Grandma teach you. I'm sure between the two of us we can....what's wrong?"

"Mom was just telling me that Dad had a dream and that Grandma came to him to say goodbye. They are both gone, Liz. Grandpa and Grandma are both gone."

"I can't believe it. Both gone? How will anything ever seem the same again?" She sat down hard, and tears flowed unbidden down her flushed cheeks. "I didn't know. How could I not know? Wouldn't you think everyone would be able to feel it? Or, at least those of us who loved them? A world without Grampa and Gramma. Oh Lord, I miss them already. Did Alec tell you about our beautiful wedding, Jana? Grandma made it the most wonderful day ever. What will we do without her?" Standing back up, she walked the two steps to her husband and snuggled into his chest. Looking up, she said, "Oh, Alec, are you okay, Babe?" All Jana needed to see was the way her son's wife talked to him and held him to know they'd made the right choice and that they would be happy together for the rest of their lives.

"I'm okay, Liz. It's just hard to believe we won't ever see them again."

"Oh Elizabeth, I'm so sorry I wasn't there for your special day. I would have loved to be there for the two of you."

"We know that, Jana. No one was angry with you. We know it's a big responsibility to save the world. All we want to do now is help."

"Well, Josh is setting up transportation back home for all the troops. It looks like we are at the end of our usefulness here, and there are people back home who will need us. And, by the way, I'm going to tell you the same thing my favorite woman in the world told me a long time ago. None of that Jana stuff for you young lady. My name is Mom to you, understand?"

"Yes Mom."

"I overheard what you were saying, Jana, and it looks like we are going to have to make ourselves useful here for a little while longer. Some of the transport planes were in their hangers, and those are okay for the most part, but the ones that were parked on the tarmac were completely destroyed by meteors, so it's going to take a little while for the guys to come up with sufficient transportation to get us all out of here. I'm sure we can find enough destruction that needs cleaning up to keep us busy, don't you?"

"So, the meteors hit in the states too? I didn't realize."

"Yeah, it seems that most of the world was hit. Much of it is still on fire. Jeff and his men also told me that a meteor the size of a mountain hit the middle of the Pacific, and the ocean surges were so high they took out miles of coastline on any continents that have direct contact with the Pacific. They also wiped out all the island chains and countries. That part of it is still playing out. We'll get more details when we get home. I'm told there are multiple millions dead from the meteors and millions more washed away by the ocean surges."

"I can't even imagine. Being here, we would never have known. I'm sure there are many who can use our help. How long do you think it will be before we can get a ride home?"

"Jeff says it'll be at least a couple days, perhaps longer, before he can accommodate us, so we'll have to make do. But, he's a good man, and I'm sure he'll make it happen as quickly as possible"

"Then we will make do. Okay everyone?"

Scott and Becca walked up behind the group. "Whatever we can do."

"Dad, Mom! I'm so glad you're okay."

"Elizabeth, baby girl, how are you doing?"

"I'm fine, Dad. It's so good to see the two of you. I wanted to be the one to tell you. Alec and I were married before we left home base."

"Oh, darlin', I'm so sorry we missed it. Was it everything you'd hoped for?"

"It was beautiful, Dad. The only thing that was missing was you and Mom, but we knew it had to be that way. Grandma and Grandpa Conyers made the day really special."

"Oh, Scott, I can't believe we missed our baby girl's wedding. I'm so sorry Elizabeth."

"It's okay Mom. The world is blowing up around us and we're standing here talking about who didn't make it to the wedding. It's all fine and we love you, now let's get some work done."

"Yes Ma'am, daughter! Love you too!"

"Does anyone know where C.J. and Angel are?"

"Yeah, Dad, they're around here somewhere helping with the wounded. We'll track them down."

"Good, I want us all on the same page, and in the same transport on the way home. I need to make sure the family is safe. Is that okay with everyone?"

"We will make that happen Scott. Don't worry. We'll all be back home soon."

"Thank you Josh. I Love you brother."

"Love you too, Scott. I'm going to make another call to Jeff and try to get more details about the equipment and the ride home."

· · · · ·

Jeff was a very good man. Josh had really only known him since coming to the high mountain base, but they'd become fast friends. Scott liked him too. He was a man's man. He'd been a Marine mechanic, when the world still allowed people to be part of the regular military services that weren't completely controlled by a rogue government.

He'd served his country for many years. But, shortly before the administration began implementing the use of tracking chips for their citizens, they'd issued a memo. The memo simply stated that the biggest threats to the safety of American citizens were ex military. That memo was one of the last nails in the coffin of gun rights in the country. Shortly after that interesting grand reveal, gun laws changed again to first, registration, and then confiscation. Once Jeff realized he was now living in a world where the only guys who still had guns were the bad guys, he and his wife went in search of the nearest resistance base.

A huge help to the resistance team thus far, he was a mechanic, and a great obtainer of things. He could haggle with the best of them, and seemed to always know the value of an item, no matter how obscure. He was most at home in salvage yards and with a wrench in his hand, or a roll of duct tape. And, he'd single handedly outfitted the base with aircraft, vehicles, and big guns. And, not only did he track these things down, he kept them running and in pretty good shape.

Jeff had wonderful parents, who trained him in the way he should go, so he always loved to worship, and he fit right in with the men on base. Whenever possible, he would sing with the camp worship group. And, though to look at him you might think he was a rough and tumble sort of guy, in reality, he had the voice of an angel and the disposition of a saint. He and Scott liked to compare tattoos, and stories of their less than wise decisions of youth, but both were grateful to God for the places He'd taken them.

• • • • •

Mike and his soldiers began to clean up what they could, to block off sections of the tunnels that had been exposed, and to create a makeshift shelter in the subway system. All of this would be integral to their survival in future events. They needed to be able to help the sick and wounded in whatever way they could, so they did what they knew to do. They served.

He kept some troops with him, but sent runners back to home base to retrieve additional supplies and Doctor Rose. He knew, even with vehicles, it would take a couple of days for their return, so he kept enough food and medical supplies with him to make a difference until then. He reasoned that there was just no way to get all the diseased and injured back to base camp high in the mountains, so they would bring as much comfort down to the plains as they were able. Mike was most alive in situations like this. An opportunity to serve and to share the Gospel, all in the same place, was certainly his idea of paradise.

When those in the area discovered the resistance had set up a clinic in the subway system of this city, they began to come. Slowly at first, and then it was only folks from the immediate area, plus a few stragglers with nowhere else to go. But once the word got out that these soldiers brought food, clean water and medical supplies, citizens who had been forgotten by their government for far too long found their way to the newly constructed, underground help center.

Citizens knew the UNGC certainly didn't care. That had been made clear for years, as cities, infrastructure, and communities disintegrated around the country and the world. Oh, there were a few districts; and those were gated, glittery havens with swarms of armed security guards; where the elite lived. Political types, with their family and friends; and a number of closed off Muslim communities operating under Sharia law, friends and acquaintances of Bahram and his cronies; which had been instituted over the past fifteen years.

These were places that belied the tragic times and drastic situations outside their gates. Places where food and clean water were available in abundance; where medical needs were met; and where there was ample security to keep the residents of these 'special' places safe. Other than those who were set apart as elite, the world suffered. But status, and justly so, had not kept these gated neighborhoods safe from the plagues ravaging the land, and it had certainly not saved a single elite neighborhood, or prominent person, from the flaming meteors that fateful day, so there was much need, even among the rich and famous.

Mike set up a triage station, and went about deciding who would have to wait, if they were able, for the arrival of Doctor Rose. He clearly wasn't a doctor himself. And, though the troops always traveled with two medics, these young men and women were trained only to remove government chips and tend to minor injuries, so many of the wounds they were seeing were way beyond what they were capable of dealing with.

These outstanding soldiers were actually kept quite busy by many who wanted their chips removed. They also helped by setting simple breaks and stitching up cuts and gashes caused by flying debris. However, there were wounds that presented challenges they wouldn't be able to foresee. Even a young woman, a very pregnant young woman, who would need assistance before the Doc could arrive. He was sure of it. She seemed to be in distress, and he didn't know a thing about delivering babies.

After consulting with the medics and others, they came to the conclusion that no one present knew anything about delivering babies by c-section, which appeared to be the direction her situation was headed.

There were also others he knew they wouldn't be able to help, that no one would be able to help. The starving they could feed, but those suffering with plague symptoms, they could only try to make comfortable and to share the Lord with them, if they would listen, until that horrible disease took them.

Mike spent his time washing wounds and perfecting his bandaging skills. As he worked, he shared Jesus, and his face radiated God's love with each word. There were so many who'd thought themselves immune to the larger troubles of the world, before being implanted years ago. They'd been sucked into the liberal, socialist rhetoric that told them it was the government's job to take care of them, and they'd made themselves vulnerable. But through the insanity of this past decade and a half, they saw things differently. Many were ready to hear the life altering message of a Savior willing to die for them, but not all, definitely not all. Even some of the Muslims from the area, who came seeking help, were open to hearing about this Son of God, Jesus; Though others used the open door policy of the clinic to try to kill infidels in any way they could, and they had to be dealt with harshly in order to protect the others in Mike's care.

Several groups of jihadists arrived only days apart, some with guns, others with knives, but killing is killing and weapons can be anything that will take a life. If a group is intent upon murder they can make anything into a weapon. One group was simply infected with the plague and intended on spreading it to as many infidels as possible before they died. So far no UNGC troops had found their location, but Mike assumed it would only be a matter of time before that occurred.

Then, as it happens, Mike started another day tending to those who desperately needed his help, and suddenly a woman stood before him. She was raven haired and olive complexioned, with eyes blue-grey as a soft winter sky. She had a slight spray of freckles sprinkled across her nose and cheeks, and lips the color of rose petals. Tall and slim, she held out her delicate, yet capable looking hand to shake his. She began to speak and he noticed an Italian accent, though her command of the English language was excellent. "Hello there. My name is Bella. The young man across the room told me you were in charge. I've come to help. I am a trained nurse."

"Oh, I, well, uh, my name is Mike. What is your name? Oh, never mind, you already told me your name. I uh, well, you said you're trained? Good, we can use your help I'm sure. Just let me, or I'll tell you what, let's go figure this out. I'm sure there is plenty we can figure out for you to do."

Her laugh was like sunshine dancing, and her smile lit up the otherwise dim space. "Good, Mike, just tell me where you want me to start." Mike, still blushing and flustered, got up from his stool.

"Well, I've already started triage, and there are quite a few whose injuries are too significant for me to deal with until Doc Rose arrives, perhaps you could start there, Bella? There may be some you can help who are beyond my meager ability."

"Very well, Mike. If you could show me where the supplies are located, and where I can wash up, I'll begin."

"Can I ask where you came from, and how you got here? Do you have a government chip? I don't know anything about you."

"Well, I'm originally from Rome, but that city has been a wasteland for some time now, and frankly, mostly a Muslim stronghold, at least since Bahram started killing Christians years ago. No, I don't have a chip. I worked at a hospital in the city for some time. They were willing to overlook my little secret, just to get an additional pair of hands, since everyone is so short of medical help these days. But I've been on the run since the government's chips became mandatory internationally.

I've recently been staying at one of the bases in the Northeast. They were giving me sanctuary from the UNGC. But the camp was discovered by government forces a while back. Those of us who weren't killed have scattered. I heard through friends that some of our comrades had been relocated to a high mountain encampment before the meteors fell, so my intention was to search for that site and see if I could be of some help there. Instead, I heard that you'd started a clinic for the sick and wounded, and thought I should stop by to see what assistance I could offer. I took cover during the meteor shower, and decided my help might be even more important now."

"Well, that explains a lot. And, I'm very happy to have your help, Bella. You are actually quite a Godsend. I'm sorry I sounded like a mumbling fool before, we aren't used to having such a beautiful…I mean capable, helping hand. Let me show you where everything is, and where to wash up. I would be happy to assist you, rather than the other way around. I'm sure you're much more experienced than I could ever dream of being without your kind of training and expertise."

Mike showed Bella around, and though he couldn't provide much in the way of supplies, she said it was more than she was used to in these troubled times, and thought it just might be enough to make a difference.

"Okay, Mike, while we work you can return the favor and tell me a little about yourself."

"There's not much to tell, Bella. I've been part of the resistance since practically the beginning. I used to host meetings in my church, preparing people for all the events to come, from our government going on a rampage, and I concentrated on getting many to safety, on secret bases that were already set up around the country."

"So, you're a priest?"

"No, well yes, in a way. I'm a protestant pastor, which is similar to a priest, but without the Catholic undertones. And I managed to become a minister much to the surprise of anyone who knew me as a kid."

"Oh, I see. So you were a naughty boy?"

"Something like that."

"Is your wife here, or does she stay in the base when you're gone?"

"I'm not married."

"Oh, is your religion similar to that of the priest? Are you not allowed to take a wife?"

"No, I'm allowed. It's just never happened."

"So, you've never been in love? You don't seem like the kind of man who is without sufficient passion to love."

"Well, there was someone once, a long time ago, but it didn't work out. I've just never found anyone else who made me feel the same way. Look at me talking about my personal feelings with someone I just met. We should get to work now that you're washed up."

"Certainly. Point me in the direction of your most wounded patients, and we will see what we can do."

"Okay, but I have one question for you. Are you married? I mean, is there someone special in your life?"

"No Pastor Mike, there is no one. But who knows what may come?"

Mike lit up inside at her answer. For just a moment he felt guilty at the reaction he felt, and then he realized that Bella was the first woman, besides Jana, who had ever caused him to feel anything at all. And, there was something nice about that. For the rest of the day he shadowed Bella, and learned many things about caring for wounded in the process. He also noticed, from the forced close proximity, that even in the midst of filth and turmoil her hair smelled wonderful, like a meadow of flowers in the sunshine.

Bella was remarkable. Her knowledge was vast, and she was used to doing much, with very little in the way of supplies, so she could fashion just about anything out of whatever available materials were on hand. Much to his amazement she could even perform some simple surgical procedures, such as: setting a badly broken bone, removing shrapnel, performing a tracheotomy, and then even a c-section. And he knew that there was little doubt she saved many lives that day, which would have been forfeit waiting for the arrival of Doc. He could hear their newest arrival crying in the background as they cleaned up and prepared to wind down for the day.

The city continued to burn down above ground, but in their tiled and reinforced portion of subway tunnel, the portion where they'd chosen to set up shop, they seemed safe and sound. Well, safe and sound as long as the UNGC forces weren't out and about. And, he was pretty sure they must be snuggled up back in their base camps, due to the worldwide panic caused by the recent meteor shower.

The underground tunnels were currently filled to the rafters with pallets and patients. White tiled walls gave off a dull reflective light in every direction, and concrete covered by grey linoleum flooring made for uncomfortable standing. But, here they were at least somewhat safe from whatever might decide to fall from the sky, so they were grateful. Every twenty feet, or so, there were small grates in the floor. Linked, of course, to whatever sort of sewer system their host city offered. This made it possible to clean up bloody messes. They were also blessed that the underground's water supply was sheltered inside giant stainless steel containers within the subway walls, and with such large reservoirs, would keep them supplied for quite some time going forward.

For the sake of keeping everyone calm and safe they separated their patients. They put patients without hope of improvement in different areas of the underground than those who had even a meager chance of survival. Those who suffered from this damnable plague would at least have a roof over their heads now, and a kind, gentle hand, in their last moments on earth, but, this way, their frequently tumultuous and absolutely imminent deaths wouldn't unduly frighten others who might recover. And, Mike made it a point to talk to each and every one who came to them about the Savior. Some were desperate to hear and listened intently, many even trusting Jesus as Lord before they passed into eternity. Some, however, even in those last dark moments of a painful death, still refused to acknowledge the King, and Mike cried for the loss of everyone who would not listen.

For some, they wondered how a loving God could allow the things which were transpiring. Many wanted to know why God hated them, and if perhaps these miserable days were a kind of punishment for them. And, even when he tried to explain the concept of choice, and a fallen world, they turned away and refused to take hold of the Grace of

God which was so eloquently offered in the death and life of Christ.

Bella watched as the man she'd just met reached out to the hurting and broken. He touched her heart as no other ever had. He was handsome and strong. She noted his square jaw, powerful frame and intense blue eyes. In her memory, not things commonly associated with the look, or life, of a man of God. At least not any priests she'd known. But this man was also a man who worked with his hands and could take care of himself. She felt drawn to his compassionate nature, and when he looked up from the latest patient he'd finished praying with, she knew there was absolutely something about him that she could love.

Mike saw something in Bella's eyes, when she looked at him, that made him smile, and he didn't remember ever feeling so happy about anything else in his life. Even in the dark, torch lit subway tunnels of a burning city, with death and destruction all around him, he was content. With the world falling in around them, there was no time to be coy. That night they shared a meal of fresh water, flat bread and canned beans; and if asked, they both would have said it was the best meal they'd ever eaten, due to the company shared. Afterward they sat by a burning barrel near the tunnel entrance, for warmth, and talked late into the evening. At some point they dozed off, and when Mike woke in the night he realized Bella had fallen asleep leaning against his chest. He was loath to wake her, so he shifted position a bit and lightly stroked her jet black hair as he watched her sleep. She was the most beautiful woman he'd ever seen, and he thanked God for bringing her into his life.

• • • • •

Bahram and Graham were in shock, when they emerged from their individual safe bunkers, after the meteor shower that destroyed everything around them was finished. Neither of them had been worried about the millions killed by plague and starvation, and they didn't care about all those destroyed by fires, earthquakes, storms, ocean surges and flooding, but the flaming rocks had hit home and couldn't be denied. Bahram was especially disturbed seeing pictures of the two prophets still walking the streets of Jerusalem even through the hail of meteors. He knew his next step had to be getting rid of those two idiots. Their every move was recorded and broadcast on the big screens he himself had ordered installed in every city, town, village and byway in the world. He'd assumed his triumphs would be recorded for posterity on those screens. Instead his failures were being flaunted for all to see.

His latest communications with the head Imam in Iran told him the nuclear weapons that were being prepared for him were almost ready. His plan, in conjunction with the leaders of the Twelver movement around the world, was to wipe Israel, the little Satan, and America, the big Satan, off the face of the earth. Once this was accomplished, and those damnable fools, the Conyers, were destroyed along with the two madmen walking the streets of a burning Jerusalem, he would be free to complete his plans to usher in the arrival of the twelfth Imam. He practically burst with excitement at the thought of being right hand man to the ruler of the universe. Once his plans were realized, he could finally rid himself of that useless idiot, Graham. In his mind, the man who'd served as UNGC puppet in the 'New World' churches had long since served his purpose, and his make believe religion saved Bahram lots of time over the years as they actively worked to rid the world of the infection of Christianity, but he believed he had things pretty much under control now. He rubbed his hands together with glee.

When he'd emerged, earlier, from his personal bunker, to assess the damage to his home city, he was shocked at the total devastation around him. This angered him even more, and somehow he blamed Josh and Jana Conyers for the loss. They'd taken Cage from him and now this. He would figure out a way to pay them back for all the loss he'd experienced in his life. For now, he would destroy Jerusalem while they were there protecting everything he hated; and he would hit them where it would hurt the most, in the heart of the country they loved. He waited for word that everything was ready for launch.

Meanwhile, the troops preparing to deploy nuclear missiles at targets in Israel and America at the direction of Amir, had some cleaning up to do. Meteors and fire destroyed most of their cities as well, and though they worked as fast as the devastation would allow, it would still take a couple of days to make ready for a successful launch of the atomic weapons.

• • • • •

Jana worked together with Elizabeth and Angel to prepare enough food for their troops, the IDF and all the wounded in the shelter, where they eagerly awaited word.

Thankfully, supplies arrived and had been unloaded into the bomb shelters before fire fell from the sky, so they weren't hungry or thirsty, but the sheer volume of food necessary to feed so many made Jana glad this wasn't her normal place in the larger scheme of things. She'd never been very domestic, and that was a fact. Elizabeth was busy making large batches of Emma's famous biscuits, and the aroma filling the place was familiar and comforting. She really would have to get together with her new daughter in law, to learn the fine art of biscuit making.

The guys were doing the heavy lifting, carrying wounded back and forth for treatments and surgeries; trying to make a difference to the sick and diseased; moving supplies to make room for more pallets; and building barricades outside, in case UNGC troops, or Muslim hordes, decided that now might be a good time for a raid.

Josh watched as his son worked. He would be leaving the world in capable hands if he left this place; and that prospect seemed more likely, and frankly, more appealing, every day. He was very proud of the young man Alec had become, and thanked God for his new daughter in law. Last night he'd watched the gentle way they touched one another while they talked, and he knew theirs was a strong, loving bond. He also knew they would be a couple who allowed the Lord into the middle of their marriage, and that they would be richly blessed for it.

Comparing his own marriage to Jana, with that of his children, he understood the strength which was contained in the bonds he shared with his wife, even though it had taken a number of years into their own union to get to this point of godly agreement. The kids, on the other hand, were starting off strong. So he was confident their union would be ironclad to the end. That was a comfort and a blessing to a dad who'd not always managed to be there for his son. He knew that for the most part he could give the credit for his son's great outcome to the Lord, and to his marvelous parents. He would miss them, and wasn't sure how the base back home would manage without any input from that godly pair. He was sure they were dancing together in heaven.

One of his men came running to tell him there was a call. He followed the soldier to the makeshift radio room and soon had a smile on his face from the excellent news. "Hey, Jana, I just heard from Jeff. They should be able to start sending transports tomorrow. Now, they couldn't come up with the number we needed to get everyone out in one trip, so the operation will be divided into two pickups. I've already told him I want all the wounded and our younger men to go first. I'll wait for the second group of transports. I want you and the kids to be on the first convoy."

"No, I will not leave without you. We came together and we will leave together. I am not going to argue about this."

"Alright, but I want the kids to leave in the first group."

"You'll likely get an argument there as well. If you remember, Scott and all the kids made a point of telling us they want the whole family together upon evacuation."

"What are we talking about? I heard my name."

"I just heard from Jeff, Scott. And, I told Jana that I wanted the kids to be on the first set transport planes. I'm sure you will agree with me."

"Actually, Josh, I don't. If you remember, we all decided that the family would stay together. That's how I vote. If you are staying until the second round, which I'm sure is how this argument started, then we will all stay and we will leave as one. We can help load the wounded for both trips."

"Fine, I swear, I'm surrounded by stubborn people."

"Well, it takes stubborn to know stubborn, so we're even."

"You know, I could pull rank on you, and order you to go, Scott."

"You might be able to pull rank on Scott, husband, but that won't work on me. We are all going together, and that is the end of discussion on the matter."

"I think you might have inherited a little more from my mom than we initially realized. Suddenly you are very bossy Jana."

"Well, I still can't make biscuits, so I'll take bossy any day."

The kids arrived in the middle of their conversation.

"That's okay, Mom. I can make the biscuits. I'm sure Alec will agree, we should all stay together. We've lost too many to split up now. God is good and He will watch out for us."

"Yes, I absolutely agree with my lovely wife."

"Thank you, Alec."

"And, thank you for that reminder, Elizabeth."

"You're welcome, Dad. I came to tell you that lunch is ready. I made soup and biscuits."

"That sounds great, and I'm starved."

"You, starved? I'm shocked."

"Very funny, Josh. I burn a lot of calories. Don't make fun of me."

"I'm not making fun, Scott. Just noting that no matter how much some things change, there are always things that stay the same. And, you're right Elizabeth. God is good all the time."

They served the wounded first, taking time to feed those who couldn't manage on their own. Turkey and vegetables in a rich broth with lots of carrots and potatoes, and Emma's famous biscuits, which should probably be renamed Elizabeth's biscuits now. She seemed to be in her element, this amazing young lady. And Jana noticed that her young daughter in law possessed all the traits that she herself had always longed for. Not only was she fierce in battle, like Jana herself, but she was congenial, quick to smile, and most unlike herself, domestically inclined. No wonder her son had fallen so completely in love with this enchanting woman. If God allowed, she had no doubt that Elizabeth would be a wonderful mother too. Jana was sure of it. But, she had to wonder if there would ever be a time when she might be a grandmother, or if their time on this earth would be too short for that.

Let no one deceive you in any way. For that day will not come, unless the rebellion comes first, and the man of lawlessness is revealed, the son of destruction, who opposes and exalts himself against every so-called god or object of worship, so that he takes his seat in the temple of God, proclaiming himself to be God.

2 Thessalonians 2:3-4

"Then I looked, and I heard an eagle crying with a loud voice as it flew directly overhead, "Woe, woe, woe to those who dwell on the earth, at the blasts of the other trumpets that the three angels are about to blow!"

Revelation 8:13

"But concerning that day or that hour, no one knows, not even the angels in heaven, nor the Son, but only the Father. Be on guard, keep awake. For you do not know when the time will come."

Mark 13:32-33

CHAPTER 6

"General Kakos, Sir, I have word from the Jerusalem front. The Christian rebels will be leaving Jerusalem soon. The two prophets are still walking the streets, and there is evidence that some there may actually be listening to their warnings."

"Quickly, help me get my reports together, I'll have to give account to Satan, and I am not looking forward to this. You'd think that meteors from heaven would cause more people to turn their backs on God, instead of bringing them closer to him, wouldn't you?"

"I would think so, General, but then I never did understand humans and their needs."

"Well, run along then. I need to report to the boss. We'll see what his orders are, and we'll go from there. Be ready to assemble more troops. Perhaps we can be done with this nasty human business once and for all."

Scurrying to the very depths of hell, where he knew he would find the old dragon, he saw him in the distance; torturing the already tortured dead, simply for the pleasure of it; and cleared his throat.

"Your eminence, I have news."

"What is it Kakos. Spit it out, can't you see I'm busy?"

"Your darkness, we have discovered that the Christian rebels will be leaving Jerusalem to head back home. The prophets are still walking the streets in the holy city, and Bahram has been doing nothing but hiding out from the latest storms."

"That's it! We need to get in there to influence Bahram's mind again, to get him to take this more seriously and take care of those ridiculous prophets! That has to be done as soon as possible, so have your men get on it. A few specially selected whispers in his ears, should do it, I would think. And, why hasn't he gotten rid of Josh and Jana Conyers? He's had that directive literally for years!"

"Yes Sir, your Royal Highness. I'm not trying to defend him, but I do believe he has tried to take them out many times. Just like General Cage did before him. That is, before the man betrayed us, and became a Christian. They are a pretty slippery couple after all."

"Don't remind me. I want this done, Kakos, get on it and bring me results that I want to hear, or you will have hell to pay! Put all of our resources on it. I know that God is planning some enormous events very soon, bigger even than all that has transpired before. I can already see things taking shape, and we need to touch as many souls for the kingdom of darkness as possible, before the end comes! I don't care what His Book says. I will not be defeated again!"

• • • • •

Home base, high in the heights, was a mad rush of activity. Their soldiers would be returning from Israel soon. Jeff and his flight commanders were on their way to retrieve those mighty fighting men and women from the fray in Jerusalem. They had managed to scrounge and repair enough ancient, military troop carriers to bring everyone home in two very crowded trips. As usual they would fly low to make themselves invisible to UNGC radar, and hopefully return without Bahram and his henchmen being any the wiser.

All residents of the mountain base had been safe and sound during the recent meteor shower, as their home seemed to be impenetrable by the flaming rock which decimated all other terrains; but, the planes were a different story. Those were stored at an old abandoned base in a nearby desert area on the other side of the mountain, and expertly camouflaged from view. But, safe from view and safe from flaming meteors were obviously two different things.

The airbase was usually very safe, as the People's Militia group who'd once made their home there had been disbanded and combined with another militia group in the city. This all happened at approximately the same time Cage's base on the mountain's plateau was dismantled about seventeen, or eighteen, years ago. Now that the UNG Council had no more use for the facility, they didn't have reason to visit there anymore. It became a perfect rally point for transporting those coming and going from the heights, when there weren't constraints on the length of travel time. The hardened desert floor made an excellent runway, and seemed to fit their needs for the limited times they were in need of international flight. The facility even boasted a couple of old hangers in which to secretly store some of the larger troop carriers. The planes which had escaped the meteors had been stored in those old hangers.

The mountain plateau, which had served as Cage's home base all those years ago, had been revamped by the resistance, and was sometimes used as an alternate runway, when quicker access to the base was necessary, and thankfully it had not been as badly demolished by the meteors as their desert location, so they would have a reliable place to land and take off for this mission.

The old desert base was a great storage space, and left no specific evidence to trace back to the mountain camp, were it to be discovered. However, it was obviously more vulnerable to proceedings of a natural disaster variety, as exampled by recent events. After all, who could have predicted the meteor storm that would destroy every aircraft not inside a reinforced hanger?

Jeff had to do some creative borrowing, and lots of imaginative repair work to make this rescue mission happen. He could only hope that the planes would stay together, with a hope, a prayer and lots of duct tape, long enough to get all their troops back home in one piece.

Even with all the various natural disasters going on around them, and the depletion of their own supplies due to help they offered other bases and citizens at large, there was still a sense of joy in the air. They would put on a party of epic proportions when their troops returned. Preparations began immediately for a huge community meal, and a worship service to honor God and those men and women who'd sacrificed so much. Of course there would also be sadness. Those at home who'd lost loved ones in Jerusalem still didn't know of those losses. Josh and Jana would handle those discussions when the time came. And, as hard as that particular task was, they wouldn't have handed it over to anyone else. Their relationships, with the troops they commanded, were very important to them; and they shared in the grief of losing the fine souls who'd been taken while fighting for God's people.

· · · · ·

Little did Josh or any of his troops know at the time, but Bahram was busily setting up further acts of aggression along with his enemy cohorts. Muslim rulers in what used to be Iran, and Russia, prepared special bases for his use. The nuclear message they were preparing to launch would destroy much of Israel, and a great deal of America. The fallout would be much more far reaching than that.

By launching two missiles at the American continent, one from the Northeastern tip of the Asian continent, which would decimate much of what was left of the Pacific coast and inland, and then into the midlands with radioactive clouds; and one from a new site on the West coast of the African continent, which would obliterate most of North America's East coast, they would paralyze huge portions of the country. Radioactive contamination, drifting into water and food supplies, would insert further carnage and death into the equation.

One might wonder why Amir was so set on the destruction of Israel and America. He was, after all, head of the United Nations Global Council, in effect, the ruler of the world. So why then would he want to destroy parts of the world he ruled? Well, the simple answer was revenge and power. Israel had never recognized his rule through the council, and he'd been taught his whole life, as part of his religious heritage, to recognize Jews as nothing but filthy pigs and dogs. His plan had always included the destruction of every Jew on the planet, and he would settle for nothing less. But, America was a little more complicated.

No matter how hard he tried to crush it, and much to his continued frustration, the Christian faith still flourished. He still didn't have a clue where Josh Conyers, his annoying wife, and all of their followers, made their residence. Most locations of the resistance bases in that country were still a mystery to him. It was as if they were covered by some sort of magical cloaking device that his troops were unable to uncover. He knew he had to do something drastic to stop those who practiced this illegal religion, to halt its fungus like growth, and his plan was to blow up most of the country and begin again. He already had many of his Muslim brothers set up in positions of power in elite cities around the country and the world; but the masses, those peasants whose lives meant nothing to him, were grumbling and revolting almost nonstop now. They seemed to complain incessantly about food, clean water, and medical care, blah, blah, blah; and he was tired of their continual whining.

Amir was most grateful that the multitudes of natural disasters, which had taken place over the past few years, eliminated much of the problem he would have been forced to deal with on his own. Wild fires, storms and storm surges, earthquakes, floods, plagues, hurricanes, tornados, and even meteors, had already eradicated billions of souls, which would make his own work easier. And, yes, many Muslims had died in these disasters as well, but it was well known among Twelvers that numerous faithful would have to make sacrifices in order to restore peace and order to the earth through the coming of the Mahdi. He couldn't wait for the joyous days to come, when the Twelfth Imam would emerge from the intricate folds of time and claim the universe as his own. For now he, a willing servant, would prepare the path.

Mike and Bella worked nonstop to take care of a steady stream of sick and injured who came down the stairs into their underground clinic. Some they were able to save, and some they weren't, but everyone who entered heard a story of hope through the Gospel of Jesus Christ. And, many were added to the Kingdom through the efforts of one man who couldn't sit by and watch a single soul go to hell if he had the power to make a difference. Of course they had no way of knowing that Josh, Jana, and the troops were on their way back. Nor could they know that a madman half a world away was set to push buttons which would destroy much of the known world.

In the evenings the two cleaned up, ate a simple meal together, and talked into the night. Mike had never felt so alive. He knew he was falling in love with this smart, strong, beautiful woman, and nothing had ever felt so right. Bella looked her whole life for someone exactly like Mike, godly, strong, intelligent, and filled with purpose. The fact that he was handsome on top of it all was just an additional blessing. She knew she'd found her soul mate, and that they would spend the rest of their lives together. She only waited for him to overcome his shyness enough to recognize this fact himself and tell her how he felt.

Runners came first thing in the morning to let Mike know that his supplies and the good doctor would be arriving by the next morning. This was a relief to everyone. Now they could stay in the area longer and minister to those in greatest need. Word had really gotten out about the makeshift clinic in the city's vacant subway tunnels. Because of that, many people found their way down to the fortified byways, and that would be a very important factor in upcoming events.

• • • • •

The ride home was bumpy and frightening, as a fleet of enormous, ancient, creaking and clanking troop carriers, badly dented, twisted, literally held together by duct tape and a prayer, and desperately in need of paint, flew barely above the ocean waves. This action was performed specifically to avoid discovery by UNGC radar and other detection devices. A trip that would have taken roughly fourteen hours in the safer years of commercial travel, was taking them easily twenty two hours or more. Jeff and his crew were working non-stop to get everyone home safely, and the last Jana had seen him, he looked beat.

They'd been warned ahead of time that the first trip back to the homeland, carrying group number one, which consisted of all the wounded and most of the younger troops, had been filled with glitches. And that upon arrival stateside, while the first group made their way to the hidden mountain base, more rolls of duct tape had been applied to rips and tears in the body of the aircraft, in order to keep the planes flying. This was said with tongue in cheek, but just barely. The crew and passengers wore pale faces covered in expressions of abject fear, and outdated life vests that they prayed they wouldn't need. Jana swore that if she'd hung out the cargo door, just a little, she could have touched the high waves which were lapping at the underside of the plane.

A distinct stench of vomit permeated the space, signaling that the bumpy ride had effected some more than others. Though, with the cargo door open, the smell of the sea helped wash away some of the offensive smell. Jana looked at Josh and a small smile curved her lips. "Are you scared?"

"If I said no I'd be lying, but God has His hand in this too, so I believe we're going to be okay."

"Good, thank you for reminding me. Look at the kids. They're all so involved in conversation that they don't even notice we're only a few feet above a choppy sea filled with shark fins."

"Okay, Jana, if you keep talking like that you are really going to scare me. You know I hate sharks."

"Alright, alright, Mr. shark wienie. How long do you think it will be before we make landfall?"

"I don't think you're a big fan of sharks either, are you? There aren't too many people who are big shark fans. Oh, never mind. I believe we're about an hour out, but I was just going to go talk to Jeff and get a better idea. You want to come, or would you rather stand here looking for sharks?"

Jana smiled at his lame fear of sharks defense. Of course there weren't many shark fans out there, but Josh didn't like to be a weakling in any area. So, on the subject of sharks, she just had to tease him now and then. "Sure, I'd love to come with you. I've never been in the cockpit of one of these old gals." As she walked behind him, she popped him on the bottom, and he turned to her with a smile. She was only kidding about the whole shark thing, and he knew it. He grabbed her, lifted her in the air and planted a big kiss on her neck, as he turned around and set her down in front of the cockpit door.

"Well, she is old, that's for sure. I won't tell you how much duct tape Jeff told me they had to use to get everything at least semi flight worthy."

"Duct tape? Flight worthy? I guess I'll just pray that we don't get rained on. I wouldn't want our magic plane repair tape to come loose."

Jana walked into the cockpit, closely followed by her husband.

"Hey, Jeff, how's it going buddy?"

"Well, we're still holding together. I've got all my fingers and my toes crossed, if that tells you anything. We should at least have enough fuel to make landfall, so that's a positive."

"Have we heard anything from the ground crew? Did the first group get on their way to home base yet?"

"They left the mountain plateau runway hours ago, but they've got a ways to go to get home. We landed without incident, or discovery, so they should be able to get all the way to the base without detection."

"Good, good, and we will be right behind them. It will be great to get home. Even though it's never going to be the same without Mom and Dad there."

"I'm sorry about your folks, Sir. It hit a lot of people pretty hard. The elders decided to wait for a memorial service until we got all you warriors home."

"I appreciate that, Jeff. Yep, we're really going to miss them."

"You okay, Josh?"

"Yeah, Jana, I will be."

"I love you."

"I love you too, Babe."

As their lead transport slowly approached the continent, and land became visible on the horizon, the slowly darkening sky suddenly lit up with an ominous blast of light in front of them. The light formed into a giant mushroom cloud backlit by a setting sun, and continued to grow, directly to the left of their forward position. It was so vast it filled the sky for miles and still continued to expand.

"What was that? Oh my gosh, Josh, what was that?"

"I'm not sure Jana. But if I were to guess, I'd say some idiot just did the unthinkable."

"What do you want me to do, Sir?"

"Just continue on course, Jeff. That blast was far enough east from our mountain landing site that we should be okay. Everyone east of the cloud is in for a terrible surprise though, because those who weren't close enough to be obliterated, will be effected by the explosion's fallout. I can't believe this. I don't know exactly how close to our sister base in the plains that explosion occurred, but we need to get in communication with them, if we can, as soon as possible. Maybe there will be something we can do to help."

"Oh, Josh, do you think our base is okay?"

"I'm sure it is, Jana. Our base is located west of where that explosion took place, and the jet stream will naturally take the fallout more south and east. Besides, we are so high up that there isn't much that can get to us in the heights. We live in sort of a natural bomb shelter, so all the people at home will be fine. Even the troops who just landed on the mountain, but aren't checked into base yet, should be fine. It's the folks out there on the plains that I'm concerned about. We're going to have to send our volunteers with supplies and try to help as many as we can, but if this was a nuclear weapon, as I suspect it is, we'll have to check radiation safety levels before we can do anything, or our troops will be exposed to lethal doses." Little did Josh and Jana know that the east coast had also been devastated by a nuclear blast that took out New York and much of the nearby coast line.

"Who do you think did this, Josh?"

"If I had to guess, I'd say Bahram. He's remained pretty tight with the old leaders of Iran and Russia, even if it was only for his own benefit. And, let's face it, they've been threatening to wipe America, and Israel off the face of the map for a long time."

"Oh no, do you think Israel has been hit?"

"I can't be sure, but it wouldn't surprise me. We can try to contact the IDF after we land. My gosh, what have these maniacs done? We need to pray Babe. Jeff, just get us home buddy."

"Yes Sir. You might want to go tell the rest of our passengers what to be prepared for."

"You're right, Jeff. I'm headed that way now."

• • • • •

Bahram was beside himself with joy. Two direct hits to America. One on the western portion of the country which decimated urban areas with large populations, and would leave a path of radioactive poisons trailing across half the country or more. Land and water would be contaminated for multiple millions of people, and would cause death and destruction well beyond damage the bomb alone had wrought.

Another devastating blast that occurred on the east coast wiped out tens of millions more inhabitants. Cities were laid waste, and those who survived the blast were wandering that wasteland looking for help. Many of those poor souls were being subjected, unaware, to levels of radiation that would continue to make them sick and eventually kill them.

The hit on Israel missed Jerusalem, but managed to destroy the area between Tel Aviv and the West Bank. Amir was sure there would still be plenty of casualties, and he felt he had made an indelible point. He was boss, and the world was his to conquer.

What he didn't count on was the counter attack from Israel. Nuclear missiles aimed at Iran, and Russia, hit their marks and the additional fallout, along with smoke and ash from the resulting explosions and fires, began to circle the globe. Nuclear winter would now begin to claim its share of victims.

As he sat in his bunker, safe from the effects of the devastation he'd caused, but unaware of the retaliation his actions had wrought, he smiled. He'd warned those top Muslim officials who were important to his plans, in plenty of time, so they'd had sufficient occasion to evacuate and find shelter. Only his enemies, and the peasants who meant nothing to him were directly affected. For any who'd thought him unsuccessful before, any who'd ridiculed his ideas, let them speak out. That is, if they were still alive to do so.

• • • • •

Mike and Bella were, thankfully, deep in the bowels of the subway system when the bomb exploded. They felt, rather than heard, the explosion. The power of the detonation, though it was many miles away from their location, pressed the atmosphere around the explosion in such a way that the air was pushed into and then sucked out of the subway tunnels for a frightening moment. The resulting effect was like weightlessness, and though it only lasted a few seconds it felt endless. The remaining space felt heavier than usual for several seconds after that. Mike thanked God that whatever exploded had not been a direct hit on their location. He hesitated to explore outside the protection of the tunnels until things were a bit more stable, but he also needed to know what to expect if he would be tasked with aiding those who would come seeking help.

When Mike emerged from the protection of the passageways he took in a sharp breath, and expelled a long whistle. Though they'd not been hit directly, the detonation had exploded out from ground zero for many miles and miles. He saw trees and buildings leveled, all pointing in one direction, away from the blast; this phenomenon was caused by wind surge related to the atomic discharge. Fires from downed power lines and gas leaks burned out of control. Further off in the distance, he could see additional smoke rising; giving evidence of cities, and suburban areas on fire all around the extended area. What had happened? Had someone finally done the unimaginable? It seemed that whatever managed to survive the meteors a few days ago, was now being destroyed by the after effects of this apparent nuclear bomb explosion.

They had no way of knowing how many would be coming for help. Thankfully they'd been fully supplied before the blast, and now that Doc was here too, they would be better able to serve those who were in need of medical aid.

Mike, Bella and Doc prayed together and prepared for the influx of new patients.

•••••

Planes made their way upward from the coast and landed on the mountain's plateau, north and west of ground zero. But, from their vantage point they could see the smoke and flames from cities on fire in the Plaines and valleys below. East of the blast site was totally devastated and would become even worse with radioactive fallout. Assuredly, water would be contaminated, and anyone drinking it would condemn themselves to a slow and painful death. There would be many who needed help. Jana felt almost guilty that they would go home to crystal clear, safe water and protection from damage the rest of the world was experiencing.

Jana and Josh were not aware that Mike and Doc were out there in the thick of it, and wouldn't know until they got home. They did know, though, that they would have to tread lightly during their future rescue missions; if this explosion was indeed caused by a nuclear device; or surely risk radiation poisoning. And they were pretty certain this was the case. The group began their trek home, wondering the whole time how badly their sister bases might be effected by the horrible tragedy. Making their way quickly in the direction of the only thing that still made sense to them in the physical world, they marched home.

• • • • •

Bahram was livid, he'd gotten word that Josh's rebels left Jerusalem before the bomb fell, so they were safely removed from the area before they could be effected by the blast or the aftermath. His sworn enemy, and that equally annoying wife of his, continued to stay one step ahead of any plans Amir could devise. He was so angry he pulled out a revolver and shot the messenger between the eyes, and then ordered his second to clear the body away.

Sitting in his enormous, brown, leather chair; face distorted with hate, and a sulking, petulant expression; he watched as men dragged the limp corpse away, leaving a trail of blood on his polished wood floors. The smell of blood mixed with urine and expended gun powder filled the room, and he took a deep breath of the familiar scent to steady his nerves. Soon, two young women in burkas scurried into the room with a pail of warm soapy water and terrycloth washrags. He watched them, mind mostly detached, as they smeared the blood into lighter and lighter circles, with the red stained cloths. Would he ever be able to make good on his promise to take out the resistance forces and all those who oppose him? If it took every bit of his strength, he would fight them till his last breath.

• • • • •

Mike woke again to Bella sleeping gently against his chest. He'd begun to grow quite used to the time they spent together and he was grateful to God for bringing this beautiful spirit into his life. If these were indeed to be his last days on earth, he could leave this place a happy man. She was everything to him. Her love for the Lord, strength in times of greatest stress, lovely disposition, and gracious nature were refreshing. She was well versed in medical procedures, and a great help to Doc; but mostly, the look on her face when they spoke about any topic under the sun, the look that said she was listening, no matter what, radiated a love for him that he'd never experienced before, and touched his heart in a way that lifted his spirits in any situation.

As he watched, Bella's face suddenly contorted in pain. She gasped for air, and tensed up as if she was trying to escape some evil entity, then she cried out. Mike cradled her in his arms and stroked her face until she opened eyes that were filled with tears of fear. When she saw that Mike was looking down at her with sincere concern, she suddenly felt embarrassed, almost as if he had caught her in a lie.

His eyes glowed with a love that made her feel warm inside, and she calmed down. Mike looked at her with a questioning gaze, and she smiled at him. "It's alright. I'm fine." She was happy to be alive, even in the circumstances that surrounded them, and she didn't want to talk about it, not now, maybe never. She heard someone moaning in the tunnel to her right, so she patted Mike's chest and reluctantly rose from the comfort of his embrace. Smoothing her shirt, and retying the ponytail which kept her thick black hair from her face, she rushed off to do her best to comfort a patient.

Mike was constantly amazed at her compassion and fortitude. She never seemed to be in a foul mood, even in situations that seemed to beg for foul moods. And, now there was this question. What had she witnessed that came back to haunt her dreams? Seconds later she returned.

"Mike, the gentleman I just spoke with told me you tried to share Jesus with him yesterday, and he shouted at you to go away. He's changed his mind and would like to talk to you. You should hurry, I don't think he has much time left. This damnable plague. There's just nothing I can do for him."

"It's okay, Bella. Only Jesus can help him now, and I thank God he's reaching out. Point the way."

"Here, follow me. There are so many, it would probably take you an hour to find him."

They reached a man who was covered with rancid sores, and clearly suffering with a neck so large, they had to wonder that he could still breathe at all. Mike took hold of the man's hand. It was already cold.

"Hello there. I'm Pastor Mike. Bella told me you were asking for me?"

In a small, strained voice, throat so huge it was strangling him slowly, "Yes, thank you for coming. I was so cruel to you yesterday that I didn't know if you'd come. I've made so many mistakes in my life. I'm not even sure if your Jesus will want anything to do with me. But, I'm hoping you will still tell me about him anyway." The man took small gulps of air after every few words, and was obviously struggling.

"We've all made our share of mistakes. But, God chooses to love us, even though we're not perfect. What's your name?"

"My name's Bob. I'm here alone. The plague took my wife, and my three kids. My parents were killed in the wildfires out west, and my brother died in the flooding down south, after the last hurricane. I know I'm dying, but I guess I just didn't want to die alone."

"I'm so sorry for all your loss. The world has certainly become a much different place in our lifetimes, hasn't it?"

"Yes it has, Mike. And most of us haven't liked it very much. I wondered if there was a way to get the chip out of my hand before I die? I'd like to know that I'm a free man in this world before it happens."

"Yes, we can take care of that right now, Bella?"

"Yes, Mike, let me just go get my instruments. I'll be right back."

"Can you tell me a little more about Jesus? My wife was always trying to get me to go to church with her, but she and the kids went to that ridiculous new 'One World' farce. I've had lots of questions, and even though I've never been much for religion, I knew I didn't want to start there."

"You were wise to stay away from that organization. It would have led you down a path to destruction. Jesus is the only path to salvation. He died and rose again to make us free. All we have to do is to believe on Him."

"So, what do I have to do now? I know I don't have very much time left."

"As far as what you must do? All you have to do is believe that Jesus is the Son of God, and acknowledge that He came to free you from your sin. Invite Him into your heart and He will walk beside you for eternity."

"Will you help me? I don't know what to say."

"Well, let me ask you this. Do you believe that Jesus is the Son of God?"

"Yes, I do believe."

"Do you know that you are a sinner, and that He came to save you from that sin?"

"Yes, Pastor Mike. I have been a terrible sinner in my life. And I do believe that Jesus has the power to save me from my sin."

"Then, ask Him to come into your heart."

"Oh Jesus, please come into my heart and save me from my wickedness. I want to live with you forever."

"And now, brother, Jesus lives in you. Nothing can ever separate you, not even death. When you leave this place, you will be with Him in heaven."

"Let me ask you this Pastor Mike. Where are my wife and kids? Are they in hell? I can't stand the thought of my kids in hell."

"Bob, I can't exactly say what might have become of your children. I know that in extreme circumstances Jesus visits people even on the verge of death, and makes Himself known to them. We serve a God of compassion. He is a God of love, because He is love. He is especially compassionate in the case of children. So, perhaps your loved ones are all waiting for you right this moment. We will pray that this is the case."

As Bella removed the chip from Bob's hand, Mike prayed with him. Moments later he took his last painful breath on this earth and walked through the door to eternity with Christ. Several other patients had died quietly during the night, and Mike sat with Bella, holding her hand, as they prayed for all those who had passed on. Then, he rose, helped Bella up, and went out to gather the day's work group for body removal and disposal.

Above, ground fires still burned, and the earth and everything in it was covered with a substantial layer of ash. It was almost dark as night, though he knew it to be only mid-morning, as evidenced by the bright circle of light from the sun, barely visible through thick clouds of smoke and ash. The men made quick work of throwing a dozen corpses into a ditch they'd been using as a mass grave, in order to return quickly to their underground space. As fresh bodies landed in the pit, rats and cockroaches; by the thousands; scurried out of the way, until they could once again return to their gruesome feast.

Mike knew their situation wasn't ideal, and that the subway system didn't offer one hundred percent protection from the poisons of radiation, which were settling over everything around and to the east of ground zero, but it was certainly more protection than they would have remaining outside.

As the day progressed new patients arrived, some who'd been protected during the blast were suffering from symptoms of the plague, or injuries from the meteor showers days ago. For plague victims, all they could offer was kindness and the Word of God. For those injured, there was medical help. But now, a new type of normal graced the steps of the underground. Those who came seeking help from the bomb blast were different.

For those exposed to the nuclear explosion, but who were not close enough to be instantly incinerated by the detonation, injuries were extensive. Skin burned so badly and so deeply in some cases, that it literally slid off of bones in large chunks , or fell off in layers. There were those who'd looked up from afar, when they heard and felt the blast, who were completely blinded by their curiosity. In many cases another loved one led them to the widely acclaimed resistance clinic for help, though they would find out on arrival there was nothing that could be done. Instances of clothing being burned off its owner; or in other cases, clothing being melted in to the patient's skin, until it was now essentially part of the skin. Open sores and hair falling out in handfuls, and teeth coming out of bleeding gums, were some of the most common consequences of the radiation poisoning that would all too soon take their lives. Many of the resulting wounds were simply those that, unless you had ever been present after a nuclear explosion, you would not have believed. And, if you'd never witnessed them, it was very difficult to know how to treat them.

Doctor Rose, and Bella, had their hands full, and then some. Mike was trying to help and fill in wherever he could, and he'd finally resorted to recruiting volunteers, from the lesser injured among their patients, to complete minor tasks.

What they couldn't see at this point were the additional masses of people who would be slowly poisoned by eating and drinking contaminated food and water. Soon, the ranks of injured and dying would swell to unimaginable levels in their little underground clinic.

● ● ● ● ●

Returning home was bittersweet. Josh thought everything looked pretty much the same as when he'd left, but knew it could never quite feel the same again. Not without his folks. Jana watched Josh's face closely, and stepped in when things looked to be too intense for him to process in his newly found grief. "Hey, let's head down to the kitchen! I'm hungry and I know you must be starved. I'll bet we can find a little something to hold us over until supper."

"Oh, I don't know, Jana. the kitchen is one of the places that reminds me most of Mom."

"I know, Babe. She wouldn't want you to forget her. She would want you to go on, until you see her again. You can't avoid every place where there might be a memory of them, because, in this place that will be everywhere. What do you say we try to make biscuits? I would say that would be a fitting tribute to Mom, wouldn't you?"

"Yeah, I guess you're right. Mom and Dad were always tough, and they wouldn't want me to crumble under the pressure. I think that's a great idea. Let's go make biscuits!"

It took several tries, and some serious direction from Elizabeth, but results of the fourth batch of biscuits were not bad. Josh and Jana were proud of themselves. With a little more work they might get pretty good at this. They sat down with big mugs of ice cold milk, crocks of hand churned butter and bowls of freshly harvested honey. And with tears clouding their eyes, they raised a glass to Emma, who would always be a bright light in each of their lives. In their mind's eye they could see Dad sitting at the table, waiting, with a cup of coffee and a big smile, for Mom's world famous biscuits. A formal memorial service was being planned for the next evening, in which both Chuck and Emma would be venerated, but for now, this small tribute celebrated with those who loved them most, was enough.

When they'd arrived home, they discovered that Mike and a troop of soldiers were out there somewhere in all the mess. It wasn't safe to follow, or to attempt a rescue mission so close to a nuclear incident. All they could do for now is pray and hope for the best. Once the radiation levels went down to safe levels, they would venture out to see what could be done.

Alec and Elizabeth, who'd not been sure they would ever see home again when they left this place, were walking through the apple orchard. It was the first place they'd ever shared a stolen kiss. They didn't know what the future might hold, but from the looks of it the world was slowly devouring itself. They weren't afraid to die. They knew they would be with Jesus in the end. But they were young, and had so many dreams for this life that hadn't been realized yet. They'd truly felt they were supposed to be warriors for Christ and the Kingdom, and now they were confused.

They didn't dare to hope they could ever be parents. Not with all that had transpired in the past few years. No one wanted to bring children into a mess like this. And no one wanted to have the responsibility of children in times like these. Tomorrow they would pay tribute to Grampa and Gramma Conyers, two of the best people that the world, and God's love, ever produced. They'd been mentors, leaders, a soft place to fall and a godly example to all those who knew them. They would be missed. But, tonight they would take some time for themselves, as man and wife, and savor the simple things.

Scott and Becca were relieved to be home with their kids. Everyone healthy and intact. They couldn't believe their good fortune, that all was well, especially when comparing themselves to Mark who'd lost his son and whose daughter had been left so broken. Tomorrow they would all come together to mourn and pay tribute to Chuck and Emma, who'd been such an integral part of their lives for so long; but tonight, tonight was just for their little family.

Mark sat outside his quarters. A concert of crickets and frogs singing in the background. His daughter was sitting beside him with her small, delicate hand in his larger one. They'd missed each other, but didn't have a clue as to what to talk about. He was ashamed that his first instinct, after her injury, had been to hand her off to Emma and run away to battle. He'd been terribly confused after her brother was killed and she was wounded. He was still confused. He knew that he should have been there for her, but he'd passed that chore along to someone better at mentoring the lost.

She was devastated over the loss of Emma, who'd been her counselor, teacher, and friend since she'd come home from battle nothing more than a broken doll. He would have traded places with her in an instant, if given the choice. But, no one had given him that choice. Instead, he was expected to man up. But, this was his baby girl. He'd already lost Tina, so long ago, then his son, and now, he feared, he was nothing more to his daughter than a distant remembrance, so he sat with tears trailing down his cheeks and falling into his lap, drip, drip, drip, as he prayed silently for an end to all the hurting.

He'd wanted to be a better man than his own dad. The man who walked out of his life when he was only four years old, leaving his mom to pick up the pieces and go on. She'd told him many times over the years, "Don't worry son, it's you and me now. And, we will always be here for each other." She'd been there for him until he graduated from high school, with all the ups and downs that go along with raising a boy, and that was all well and good. But, when she was diagnosed with breast cancer, he discovered that he was not nearly so good a friend to her as she'd been to him, and instinctively ran away into anything that would consume his time and attention.

Friends and relatives chastised him, and shamed him into doing the right thing. Now it was his turn to be there for her. He watched as the chemo treatments took her hair, and then reduced her once ample frame to skin and bones.

Her eyes became hollow and her skin yellow, and he found himself resenting her so much he could hardly stand being in the same room. How dare she get sick and subject him to all of this. And then, soon after, how dare she leave him.

He found himself being the same kind of husband to Tina, as he was a son to his mom. As long as she was keen to do for him, he was a willing participant. But, if she needed something in return, he shut himself off. She was patient with him. One day he finally acquiesced, and accompanied her to church, where he discovered a Father, in God, he'd never known existed. This was a Father who wouldn't, couldn't, disappoint. From that day forward their shared love grew around Christ, and flourished. Once they had children, he was frightened, but knew that with the help of the Lord, and Tina, he could be the kind of dad his children needed. When God allowed his beloved wife to be snatched from his grasp, he was angry and bitter. He'd learned to adjust, but it was impossible for him to be the kind of cheerleader for God that Josh was.

Part of his faith was restored when he arrived at the high mountain sanctuary, to find that his sister in law had managed to get his kids to safety. Nothing could ever replace Tina, but having his children back was a step in the right direction.

Mark knew his faith wasn't as strong as Josh's, Mike's, or even Scott's, but God had been working on him. Then, when his son was killed in battle, and his daughter returned to him a broken mess, he was angry and bitter again. He'd been told that God only allows things to come into our lives that we can handle, but he didn't feel that he was 'handling' this very well. Now that Emma was gone, he would have to be here for his daughter, and he really wanted to be the dad she needed. He wanted to be a better dad, than he'd been a husband, or son.

"The Word of the Lord came to me: And you, O son of man, thus says the Lord God to the land of Israel: An end! The end has come upon the four corners of the land. Now the end is upon you, and I will send My anger upon you; I will judge you according to your ways, and I will punish you for all your abominations. And My eye will not spare you, nor will I have pity, but I will punish you for your ways, while your abominations are in your midst. Then you will know that I am the Lord."

Ezekiel 7:1-4

"Finally, be strong in the Lord and in the strength of His might. Put on the whole armor of God, that you may be able to stand against the schemes of the devil. For we do not wrestle against flesh and blood, but against the rulers, against the authorities, against the cosmic powers over this present darkness, against the spiritual forces of evil in the heavenly places."

Ephesians 6:10-12

"Hear this, O house of Jacob, who are called by the name of Israel, and who came from the waters of Judah, who swear by the Name of the Lord and confess the God of Israel, but not in truth or right. For they call themselves after the holy city, and stay themselves on the God of Israel; the Lord of hosts is His Name."

Isaiah 48 1-2

CHAPTER 7

Reports from Israel were disturbing. As the Jews suffered devastation beyond anything they'd endured in their previous eons of history, they were also coming to Christ in numbers never seen before. Bahram was inconsolable. Nothing could have prepared him for this kind of revolting news.

• • • • •

"Kakos, come here, immediately!"

"Yes your magnificence. What can I do for you Sir?"

"I'm hearing reports that the Israelites are turning to Jesus by the hundreds of thousands! Is this true?"

"Well, yes Satan, but if you'll let me explain."

"There is no explanation, no excuse, for this. What is going on with Bahram, and that sidekick of his, Graham? What has he done with the two prophets in Jerusalem? Are the Christian rebels contained yet? I need results. Evidently your minions aren't doing their jobs. I need you to know, them to know, that I can make their God forsaken existences even more painful and hideous than anything they've experienced before. Right now, the earth is mine. I will not lose that advantage to heaven. Not after the humiliation they've already put me through. Do you understand me? If I have to go upstairs and take care of this myself you will not like the outcome. They don't call me the dragon for nothing."

"Yes Sir, We will put more pressure on Bahram, to take care of his obligations. I promise, Sir, you will have your results soon."

"I want reports, daily reports, do you hear me?"

"Yes Sir, I will see to it Sir."

Satan's head demon knew he didn't have a handle on what was going on. He could only pretend for so long. Since the beginning of time, just the mere suggestion of sinfulness or a slight nudge in that direction, whispered into the ear of a human by one of his many minions, could send the victim of that suggestion to a dark place, eager to do the evil bidding of the underworld. That is, unless they had trusted Jesus for salvation. These humans were so much easier to control when they weren't anchored to the Rock. Some of the Christian rebels had begun sharing the sickening love of Jesus so much, that Satan's percentages of new souls added, were falling dramatically in recent years. And, as demonstrated, he wasn't at all happy about that. Kakos knew he had to come up with a plan.

Keres watched Kakos leave Satan's presence shaking his head. "Is everything okay, Kakos?"

"I don't even know where to start, Keres, but no, everything is absolutely not okay."

"Can I help? Just tell me what to do."

"Unless you can figure out a way for me to get control of our numbers on earth again, there probably isn't anything you can do. I'll get it straight, I have to, because if I don't, I doubt you'll see me around much anymore."

"Just let me know if I can help. I'll do anything you need me to do."

"Any ideas you can give me about how to turn the heads of these humans, so that they will once again willingly come to us, would be appreciated. Some of the old tricks, even the really good ones, have stopped working."

"Let me see what I can come up with. I believe we can still deceive them. We just have to be more creative, and appeal to their egos even more than ever before. Especially the young ones. They are so wrapped up in themselves. Everything is always about me, me, me with them. Most humans only listen to what they really want to hear, so all we have to do is tickle their ears, tell them whatever they want, and convince them that if they want it badly enough, it must be okay. I'll work on a few things. Let me get back to you."

• • • • •

The celebration was in full swing. It began with a worship service to give glory to God, and to thank the men and women who'd sacrificed so much. Chuck and Emma were honored with eulogies and songs. They paid their respects to the twenty two soldiers who'd been lost during the missions in Israel, and the thirty four who had sustained injuries there. During the same service the camp honored seventeen who'd recently lost their lives during battles in America, and another twenty three, including Mark's daughter who were wounded in those same conflicts. The whole camp praised the Lord together and sang. Beautiful music echoed throughout the mountain, thoroughly stirring every soul. Most everyone in the congregation left the two hour long service with tears dampening their cheeks, and a gratefulness in their hearts for all the ways in which they'd been blessed.

The food was great. Elizabeth entrenched herself in the kitchen, much to everyone's delight, and seemed to have a gift for baking that rivaled even that of the beloved Emma. All the other women loved her, and gave her free reign, just as they'd always done with her grandmother. Today's menu included chicken and noodles, naturally with homemade egg noodles; mixed vegetables in a light, white cream sauce; fresh fruit salad; lots and lots of Emma's famous biscuits with hand churned butter and fresh honey; three types of pie: apple, cherry, and strawberry rhubarb; plus pitchers of ice cold milk, hot coffee and tea, and freshly squeezed lemonade. People raved about the deliciousness of the food, and Elizabeth was bombarded with compliments.

Jana remembered the reward of compliments she'd received when she'd spent a season learning a certain degree of domesticity from her sweet mother in law; but her first love would always be doing battle against the enemy, side by side with her husband.

"Looks like our boy has married a winner, don't you think?"

"I think she's wonderful, Josh. Alec seems so very happy. Do you ever wish I was more domestic?"

"I wouldn't change who you are for anything in the world, Jana. And, I think you're a pretty good cook too. I don't look like I'm starving to death, do I? Besides, with as many missions as we've been on in the past decade and a half, when would you ever be doing a lot of cooking?"

"I know. I just want to be the best wife to you that I can possibly be, and I think there are probably lots of ways that I've missed it over the years."

"Oh, don't be silly. You are perfect, and you are mine. As I said before, lovely lady, I wouldn't change a thing about you. God brought us together, and I think He did a pretty good job of turning us into exactly who He needed us to be, in order to do His will out there on the battle field."

"I know you're right. But, I sure am happy to see Alec and Elizabeth so filled with joy. We couldn't have ever given them a gift so great. There is a part of me that wishes they were going to get a chance to live a normal life, have babies, and grow old together; but I believe God has other plans."

"I agree. I think the end of this life as we know it will be coming to a conclusion very soon, and that doesn't make me unhappy at all. I can't wait to see what the Lord has in store for us. We should get back to the celebration. Time for thinking about all of that will come soon enough. We will have to put together a contingent to see what we can do for those poor souls who were caught out in the middle of those bomb blasts, and that will present a whole new list of hurdles to overcome."

• • • • •

"Come here wife. I've hardly seen you all evening."

"Oh, I know, Alec. I've been so busy getting everyone fed, I've hardly had time to breathe."

"Well, come with me and I'll give you a little mouth to mouth."

"Very funny, husband. Just let me help with the clean up, and I'll meet you back at our place. You can have me all to yourself then."

"Hey, you did the cooking. You can leave the cleanup to the other ladies, can't you?"

"Okay then, let me go in and say good bye. I'll be right out."

When Elizabeth emerged from the kitchen area, removing her apron, Alec swept her up in his arms and carried her off to their housing unit; all to the amusement of anyone watching. Afterward they lay content in each other's arms. "I wonder what it will be like?"

"What do you mean? What will what be like?"

"When we're taken up to be with the Lord?"

"I don't know, but I'll bet it will be beautiful."

"Do you think it will be soon?"

"From the way my folks talk, it looks like it will probably be very soon. But, I don't have any idea. I'm going to keep fighting, and do everything I know I've been called to do until that time, including being a husband to you gorgeous lady!"

"Good, because I can't think of anything I'd rather be than your wife."

• • • • •

"I love to see them so happy, don't you?"

"Yes I do. We missed so much of her life while she was growing up. I have nothing but gratitude for Chuck and

Emma, stepping in and taking care of her for us when we were gone, but it would have been great to be here ourselves."

"Well, we're all together now, so let's just be happy with that."

"We're not exactly all together. Not when he is picking her up and carrying her off to do who knows what."

"Oh, I get it now, Daddy. You're a little jealous that she isn't your baby girl anymore?"

"She'll always be my baby girl."

"Yes, she will, but she's married now."

"I guess it doesn't feel like she's married, because we didn't get to be part of the wedding. But I know I have to get over it. Alec is a good boy."

"Good man."

"What?"

"Alec is a good man. They are all grown up and married now, remember?"

"Yeah, yeah, I know. I hope she doesn't forget about us, that's all."

"Let's go home. Maybe we can play a board game, until C.J. and Angel go to bed."

"What do you want to do once they go to sleep?"

"We'll think of something."

Right in the middle of a rousing game of Monopoly, there was a knock on the door and suddenly Elizabeth and Alec were making their way into the living room. Elizabeth brought homemade chocolate chip cookies, Angel ran to get milk and glasses to go with the cookies, and then there were hugs all around before someone thought of charades, a game that everyone could play. Scott remembers thinking, maybe his baby girl hadn't forgotten about him after all. And, all was right with the world.

• • • • •

Tina would be proud of her. Eva had grown into a fine young woman. Mark believed she was much more independent than he would have been in similar circumstances. He'd watched her helping in the kitchen tonight, and if he hadn't known she was blind, he wasn't sure he would've believed anyone telling him so. Jr. was gone, and they both had to live with that, but maybe they could make this work. He liked to think so anyway. And, yeah, Tina would be very proud.

There was a soft knock at the door. "Come in."

"Hi, are you two busy?"

"No, Rachel. We were just resting. Eva worked her little bottom off in the kitchen tonight."

"I know. I saw you out there, Eva. You've become quite the culinary expert."

"Emma was a good teacher."

"Yes, she was much better at all of that than I was."

"But, you were always here for us too, Aunt Rachel. I don't know what I would have done without you when we were growing up."

"I'm just glad I could be there for you. I didn't mean to interrupt the two of you. I was just feeling kind of lonely."

"Why don't you two go for a walk? I was going to get ready for bed anyway."

"Are you sure, Eva? You don't want to come along?"

"No, I'm sure, Dad. Get out of here. Boy, a girl has to practically drop a house on your head to get your attention, doesn't she?"

"Oh, I don't know. Do you want to go for a walk, Rachel?"

"Yes, I'd love to."

At this, Mark blushed. He'd always thought of Rachel as a kind of sister, even when she was taking care of the kids. He'd loved Tina so much that when she died, a part of him died too, and the grief all but swallowed him up. But that had been so long ago now. Had Rachel been waiting for him to come out from under his grief all these years? How had he not seen? Well, he'd always been a bit selfish, so it was easy to look past everyone else's pain and concentrate on his own.

They walked, quietly at first. Then, "The party tonight was fun, don't you think?"

"Yes, it was good to see everyone again. It's been too long."

"I agree. It was terribly lonely here while all you soldiers were off in battles around the world. Some of us women met in the kitchen every morning, just to have a little human contact."

"Well, most of us are back now."

"It was good to have Jr. honored tonight."

"Yes."

"I'm sorry, we don't have to talk about it, if it bothers you."

"No, I guess I'm just kind of a selfish jerk. I guess I never stopped to think about the fact that you helped raise the kids from the time they were small. You were even the one who climbed a mountain to keep them safe, and the one who was watching over them every time I went off on a mission, so I know you had to be very close to Jr. I guess I've been so wrapped up in my own misery that I never thought about anyone else's feelings."

"Well, your daughter thought it was about time we started spending some time together as friends, instead of just the 'survived by' of Tina. And, I have to say that I agree with her. You know I loved my sister very much, and I would have done anything in the world for those kiddos, but I've grown to care about you over the years as well."

"And selfish me, I just figured you'd always be around. I suppose you could have had your pick of most of the men in camp."

"Oh, I don't know about that, but just so you know, I pick you."

• • • • •

Fires still burned throughout the city, and in every other city, town, and village from the coast, to the plains, and then again on the other coast. Though, as gas and oil reserves in those stations and storage facilities, were used up they were beginning to wind down in the lesser populated areas.

Victims of the plague, and of multiple natural disasters, added to the fatalities caused by the atomic explosion and its aftermath. Bodies littered roads, streets, sidewalks, and every open space imaginable. Scavenger birds and animals had their fill of rotting flesh. The sky was still thick with smoke and ash, so there was almost no discernible designation between day and night.

All of that said, it simply wasn't safe to be outside. Many who'd escaped the ravages of nuclear bombs, or various other disasters, decided within themselves to take advantage of those who'd suffered even more. Gangs of thugs roamed the streets looking for victims, hell bent on profiting from the tragedy of their fellow man. They were subsequently beating, robbing and killing any that seemed to have more than they.

Tunnels in the subway were filling up daily with more of the wounded and near dead. Mass graves were heaped to overflowing. Another jihadist group had broken in and murdered multiple patients and caregivers alike, not discriminating between Christians, Jews, and Muslims. It seemed they just wanted to go out shooting and didn't care who they took with them. Quite possibly to assure themselves a place in their idea of paradise. Rats, looking for a warmer place to spend the chilly nights, were flooding into the clinic, and had to be herded out, or killed, by volunteers.

So far their supplies were holding out, though many of their guests complained that portions were meager. The underground's walled in water tanks had been filled shortly before the conflagration, so they would still have a pretty good supply of uncontaminated H2O left. Mike and Bella had been called to duty, from a short night's sleep, more times than they could count, and they were getting pretty tired. Forming a tight bond throughout a series of ordeals, Mike didn't know if he could have withstood all that occurred recently without his beautiful Bella. It seemed that as she became more exhausted, she was suffering from more nightmares, and he'd held her as she shivered from the after effects of a dream on many occasions. Still, she claimed she didn't want to talk about it.

After a particularly dreadful day, where somehow Bella still managed to end the evening with a smile on her face, though a fatigued one, they decided to wash up and catch an early night. Mike checked in with the guards he'd posted for the evening, being sure they had water and coffee; as Bella took a last minute walk of the tunnels to check on patients. Doctor Rose was sitting with an especially young plague victim that he didn't expect to make it through the night, the girl was only seven years old. He missed his family, and felt drawn to this little girl who was the same age as one of his granddaughters. "You okay, Doc?"

"I suppose. Though I don't know how anyone can really be okay these days, with all that's going on. I guess I'm missing my family."

"I'm so sorry you got stuck out here with us, Doc. If I'd have known about the bomb, I never would have sent for you."

"Don't worry about it, Mike. There's no way anyone could have known. Besides, as long as I know Cathy, the kids, and my grandkids are all okay, how could I ever want more than that?"

"I suppose you're right. But I still feel bad."

"You know, Chuck and Emma figured we'd all be heading home pretty soon anyway. So, if things continue to pan out the way they have, we will all be together with Jesus quicker than we ever thought. What a reunion that will be, huh?"

"How is your little patient? Did we ever figure out where her parents were?"

"Her folks died on the road. She came in with her sister. We lost her yesterday. But, before she died, she trusted Jesus for salvation, and then this little one followed suit. So, I guess they will all be together soon anyway."

"Well, we can praise God for that. I swear that there is no better feeling in the world than when one of these little ones decides for Christ. If we take nothing away from this but the knowledge of a sure eternity, it will all be worth it."

"Yes Sir. I agree. And when all is said and done, we will all be together in heaven."

"I'm going to go get a little rest, Doc. Call if you need me."

"I will. Have you said anything to her yet?"

"Said anything to who?"

"To Bella. Have you told her how you feel about her yet?"

"Well, kind of, I guess. How did you know?"

"Oh, come on Pastor Mike. Everyone knows. It's as plain as the nose on your face. But time is short. You need to let her know how you feel. I'm sure she's been waiting to hear."

"Okay, okay. I'll say something to her. Though I'm pretty sure she already knows too."

"Goodnight, Mike."

"Goodnight, Doc. Thank you for being here. I know that a lot of lives have been saved, in more ways than one, just because you're with us."

"Thank you Pastor Mike. I'm sure I can say the same about you."

"Praise God, and to Him be the glory."

Mike washed up and made his way to his pallet, checking it for guests of the four legged, and the six legged kind. Then he shook out Bella's blankets as well. As he was making up her bed, she walked up behind him and patted him on the back.

"Thank you, Mike. I can always count on you to take care of me."

"Can you?"

"What?"

"I mean, I don't think I've ever told you how much you mean to me. I don't think I could do this without you."

"Well, I beg to differ, Sir. You were doing it without me before I got here."

"I guess what I'm trying to say is that I've come to care a great deal about you. I love you, Bella. You mean the world to me, and I don't want to ever be without you. I think I've been afraid to say anything, because I didn't know if you felt the same about me."

"Well, Pastor Mike, you'd have to be dimwitted to not see that I feel exactly the same way about you. I've been waiting for you to tell me this for a long time."

"Just call me dimwitted then. You know, I don't know how much time we'll spend in this place, or, for that matter, if we will ever leave, but I don't ever want to be without you here or anywhere else. You are the most beautiful, intelligent, strong, capable, godly woman I've ever known. Would you please do me the honor of being my wife?"

"Yes, Mike, I would be honored to be your wife. I have waited my whole life for a man as caring, and loving as you. You are everything I'd ever hoped for in a husband. But, there is one thing you haven't thought of. You are the pastor, so who would marry us?"

"I'm sure Doc would do the honors."

"Would it be legal?"

"Well, as legal as it can be, I guess. Besides, out here we don't have much choice."

"For now can we get some rest? We can talk about the details tomorrow."

Mike could hardly settle down enough to sleep, though he was dead tired, with so much excitement on his mind. However, Bella dropped off right away. While she slept he lightly traced her features with his finger and stroked her hair. Her face seemed to relax, and when he saw the stress on her face release, he finally drifted off to sleep too.

He was awakened in the middle of the night as Bella cried out in fear and fought to sit up. He held her tight, and when she opened her eyes he said, " It's me, I'm here. Don't be afraid." As her eyes focused, and she realized where she was and who held her, she calmed down. Then Mike said, "Tomorrow we will talk about this, once and for all. I love you, Bella, and I want to share everything with you. The good, the bad, and everything in between, and I need to know what frightens you so."

"Okay, I promise, tomorrow we'll talk. I love you Mike."

"I love you too my beautiful Bella."

• • • • •

"Did you get a chance to talk to Bella last night?"

"Yes, Doc. I finally pulled on my big boy pants and told her how I feel. It seems you were right. She'd been waiting quite some time to see if I felt the same way she did. What do you think about performing a wedding ceremony?"

"I'm good with that, if you can tell me what to say. That's usually in your wheel house."

"We'll figure something out. How's your little patient?"

"We lost her in the night. Though it was kind of a beautiful thing. She was in a coma at the end, but right before she left us, she sat straight up and was wearing a huge smile on her face. She reached out in front of herself, like she was going in for a hug. When she did that she said, "Oh, Jesus", and then she was gone. Somehow it didn't hurt quite as badly as I'd thought it would. Knowing that she's safe in His arms. I guess the older I get, and the more I know about Him, the less objectionable death seems to me."

"I know what you mean. Heaven sounds pretty good these days. I just want to take as many people with me as possible, you know?"

"I do know. But, you'd better run along and get your rounds done. It seems that we have a wedding to plan."

· · · · · ·

Bahram called for his limousine. He'd decided he just couldn't watch one more news feed centered around those infuriating prophets walking the streets of Jerusalem. He determined he was going to take care of this situation once and for all.

When he arrived at the intersection where the two men in sackcloth were last reported to be seen, he got out of his vehicle carrying a military grade rocket launcher. The two men didn't try to run. They would stand their ground warning of God's wrath until the bitter end. Amir shouted for them to stop, but they looked him directly in the eyes and continued to prophesy. Bahram took aim; this was one chore he didn't leave for his lackeys to accomplish; and he pulled the trigger. The blast knocked him back hard. Upon impact with the ground the breath was knocked out of him, and it took several seconds for him to recover. When he stood, with help from his obviously shaken driver, he noticed that the two men were laying face up on the street. He called for a medic. Once it was confirmed that the prophets were dead he nodded his approval and walked toward the car.

Two of his subordinates asked if he wanted the bodies removed to be burned. "No, we aren't going to burn them. We will leave them there, for everyone to see, as a warning to anyone who would stand in the way of the 'New World Order'."

Many millions of viewers watched the exchange on jumbo screens around the globe. No matter what tragedies or natural disasters took place, those satellite powered television screens, though banged up, scratched and dented, still worked, and sent out messages to the world. The message they sent out today was, "Don't heed warnings about God's wrath, worry about the wrath of Amir Bahram instead!"

Sadly, when the bodies of the two witnesses dropped to the ground, most of the earth rejoiced. Those who didn't know Jesus were tired of hearing about God's judgment and wrath. They wallowed in their own sin, and they didn't need to be reminded of it on a daily basis, by a couple of crazy, old men in sackcloth. They'd heard about right and wrong their whole lives, and nothing had made them search out a God of Grace thus far, so why should this sign have made them come to their senses? For the most part, the warnings of the prophets had gone unheeded by a dark and broken world. But a day would come.

"Kakos, I have good news! The prophets have been dealt with! It was classic, beautiful. Bahram walked up to them right out there in the open and blew them away with a rocket launcher. The overwhelming response from the jumbo screen ratings showed that humans, by and large, were in favor of the action. We just might be back on track to get our numbers up!"

"This is just the kind of news I've been waiting for! This will be the first positive report I've taken to the big guy in a long time. Help me pull up the footage, so I have some evidence. I think he's going to be pleased with this news."

"Well, I'm glad you are pleased, Kakos. Perhaps this time we can talk about a promotion?"

"Right now I'm more concerned with keeping my head. Now help me with the footage."

Kakos knocked to get Satan's attention. "What is it Kakos, can't you see I'm busy?"

"Yes Sir, your royal highness, I know that you are always busy with the work of the underworld, but I've come with news that I think you will welcome."

"What news is that, Kakos. None of your news of late has been of particular interest to me. What great message have you brought this time?"

"Your Honor, Bahram has killed the two witnesses. And, it seems that the response from humanity has been overwhelmingly positive about the whole operation."

"You're kidding. I don't believe it. Bahram finally got off of his laurels and did something for the cause? Do you have proof of this?"

"Yes Sir. We've brought a digital recording of the event. Would you like to see it?"

"Of course I'd like to see it."

Satan watched the recording several dozen times, and laughed harder each time it played.

"And you say the humans approved?"

"Yes Sir. Evidently, by and large, most humans aren't big fans of being told they are sinners and that God's judgment and wrath is coming soon. After all, they've been hearing the same message for eons, and they've never heeded it yet."

"Excellent! Now, perhaps things will begin going our way again. We need to get those numbers back up. Has Bahram done anything about those damnable Christian rebel leaders yet?"

"Not yet, Sir, but I'll keep you posted on any progress in that department."

"Keep it up, General Kakos. Perhaps you will give me reason to let you keep your head."

• • • • •

Josh sent out another crew, he'd been checking safety levels since a week after the nuclear blast. And the latest tests showed radiation levels on the plains were still too high to risk men's lives on a possible rescue mission. They only possessed three radiation suits, and those were ancient by industry standards. Not knowing if Mike and his men were still alive was the key. He couldn't allow more lives to be put on the line with no proof of life from the field. Jana hadn't been able to reach anyone from the other three existing bases either, so there was a good possibility, due to the location of the nuclear detonations, that those camps had been wiped out. It was a lonely feeling, not knowing if the friends they'd made in all those camp locations were dead or alive. They could only hope that more people found refuge in places where they would be safe.

Mark announced in an elder's meeting that he and Rachel would be getting married. That was a welcome piece of news in the midst of so much sadness, and it appeared his daughter Eva was completely delighted about the pronouncement. So, now there was a wedding to plan. Jana and the other women of the resistance camp had known for years that Rachel loved Mark. It was frankly very plain to see. And, after all, she had practically raised his children single handedly.

But then, as years marched on, it seemed she'd all but given up on the idea of love or marriage. That is until the death of Jr. and the results of Eva's battle wounds affected her as profoundly as they'd affected Mark, and she could see him slipping further into himself. Even then, it seemed he was never going to get the message, and the possibility of a union between those two had gone to rest in the back of everyone's minds, so the news of their impending marriage was a delightful surprise.

While the entirety of the world burned, their camp in the highest heights seemed to be the only safe place left on planet earth. Rising each day to this glorious community made it hard to imagine the horror that was going on below. Jana and Becca helped Rachel with her plans and they were able to come up with a very nice little ceremony to celebrate the coming together of two of their best friends.

Mike wasn't available to conduct the nuptials, but Josh would fill in. He was nervous because, though his rank gave him authority to perform a wedding, he'd simply never done it before. He was used to leading worship services on Sundays, however, so he thought he might be able to manage.

After commenting that she didn't want to wear a dress designed for someone half her age, Rachel decided on a cream colored long skirt and blouse. She borrowed a heart shaped necklace from one of the ladies in the kitchen; and carried blue forget me not's, mingled with baby's breath, and tied with cream colored ribbon. Her dark auburn hair was tied up on her head in a becoming fashion and interlaced with ribbon and more forget me not's.

Mark wore a blue suit and a simple boutonniere of baby's breath and forget me not's. He was nervous. He hoped he might be a better husband to Rachel than he'd been to Tina. They'd written their own vows. Josh helped Mark with his. And they went like this.

"Rachel, I've always known you were a treasure. I guess I'd just never realized you could be my treasure. After the loss of Tina I sank into a depression that lasted for years and made me pretty unpleasant to be around." At this point there was a loud, "I would say so", from Scott in the congregation. Several people laughed. "I just want you to know that your smile, your positive influence, your patience, and your 'never give up' attitude, are the very things that brought me back to life and caused me to love you. You have been my partner in raising the children, my shoulder to cry on during hard times, and my best friend. And, now I can say that I will be the most blessed man in all the world to have you as my wife. I will do my best to let God lead me, so that you might also have the husband you deserve,"

"Mark, It has been an honor to walk beside you to raise the children, to carry your burdens, and to have you as my best friend. I'm certainly glad you've awakened, because I've loved you for years. I will do my best to be the wife you deserve, and to allow Jesus to be at the center of every decision we make together. You are the man of my dreams, and I can't wait to live with you and grow old with you."

"Mark, do you take Rachel as your lawfully wedded wife; to have and to hold, in sickness and in health, for richer or for poorer, until death parts you?"

"Yes, Josh, I do."

"And Rachel, do you take Mark as your husband; in sickness and in health, for richer or for poorer, to have and to hold, until death parts you?"

"Yes, I do."

Josh read several scriptures, some from the book of Ruth, and the love verses from 1 Corinthians 13. A solo was delivered as the couple lit candles; including Eva in this intimate portion of the ceremony; and the entire congregation had tears in their eyes when Eva told Rachel, "I've waited a long time to be able to call you Mom," before she hugged the woman she'd loved for so long.

What followed caused the entire congregation to erupt in applause. Josh said, "You may kiss the bride. Congregation, may I present Mark and Rachel Randal, man and wife! Now, let us say a prayer before we go in to eat. Dearest Lord, thank you for the wonderful food we are about to eat, for the celebration of life amid all the daily reminders of death that assail us, and for this wonderful couple. We ask you to bless them and walk with them all the days of their lives, as they faithfully serve you."

Elizabeth and the other ladies had outdone themselves. Roasted chicken with cornbread stuffing; light and creamy mashed potatoes, with gravy so smooth it glistened in the candle light; baby peas with tender pearl onions; assorted fruit plates with a delightful cream cheese dip; stacks and stacks of Emma's famous biscuits; and the piece de resistance, a three tiered masterpiece of moist white cake with butter cream frosting, decorated all around with tiny, blue forget me not's.

It was good to be able to celebrate joyous moments with the same friends and family they'd met with so recently to mourn the lost. Somehow it made sense in the larger scheme of things. The circle of life if you will. "Hey, do you want to go for a walk with me?"

"Anything for you, my beautiful wife."

"You always make me feel good about myself, Josh. I hope Mark will do the same for Rachel. She really needs some positive affirmation."

"I'm sure he'll do fine. He seems to have turned over a new leaf. Not quite so sour and dour anymore, if you know what I mean?"

"Good, it's about time. I never begrudged him mourning his wife, but eighteen years? I know it was really hard on the kids. I'm glad you think he's doing better."

"Yeah, Jana, I think they'll do just fine. And I know Eva is happy about the way things turned out. I think if she'd had her way this would have happened years ago."

"I'm sure you're right. Boy that was good wedding cake! Our daughter in law has a real talent! If this were a different time and place, I would have said she should open a bakery."

"If only, Babe. If only."

• • • • •

"You know you're going to make me fat, right?"

"I don't think you could get fat if you tried, Alec. Too much muscle on that great body!"

"You think I have too much muscle? Well, I know I can do this." Alec exclaimed as he picked Elizabeth up and held her over his head.

"Hey, put me down. I think you have just the perfect amount of muscle my handsome husband."

"And you have the perfect amount of everything! You wanna go for a walk?"

"I can't leave the ladies with all this mess again. Why don't you head home, and I'll follow you in a few minutes."

When Alec arrived back at their quarters he lit candles and fluffed pillows while he was waiting. He'd really been blessed, and he knew it. Elizabeth was a perfect wife: smart, beautiful, compassionate, loving, a great cook, and his best friend. He also knew the world was collapsing around them, and that at some point this would all come to an end. He looked around the room he shared with his bride. She'd added small touches to make the space more personal and homey: hand sewn pillow covers; delicate vases filled with wild flowers; a lovely pitcher that she kept filled with fresh water, right next to the bed; and small dishes of fragrant rose petals. How did he get so lucky?

As he contemplated his good fortune, he heard the door open in the other room and Elizabeth's voice as she walked into the bedroom. "Oh, you lit candles. You know I love candles."

"Come here you. I'll give you a back rub. You really worked hard today getting all that food ready."

"I did have help you know. But, my back is a little sore."

Alec laid her on the bed and began by rubbing her back, and kissing her neck.

Mike was awakened again by Bella crying out. This time she seemed truly frantic, trying to get away. He held her and called her name. "Bella, you're safe. It's me, Mike. I've got you."

When she realized where she was, and who held her in his arms, she began to cry. "I'm sorry, Mike. I don't mean to...."

"Don't mean to what? Be frightened? You don't have to be frightened anymore, Bella. I will watch out for you, no matter what. Once we are married I will hold you every night, and whatever it is that's been haunting your dreams will just have to go away."

"I know you want to know why I have nightmares, Mike, but there is a part of me that's afraid to tell you."

"Afraid to tell me? Why?"

"I'm worried that you will think I'm dirty, and you won't want me around anymore."

"Nothing could ever make me think that about you, my love. I promise. Tell me the things that are eating at you, and we will face them together."

"Okay. It's probably better that you know now, so that you can back out of the marriage if you want to. I know I haven't told you much about my life, but there are many reasons for that. I grew up Catholic. I was an only child, and my parents loved me very much, though probably the only thing they loved more than me was the church. I was fine with that. I was very active in the church, and as a family we attended services whenever the doors were open. When I began Catechism classes the priest asked me to stay after one day, and, well, I won't go into detail, but he molested me. Then he told me that because he was a holy man, if I told anyone what he had done, my parents would go to hell. I was scared to go back, but my parents were insistent. They couldn't understand my change of heart. During that two years of classes, he attacked me many times, and I couldn't understand why God would let that happen to me. I became very confused, and rebellious.

"When I was fourteen my mother became ill, and I was tasked to care for her. Each day I would go to school, come home, prepare the evening meal and undertake the care of my mother's needs. In the mornings I would wash and dress her before I left for school. My papa was devastated. He prayed and prayed to Mary. And he prayed for God and all the saints and angels to heal her, but she didn't get any better. She died when I was only fifteen years old.

"When the government began to press people to get the GHO's chip in their hand he was fine with that. I didn't agree and wouldn't go with him, so he decided to do some investigating by talking to others who were already implanted. A cousin died trying to remove the chip, and others claimed that it wasn't just an information chip, it was also a tiny GPS device, so that the authorities could track our movements. He didn't like the idea of that. We talked about it, and like many others, we ran.

"We managed. We stayed in a small cave in the hills of Tuscany for quite some time, and lived off of grapes, olives, and wild game. He was my best friend, and since it was difficult for him to stay angry at God, even over the death of his beloved wife, we prayed and for the first time in our lives we began to read the Bible. You see, in the Catholic church we were provided with small booklets in the back of each pew. These were used as a guide in order to follow the service, but the average congregation member didn't read the Bible. That was the priest's job, and many people in our church didn't even own a Bible, or if they did it was used for decorative purposes. You know, a place to inscribe family names, births, deaths, marriages and so on. When it became illegal to own one, we counted ourselves fortunate that we didn't have to worry about that, but when we wanted one later, it proved to be very difficult to come by the precious gift.

"It became a precious ritual for us, reading the scriptures together. But, we discovered that the things we were reading didn't match up to the tenets of the Catholic faith, so out of a desire to know more, and a sense of confusion, we continued to read, dug deeper, studied and learned. Somewhere along the way we both came to faith in Jesus, and we knew we could never go back and worship in the Catholic church, or the 'New World' churches the government had set up. We were determined never to allow the authorities to implant us with chips, so we decided we would live as hermits, nomads if you will, just a few steps ahead of the UNGCs soldiers.

"One day the soldiers found us. My father told me to run, and I did. I didn't realize until sometime later that he wasn't behind me. He had sacrificed himself for me, allowing the UN goons to capture him so that I could get away. They took him to Rome. I knew this because all prisoners were taken to Rome. The government had taken over Vatican City when they outlawed the practice of the Christian religion. I hid, and I followed, traveling only at night, sleeping during the day in whatever hole or crevice I could find. I ate what I could dig up or kill, often grubs, or other insects, sometimes fruit when I could find it.

"I was filthy, and starving, but so were most of the citizens of Italy in those days, once the UNGC took over. I made it to Rome in time to watch the mass execution of twenty enemies of the state. My father was one of them. I shouldn't have stayed to watch, but I felt like he was all alone, and I needed to be with him. At one point when he looked up, he saw me in the crowd and the expression on his face was one of pure horror when he discovered that I'd followed him. I know he was afraid that I would be discovered.

"All twenty of the prisoners were forced to kneel on the concrete, with their hands tied behind their backs. At once, the soldiers standing over each detainee raised their swords in the air, and at a signal the blades came down as one. My father's head fell from his body and rolled several feet. It took several minutes for his body, twitching and spewing blood, to realize it was no longer in possession of his head. Then, it took me a moment to realize I was screaming at the top of my lungs. People all around me backed up a few steps. I looked up and saw a soldier walking toward me, so I broke free from the crowd, and began running as fast as I could. I was able to evade authorities because of the crowds, but when I finally stopped to hide, I found that I was shivering so badly I was made to vomit.

"I pilfered a change of clothing from a laundry line, and though they were ragged, they were at least clean. I was hungry and tired, scared and in shock. I knew I couldn't stay in the city, there would be too much chance of being discovered in Rome, so I decided to travel back to the rolling hills of Tuscany. However, a hundred and forty miles is no short hike, and I had UN soldiers hard on my heels.

"I'd made it almost back to the rolling hills when someone in a small town where I'd begged for bread turned me in. I was captured and taken back to Rome. The captain of the guard decided that I was too pretty to kill right away. They passed me around for months. I felt so dirty. No amount of prayer, or begging, helped. I would rather if they'd taken my head. Every humiliation, every filthy imagining, beatings, and whatever they could do to degrade me; from making me walk naked, with a leash around my neck, from one soldier's chambers to another; to servicing all the new troops. I begged for death. At least that would release me to be with the Lord, and I could see my parents again, but they wouldn't kill me.

"One day, a cleaning lady who'd come to pity my situation took a chance. She brought me clothing and helped me to escape. She hid me in her home, and eventually found a group of rebels who were leaving by boat to go to America. Obviously she wasn't aware that this country was in as much turmoil as the rest of the world. But, at least here no one knew who I was. I can never thank her enough for the things she did for me." At this, Mike noticed that Bella's eyes were shining with many unshed tears.

"Go ahead Bella. I'm still listening."

"Once in the country I found a hospital in the city that was looking for help. They were desperate and I lied to them. I told them I'd been a student nurse in Italy, so they took me on, teaching me, and letting me learn. My supervisor discovered I had no chip in my hand, quite by accident, but chose not to turn me in. By that time I was experienced enough, I'm a pretty quick study after all, so that she really didn't want to lose the extra pair of hands. I worked there until some unknown person turned me in again. Then I moved on. At last I found refuge with the rebels at the northeast resistance base, until it was discovered and destroyed. I'd been on the run again, until you took me in. I guess that's it. I understand if you want me to leave, and I also understand if you no longer want to marry me."

"What are you talking about, Bella? I love you. You are my life."

"You mean you don't think I'm a whore?"

"Bella, what those men did to you was a tragedy, but it wasn't your fault. How could you think I would ever stop loving you because of something horrible that others did to you?"

"I just didn't know. I've always felt so dirty. Ever since they touched me I haven't been able to look in a mirror."

"Oh, Bella, God loves you, and because you know His Son as your Savior, when He looks at you all He sees is the blood of His dear Son, Jesus. When I look at you, all I see is the beautiful woman I've fallen head over heels in love with. I couldn't imagine my life without you. And, I wouldn't want to. Doc has already agreed to marry us. Shall we go see him?"

"Is it legal for a doctor to marry a couple?"

"With all that is going on in the world these days, I think we'll be fine with the doc performing our ceremony."

"Okay, let's go see him."

The bride wore a charming layer of dust and ash, and carried a single plastic rose that someone found in one of the subway tunnels. She washed up as best she could, and pulled her hair, which still, strangely, smelled to Mike of flowers, into a loose pony tail.

The ceremony was witnessed by Mike's troops, and the clinic's patients alike. A cheer filled the tunnels when Mike was given permission to kiss the bride. Supper would be simple, and sparse, but someone had taken an extra can of k-rations, and inserted a small candle, to serve as a wedding cake. They both smiled when they saw it, and realized how close they'd all become down here in their white tiled sanctuary. Mike wished there was a way for his beautiful bride to meet his family in the high mountain base, that is, if any of them were still alive.

"Then they will deliver you up to tribulation and put you to death, and you will be hated by all nations for My Name's sake. And then many will fall away and betray one another and hate one another. And many false prophets will arise and lead many astray. And because lawlessness will be increased, the love of many will grow cold. But the one who endured to the end will be saved. And this Gospel of the kingdom will be proclaimed throughout the whole world as a testimony to all nations, and then the end will come."

Matthew 24:9-14

God is our refuge and strength, a very present help in trouble. Therefore we will not fear though the earth gives way, though the mountains be moved into the heart of the sea, though its waters roar and foam, though the mountains tremble at its swelling.

Psalm 46:1-3

CHAPTER 8

Amir was livid at the news. Troops, clad in somewhat protective clothing, returned from scouting missions out in the radioactive wastelands. It seemed that resistance bases were destroyed, and many of the rebels were dead, but no one could account for the whereabouts of Josh and Jana Conyers. Was it possible that they'd managed to escape extinction even after the assault by nuclear warfare which had recently been launched? How could this be? There was evidence that many of the resistance soldiers escaped, and no one had been able to track them down. "What do you mean you haven't captured them yet, Sergeant? What is going on? Where could they have gone? I'm sick of this. It's as if they walk through a secret portal and disappear into the universe. I want answers, and I want them now!"

"Sir, while we were searching we came across a couple of individuals who were willing to give us a little information, in exchange for food and water. They spoke of a secret clinic somewhere in a city on the plains, which is run by resistance rebels. Though it was just a rumor, and even when tortured they couldn't give us information about location, we believe that some of the people you're looking for might be found there. We searched for a time, but the smoke and ash is still so thick out there that it made the quest impossible at this time."

"Listen, I want every available soldier out there searching, do you hear me?"

"Sir, we don't have enough protective clothing to cover every soldier, and even what we have isn't of much help. If we send men out there in this fallout, without protection, they will get sick and die."

"I gave you an order, Sergeant. I want that clinic found, no matter the cost. Do the men know the consequences of radiation poisoning?"

"Some do sir."

"Then put those men in the protective clothing. For the ones who don't know the difference, send them out as they are."

"But, Sir, you'll be essentially sentencing those men to death."

"Well, war is hell, Sergeant. We all know that sacrifices are made in times of war. I gave you an order. Is there another question?"

"No Sir. Right away Sir."

"I want regular reports. Do you hear me, Sergeant?"

"Yes Sir. As soon as I hear anything, you will be the first to know."

"Very good. You're dismissed."

• • • • •

"What is it Kakos? What do you want now?"

"Well, your highness, we have just gotten word that the bombs Bahram unleashed on Israel and America have destroyed all of the Christian strongholds. It seems the resistance bases are wiped out."

"So, what about Josh and Jana Conyers? Were they dealt with?"

"Now, that's another story, your eminence. It seems that no one can corroborate any information having to do with the deaths of those two."

"How can that be? Where are they hiding? What is Bahram doing to adjust this narrative? I'm tired of excuses. I want results!"

"Yes your un-holiness. I have it on good authority that Bahram is sending troops out to search for a secret clinic. A clinic which is being run by resistance troops. If any of those we've been looking for have anything to do with this effort to reach out to the masses effected by bombs or natural disasters, we will nab them. I believe we have a higher than average chance of getting our hands on them this time, Sir."

"I'm counting on you, Kakos. Bring me a good report, or all hell will be let loose."

"Yes Sir, we will be on top of it, Sir. I really believe this will be it, Sir."

$$\bullet \ \bullet \ \bullet \ \bullet \ \bullet$$

"Okay, I'm ready to learn, Elizabeth. I'm hoping you can help me master these biscuits once and for all. I'd like to surprise Josh."

"I think you're almost there, so we're just going to work on the finer points, is that agreeable?"

"Yes, daughter. I am all yours. Mold me at your will."

"Here we go, Mom. Just follow me."

At the end of the baking session, which included lessons on handling the dough lightly, and not adding too much flour to the kneading board, Jana produced a batch of delicious biscuits that would rival even those of the beloved Emma. "No one has ever been able to get these lessons through my thick scull daughter, until now. I don't know what to say. I think I might actually cry. I know this might sound crazy, but especially since Mom died, I've wanted to be able to give Josh biscuits, good biscuits, and I think I've finally done it. However, I couldn't have done it without you, Elizabeth. Thank you, from the bottom of my heart."

"Anything for you Mom. I had fun working together with you, and I'm very proud of you. And, no, I don't think it sounds crazy at all. Since Alec and I have been married, my greatest desire has been to please you. So, I feel as though we've both had our wishes granted."

"You wanted to impress me? Elizabeth, I think you are a remarkable young woman. And, I think that the best thing that has ever happened to my son, in this lifetime, besides Jesus, is you." The women hugged and promised to do it all again. Then Jana ran off with a basket of her very own, famous, homemade biscuits, to share with her husband.

• • • • •

Thunder and lightning storms became a regular phenomenon on the plains. Not the ones that used to supply the farmers with much needed rain for their growing crops, but the unproductive kind that made noise and lit up the smoke and ash clouds, which had become part of their everyday lives. Evenings were worst. It was as if all the electricity in the air collected together during the daytime hours, and at the exact prescribed time, it let loose in the nighttime sky.

As lightning lit up the dark with an eerie glow that appeared as a flash of glowing spider webs in the static filled air, the very atmosphere crackled and caused hair to stand on end. Then a boom of thunder, so loud as to shake the very foundations of the earth, would echo through the tunnels of the white tiled subway. Sunlight ceased to warm the earth in those days. And where no sun warmed the earth, the planet became cold. Mike and Bella kept fires burning in the tunnels, and they checked every day to see if the clouds were dissipating, but so far they were greeted with only dark and dreary landscapes and more wounded people wandering in to seek care.

Supplies were running short, in spite of their harshly implemented rationing. And residents, even the ones whose lives had been saved by the clinic and those who ran it, were beginning to rise up in anger, doing what humans often do and demanding what they believed was theirs. It had become easy for them to sit back and depend on Mike and Bella for their subsistence, and when their demands were not met, they often formed mobs that had to be dealt with. It became a daily struggle to keep peace among the patients, and to guard what foodstuffs remained.

Conditions weren't getting better. More were dying from plague and other illnesses; many were still arriving with symptoms of radiation poisoning, in different stages of dying from the effects; and though Mike and Bella were kind to them they knew there was nothing they could do to save their lives. Hard decisions needed to be made. The couple sat with Doc and came to the conclusion that those in the tunnels who were simply living on borrowed time would receive only half rations of food and water. What was left of the bulk of their supplies must be put aside for those who might be saved. However, Mike, Bella and Doc all decided to go on half rations of food themselves, just to alleviate a bit of the guilt associated with making life and death decisions for others. And, now, along with the dead were some of the troops Mike had brought with him. Mostly the fellows who were on body detail, and errands causing them to go out into the contaminated city, but others were following.

They waited for word from home. Hopeful that the conflict in Israel had been settled. Hoping too that the people they loved and cared about were still alive. Would there be a rescue team? Was it still too dangerous to walk the wastelands? They watched each day for the skies to clear, for the clouds of smoke and ash to blow away. Instead, a film of grey filtered down on everything and everyone who ventured outside.

• • • • •

Mark was happier than he'd been in years, and Rachel loved their little family. Eva could feel the peace that filled the home they shared, and she was glad her dad had finally seen the light. Men could be so stubborn. It became a family tradition, after the ladies helped in the kitchen, and Mark worked in the fields, to sit and eat their evening meal together with friends, and then go home to sing, tell stories, and enjoy the company of family.

Jana saw a real improvement in Mark, and the obvious joy of her friend, Rachel, as she reveled in the delight of a healthy marriage. It was good to see them happy here, as times would likely become harder when the end drew nearer.

Alec had become as good a farmer as his dad, and his grandpa before him, and after a hard day's work they often walked together with Scott and Mark to the kitchens, to eat supper with their wives before going home to shower. Even C.J. now had his eye on a lovely young woman who was daughter of one of Josh's sergeants, so he was quick to join them when he discovered they were headed to the kitchens where she worked.

Of course it was essential to spend a certain amount of time each week honing their warrior skills, but they wouldn't have dared go off to train without their wives, so that became something they all did together as well. Josh and Jana, Scott and Becca, Mark and Rachel, and Alec and Elizabeth, would entertain themselves with competitions of all sorts: Hand to hand combat; bow skills; knife and staff; marksmanship; running and jumping; and even swimming. Hands down, Jana always took bow skills, with Becca and Elizabeth a close second. And, Jana held her own quite nicely in knife and staff, as well as marksmanship, with her daughter in law a close second. But, they were usually bested in all the other skills by the men. Josh and Alec were often neck and neck, but Scott was no slouch either and he normally came in a quick second in all the disciplines that required strength and speed.

With so much time spent together as couples, they became closer than they would have ever imagined possible. When they weren't working together, they were playing together. Jana felt very blessed to have so many good friends. When she looked back on her life, she remembered being a loner for much of it. After the death of her parents and then her grandmother, she'd tended to focus all her attention on getting ahead. Proving herself to all those around her. She wanted others to see that she was good enough, and deserved better than she'd gotten as a girl. Then she met Josh, her wonderful husband. What a difference he had made in her life. A difference he still made today. God was truly good to bring them together, and she would be forever grateful for His blessings in her life.

• • • • •

The entire base wondered about Mike and Doc. Were they still alive? Had they managed to hide somewhere safe during the atomic blasts? Why hadn't they heard anything from them? Obviously, if the wastelands were still too hot for their own troops to risk a trip out into the plains, Mike and Doc would be smart enough not to endanger their own men either. Jana realized they might never know what happened to their friends, and Doc's family waited and prayed. The camp tried to be there for Cathy, their kids and grandkids as much as possible, and they continued to include them in every aspect of daily life in the base as they always had, but nothing really takes the place of the one you love.

Doc and Cathy had been through this before. When Doc was captured and hidden away in the mountain's prison cells, by Cage, he'd been away from his family for quite some time, so Cathy was holding on to hope that her husband might still be alive somewhere out there with their friend Mike.

She'd known Jim since they were in college. He with his aspirations of being the world's best surgeon, and her desire to teach. He'd accomplished his goal, but she'd given up teaching in private Christian schools, willingly, in order to home school their own children.

After Jim was threatened with death when he found out about secret government experiments going on at a local college; using live flu vaccine to thin out what the regime considered undesirables; he'd refused to take part in those experiments anymore. When it seemed that they were being watched and followed in every aspect of their lives, they moved, and tried to start over again several times.

After the ruling administration began to use the GHO to implant citizens, the whole family agreed they wanted no part of it. And when Pastor Mike began holding meetings at his church, and Doc, as everyone called Jim, met Josh and Mark at one of those meetings, they decided as a family to escape together to one of the region's resistance bases. It was on their way to a meeting with resistance members who would take them on to safety, that they'd been separated. And Cathy, along with the children had come to the heights. She was told that her husband was dead, but she refused to believe that information then, and he had come back to her. So, today she would wait patiently, and pray daily, for the safety of her husband, hoping that he would once again come home to her.

Jana especially felt the loss of Mike. They'd become close during their time in the cave, after she'd wounded him so badly on the mountain plateau. He'd mentored her in the Bible, and she'd learned so much from him. She also knew he loved her. Suspecting he chose duty assignments as far away from her as possible, to save his wayward emotions, she never questioned his absences. A part of her always felt especially bad that he'd never married. But, she tried to keep those thoughts and concerns to herself, so as not to embarrass him unduly. Now though, was he alive? Had he died never knowing love fulfilled? If he was dead, she hoped it had been quick, and that he hadn't suffered.

• • • • •

Scott and Becca knew, just as their group of friends did, that the beginning of the end was surely near, and they were so grateful that their whole family was together. Scott knew that besides Jesus, Becca was the best thing that ever happened to him. He'd been alone his whole life, even while married to Virginia, until his beautiful bride came and filled his heart. And every moment with her had made him smile. He couldn't think of a single argument in which they'd ever indulged, in all their years of marriage; and he didn't think he'd ever seen a day go by where his amazing wife didn't have a smile on her face. He was truly blessed. Now to be home with her, C.J., Angel, Elizabeth, and all their friends was a bigger blessing than he'd ever thought possible.

"Hey, you all want to play some board games when we get home from supper?"

"Dad, we all know you've had your eye on that Monopoly board all week."

"Yeah Angel, that one is my favorite, but if you want to play Scrabble, Aggravation, or even cards, I'm up for that too."

"Sounds fun to me, Scott, but you have to promise to go easy on me when you start buying up all the property. You can be quite a Mr. Meany when it comes to collecting rent."

"I am not a Mr. Meany, Becca. I'm just a good business man."

"Well, when I run out of money, the game is over, so I'm just saying."

"Can I invite Candice over for games?"

"You mean Candice from the kitchens, C.J.?"

"Yes, Dad, Candice from the kitchens. Can I invite her?"

"Do you think she'd really enjoy an evening with your parents?"

"Actually, I've kind of been seeing her, and she's been anxious to spend some time with the family."

"Well, well, well, does this mean that things are starting to get serious?"

"Oh, Dad, if you're going to make a big deal out of it and make her feel uncomfortable."

"No, no, I promise. I won't embarrass you, or make her feel uncomfortable. Go ahead and ask her over."

"Yes, I'd love to get to know her better, C.J. I think that would be nice. And I will keep a tight grip on your dad, so he will keep his promise. I think this will be fun, don't you Scott?"

"Yes Dear. Though I have to say, you're taking all the fun out of it."

"Thanks, Mom. I'll go get her. I'll be back real soon."

"You know, I've actually been talking to Candice quite a bit. She's very nice, and even though she's younger than C.J., she's very mature for her age. I think you'll like her, Dad."

"Okay, Angel, if you say so. I just hate the thought of giving up our family time."

"Well, if C.J. has anything to say about it, Candice will be family soon enough. So you'd better make a little more room in your heart for the inevitable."

"I guess it will be okay. They've just all grown up so much, and I feel like I missed most of it while we were away at war."

"You did, Dad, but we understand. Our lives weren't much different than anyone else's here at the base. But, we had Chuck and Emma to help us out. I think we all turned out fine, and we still love you."

"Boy, I sure do miss those two. The place seems kind of empty without them. I know Josh sure misses them too."

"Hey, Dad, Mom, this is Candice. And I think you already know my sister pretty well, don't you?"

"It's nice to meet you all, and, hi there Angel. Thank you everyone for inviting me over."

"Glad to have you. Any friend of C.J.s is a friend of ours."

• • • • •

"Hey, I thought we were going for a walk?"

"I'll be right there. You know I helped your mom work on her biscuits today. They turned out pretty good. I think your dad will be surprised."

"You two have been getting pretty close, haven't you?"

"Yes, it feels nice. I think she really likes me.'

"I know she does, Dad talks great about you too. I'm lucky. I get to have the girl of my dreams, and my parents don't hate her. How blessed is that?"

"Well, my dad finally likes you. It took him a while to get used to the fact that I was going home to bed with you, instead of coming back to the family place. He was gone so much while I was growing up that he feels like he missed most of it. I know he still thinks of me as his baby girl."

"Yeah, my parents feel the same way. They're grateful that Grandpa and Grandma were around to take care of us, but they're sad they missed most of our growing up themselves. They're especially sad that they missed our wedding."

"Perhaps we could renew our vows for our anniversary? Then they would feel more like they'd been there for us all along."

"That would be great. I'll say something to Dad and Scott at work tomorrow, and maybe you could say something to both our Moms while you three are working in the kitchens? I'd love to make both sets of parents feel better about the whole thing, and I'll bet they'd even get a kick out of the whole thing."

"I will. Okay, let's get out for our walk before it gets too late."

"I'm right behind you beautiful lady, and I can't say that there's a better view anywhere around."

"Oh, you. You flatter me. I love you, Alec."

"I love you more, Babe."

• • • • •

Bella noticed one of the first signs when she tried to fix her tresses that morning, and her brush came away filled with hair. She'd been tired, and not very hungry, but had thought they were mostly protected in the tunnels. However, it seemed that enough of the residual radiation from fallout had managed to creep into their living space, to cause poisoning.

She'd seen signs in others, but those had been out in the open where the contamination was at its highest, or had walked through high radiation levels to get to their clinic. It just never occurred to her that their patients were probably tracking the poison into the caves upon arrival. She wondered if she was the only one, or if others had noticed symptoms of the same radiation poisoning.

When she saw Mike, she showed him her brush. "I wondered if I was the only one, Bella. I didn't want to scare anyone, so I didn't tell. How are you feeling?"

"I'm okay, Mike. A little tired is all. I wonder if Doc has noticed any changes?"

"We'll have to check with him. You know there's nothing that can be done, don't you?"

"Yes. Pretty soon our gums will bleed, teeth will become loose, and we will begin to get sores. Those are usually the next symptoms."

"I'm so sorry my beautiful Bella. If there was any way that I could take this from you I would."

"I know that my darling, and I would do the same for you, but this is the hand we have been dealt, and we must do the best we can with whatever time we have left."

"I'm going to go see how Doc is doing. I'd like to know if he's started realizing the same symptoms we've seen."

"I'm coming with you. I've already checked on my tunnels. We can wait to remove those we lost in the night until we return."

Mike and Bella made their way, to the section of subway, where Doc was taking care of the more seriously ill and wounded among them. When they arrived they didn't have to ask Doc if he'd noticed anything changing with his own health, because they both saw the places on the back of his head which were devoid of hair. So, obviously he'd realized the truth and hoped to spare others from the inevitable truth of the situation.

"Hi Doc. How's it going?"

"Things are going pretty good on this side of the tunnels. I would ask how you two were doing, but from the look on your faces that's an unnecessary question."

"How long have you known, Doc?"

"I think I've known since right after the bomb dropped. The subway isn't airtight; we had to take trips outside each day to remove bodies; and with new arrivals each day, tracking radioactive particles into our space, it was just a matter of time. If it makes you feel any better, there's nothing you could have done to prevent this, so none of this is on you. I'd have to say that if I have to go out, I'm okay with going out helping people, and sharing the Gospel."

"I agree. We knew that this old world was winding down, so I'm okay with winding down a little earlier than the rest. I have to say that these past days, after meeting the woman of my dreams, have been the best days of my life. And Bella, I wouldn't trade any of this if it meant I wouldn't have met you."

"I feel the same way husband. You have made me very happy, and I could never regret my time here, since it led me to you. But, my heart breaks for you, Doc. We have each other, but you don't have your family with you."

"That is my only regret. Not being able to tell Cathy and the kids goodbye. But, knowing they are safe from all this is comforting enough. We will all see one another again. Probably sooner than anyone could have predicted. For now, I'm content to continue taking care of those who are sicker than I am, and sharing Jesus with anyone who will listen."

"Amen. And we will do the same. Let us know if you need anything, Doc. We'll head over to the other side. I need to put another detail together. We've got some bodies to move, and patients to take care of."

• • • • •

"I sure wish I knew if Mike and the doc were okay out there. We don't even know if they're still alive. I'm sure we are coming closer to the end, and I know we will see them again then, but I can't stand the thought that Doc is away from his family."

"I know, Josh. I feel the same way. Here we are safe and sound, Alec and Elizabeth are fine, and so many of our friends are here with us. I can't imagine what it must be like out there, for any who made it through the blasts."

"I can tell you what it's like. Radiation poisoning is no joke. Anything exposed to the blast, or the fallout afterward, is contaminated. Food and water are not safe to eat or drink, but you have to have water. People who suffer from radiation poisoning, meaning those not immediately killed by the nuclear explosion, who are not in a fallout shelter, will begin to lose their hair and teeth, sores will form on their bodies as the poison eats its way from the inside to the outside, and they will die a slow agonizing death. The thought of either of our friends dying like that just breaks my heart."

"I guess I didn't know all of that. There must be thousands and thousands of people wandering the streets in areas where the fallout has drifted. They don't know what is happening to them. They're scared and searching for help. How many of them don't know the Lord? What a terrible way to go."

"Well, as far as I'm concerned, any way is a terrible way to go if you don't know Jesus."

"You're right, Josh. But, if I know Mike, and if he's still alive, he is sharing the Gospel with anyone who will listen. Don't you think?"

"I absolutely believe that. Doc too. I wish we could get out there and look for them."

"I thought you said that the last readings were still too high?"

"They are, and I can't justify sending men out into a situation that is certain death, when we don't know if Doc and Mike are even still with us. No, we'll have to wait. From here we can only pray, but God will hear our prayers, and He will decide how all of this plays out in the end."

"Until then, we will take care of those who are in the camp. I know I should be praying for everyone, even Amir Bahram, but I'm having a hard time with that. He's turned the world upside down and set it on fire with his twisted religion and ego. How can I forgive someone like that?"

"Jana, you know that we are to forgive, as we've already been forgiven. God will deal with the Bahram's of the world, and everything will end up exactly as He designed it to work out before the foundation of the world. It would be great, or perhaps scary really, if we got to decide what to do with anyone who crossed us; but I wouldn't even want that responsibility. I might end someone's life, just because they made me angry. And they could do the same to me. I don't think I'd want to live in a world like that."

"So, what do you think it's going to be like, Josh?"

"What?"

"The end. What do you think the end will be like?"

"Well, I believe Jesus will return and take us with Him. Much of the book of Revelation is hard to decipher. There are scriptures in Isaiah, Ezekiel, Jeremiah, Daniel, and the Gospels, among others, that speak to the end times, but some are deeply spiritual, so who knows if we've discerned them correctly. I guess we'll know more when it happens. I do know scripture tells us that those of us who belong to Him, will be with Him, so I'm satisfied with that. Whatever my role is after that, I'm sure Jesus will let me know. You know I'd be fine with riding into battle and taking on the enemy. I think it would be pretty great to fight alongside the Savior of the world."

"You can sign me up too! How wonderful that would be to go to battle with the enemy, right beside the Lord. I'm not afraid to die, you know. I know where I will be, and I know that you will be there too. Everyone we know and love will be there, so it will be a reunion like no other in the history of the universe."

"Hey, now you've got me all excited, and let's remember that we really don't know when the end will come. Not even Jesus knows, but only the Father. Yeah, I'd have to agree with you. That will be pretty exciting. For now we have work to do here. Perhaps we will hear something from one of the other bases soon, or maybe even Mike and Doc. We will just continue to pray."

"I am the Lord, and there is no other, besides Me there is no God; I equip you, though you do not know me, that people may know, from the rising of the sun and from the west, that there is none besides Me; I am the Lord, and there is no other. I form the light and create darkness. I make well-being and create calamity, I am the Lord, who does all these things."

Isaiah 45:5-7

"Behold, I have created the smith who blows the fire of coals and produces a weapon for its purpose. I have also created a ravager to destroy; no weapon that is fashioned against you shall succeed, and you shall confute every tongue that rises against you in judgment. This is the heritage of the servants of the Lord and their vindication from me, declares the Lord."

Isaiah 54:16-17

"How you are fallen from heaven, O Day Star, son of Dawn! How you are cut down to the ground, you who laid the nations low! You said in your heart, I will ascend to heaven; above the stars of God I will set my

throne on high; I will sit on the mount of assembly in the far reaches of the north; I will ascend above the heights of the clouds; I will make myself like the Most High. But you are brought down to Sheol, to the far reaches of the pit."

Isaiah 14:12-15

"The Lord God said to the serpent, "Because you have done this, cursed are you above all livestock and above all beasts of the field; on your belly you shall go, and dust you shall eat all the days of your life."

CHAPTER 9

Sir, I've come with good news."

"That's great, because I could use some good news for a change. Have you located that damnable Josh Conyers?"

"Sir, our trackers have located a position. We have confirmation that the resistance has been running a clinic on the plains, and we think we've established that the place is being run by Conyers and his team."

"How are they surviving on the plains? That whole area has to be hot with radiation."

"Yes Sir, but evidently their operation has been holed up in a subway system beneath the city, which would keep them safe from a certain amount of radiation poisoning."

"Have you organized your men for a raid?"

"Well, Sir, there will be a certain amount of preparation that needs to be done. After all, as you just mentioned, the area is still hot. We're trying to get the troops fitted with protective gear now, and then we're just waiting for your word."

"Gear or no gear, you have a word from me. The word is, 'go', get them. Do whatever you have to do to shut them down. Destroy it all! However, I don't want you to kill Conyers and his woman. That will be my pleasure. Just bring them here to me."

"Yes Sir. We will be heading out within the hour."

"I want hourly reports. Is that clear?"

"Yes Sir. I will see to it myself."

Bahram leaned forward in his leather chair and slapped the top of his desk with a flat hand. "I've got you Conyers. Now we'll see who has the last laugh."

• • • • •

"Josh, Becca and I were talking and I'm thinking of going down the mountain to see if I can track down the Doc and Mike. I know we have no idea if they're even still alive, but I can't help thinking that they might have found shelter, and they're just out there waiting for help."

"I've been thinking the same thing myself, Scott. I know the levels still aren't safe, but I think if we put on enough protective gear we might still manage."

"I've already told Becca she can't come. I'm hoping you'll say the same thing to Jana. We don't have enough suits to accommodate everyone anyway. We'd be traveling with the bare minimums."

"Let me see what I can do, buddy. I'll go talk to her now."

"What do you mean? Why wouldn't I be able to go with you, Josh?"

"Jana, the radiation levels are still high enough to cause serious harm. It's just going to be Scott and me."

"So, you're immune to radiation now? Don't be ridiculous. You are not leaving here without me, do you understand?"

"Of course I'm not immune, but we do have a couple of protective suits here at the base. We can wear that protection and tread very carefully."

"Josh, those suits are ancient. And, if I'm not mistaken, there are three of them. So explain to me again why it's okay for you to go out there and risk your life, and I can't come? And, "because I said so", is not a reason."

"Scott isn't going to let Becca come."

"Good, then I'll use the third suit. I wouldn't want to have to worry about her anyway. What's wrong with Jeff flying us in as close as he can to the biggest city on the plains? The less time we spend, walking through radioactive dust, the better. We all know that if they got caught out in the open during the nuclear blast we'll never find them, because they would certainly be dead by now. But, if they found shelter in the city, there's a possibility they've survived. We could be in and out of there much quicker if we fly in. Also, there's a chance we can fly low over the locations of our sister bases. We might be able to put to rest the question of their viability. Wouldn't you like to know if any of them made it, or if there is a way we can help them? Perhaps the explosions only knocked out their communications. It would be nice to know."

"You are maddening woman! Why do you always have to make so much sense? Fine, I'll talk to Scott and we'll start making some plans."

"We need to be mindful of Jeff too. We don't want him to land and kick up all that radioactive dust and ash if he doesn't have to. I know there are some old parachutes in the storage room. We'll check them over and be sure they're at least passably safe. We can jump in and save him from the chances of exposure."

"Okay, that's a good idea too. I honestly don't know why I ever think of going anywhere without you."

"I don't either. So, never do that again."

"You know Becca is going to be angry about you coming with us."

"She'll get over it."

"Why don't you go tell Alec what's going on while I talk with Scott?"

"Sure, I can do that. But, you know he's going to want to come, don't you?"

"Well, there are only three suits, so that settles that without an argument. Besides, someone needs to be here to help out on the base. Just be firm with him, Jana."

"He isn't going to be satisfied with the idea of being a babysitter, so I'll jazz it up a bit. And, why is it that I always have to be the firm one?"

"You've always been better at it than I am, at least with Alec. Just tell him that we need his leadership here. We don't know what else Bahram might have up his sleeve. He needs to keep the troops at the ready in case of trouble."

"Good, that should work. You know anytime we go out on missions like this I wonder if this is the last time we will see our son."

"Hey, you don't have to go. You can stay right here and keep an eye on Alec and Elizabeth for yourself if you'd like. I probably wouldn't get so much flak from Scott if you stayed behind."

"Nope. As much as I always want to make sure Alec is okay, I would die if anything ever happened to you on one of these missions. I could never forgive myself for not being there to help if you needed me. Besides, he's young."

"Oh, and I'm old? Is that it?"

"You said it old man."

"Come here, you, I'll show you who's old."

"Josh, not right out here where everyone can see!"

"I'll kiss my beautiful wife anywhere I darn well please!" Josh picked her up and kissed her soundly, before setting her down and giving her a little pop on the butt. "You go tell Alec what's going on, and I'll go talk to Scott. I'll meet you in the kitchens and we'll get some supper, okay?"

"Sounds good to me."

Alec balked at first. Not wanting to be treated like a kid.

"There are only three suits, Alec, and we are going to have to take extra precautions as it is. You will be needed here, so use the time to keep the troops ready for anything."

"Okay, Mom, but I'm staying under protest."

"Your dad trusts you and so do I. These are dangerous times, Alec. We never know when the enemy will be knocking at the door, and we can't go unless we have someone here that we can depend on."

"Fine, Mom. But you two better be careful. I know the radiation levels are still not back to normal."

"We're going to take the proper precautions. Don't worry about us son. We'll be home before you know it, and hopefully, with Mike and Doc in tow."

"I'm sure Cathy and the kids will be excited about that. What if you can't find them?"

"I don't know yet, but we have to try. We need to know if they're out there somewhere waiting for help."

"I understand. I'll do my best to keep things running smoothly here. Do you want me to put together some supplies for the trip?"

"That's great. We'd appreciate it, Alec. Remember we'll be traveling light, so just the basics. I love you son."

"I love you too, Mom."

Josh found Scott in the fields working hard. He watched him for a moment, and wondered what would have become of them all if Scott hadn't come into their lives. God's timing was perfect, and this man had become a true friend over these past years.

"Hey, grab a hoe."

"I just came to tell you about my conversation with Jana."

"Well, I can already tell by your tone, and the look on your face, that we have our third."

"You know me way too well, buddy. Yes, she's coming, but she really had some great ideas. You know she can pull her weight on any mission, Scott."

"I can't deny that. It's your decision, Josh. I didn't want Becca to come because I figured it was too dangerous for her, but if you two have talked about it, and you aren't worried, then I'm fine."

"Jana went over to tell Alec. He'll be upset, but we're going to ask him to take care of the troops while we're gone. That will give him something productive to do, so that he won't feel as though he's of no use to the cause. We only have the three suits anyway, so we'll all make do where we have to."

They would leave at the first sign of sunlight through the mountain's dense clouds.

• • • • •

"Boy, we're a pair aren't we? If I wasn't so exhausted, I wouldn't even want you to see me like this."

"Don't worry about it, Bella. Hair is a highly overrated commodity. Besides, you are so beautiful you could carry off any look, including bald. I, on the other hand, was definitely not meant to have a bald head. "

"Go on with you, Mike. I'm glad that love is blind. And, I for one think you are quite attractive as a bald man. I especially love the little tufts of hair right above your ears."

"Oh, good, I'll try to hang on to those for you. I wouldn't want to lose my appeal."

"Oh, Mike. We've lost so many over the past few days, and there really isn't much we can do for those who are left. My heart is breaking, especially for the little ones."

"Yeah, I checked in on Doc earlier and he's running into the same situation in the other tunnel. He didn't look very good. I'm worried about him."

"Oh yeah? Have you looked in a mirror lately? We aren't exactly at our healthiest, or most attractive, these days."

"You know what I mean. There aren't really any men left with the strength to help me carry bodies out to the mass graves. The tunnels are filled with the dead and I haven't got the strength to chase off the rats. There isn't much left for us to do, Bella. I'm so sorry that you've had to endure all of this."

"Don't be ridiculous, Mike. This time in the tunnels with you has been the happiest time of my life. I have been useful, and cherished. If I hadn't been here with you, I probably would have died in the blast, so my existence has been blessed with the time to love the man of my dreams. I will never regret these days."

"Well, I don't know what I would have done without you, Bella. I didn't think I would ever have love, that this part of my time here on earth just wasn't to be. But God gave me you when my life was in its darkest moments. If this is it; if this tunnel is where we breathe our last, I will die a happy man. And, we will always have eternity."

Things in the tunnels had become more bleak by the day. Radiation poisoning, plague and injuries had taken so many. They'd done what they could. They'd shared Jesus with any who would listen, and many had been added to the kingdom through their ministrations. They knew that trying to make it from the city to the mountain, through the poisoned wastelands, would simply be a suicide mission. Besides, there were still people here who needed them. They would try to be present for their patients until their last breath.

$$\bullet \; \bullet \; \bullet \; \bullet \; \bullet$$

For those who lived in cities, towns and villages around the world, who still had functioning satellite jumbo screens, the events which transpired this day would act as proof positive that God was still alive and on His throne. Amir had his men in Jerusalem focus all available cameras on the fallen prophets, after he'd killed them with a rocket launcher three and a half days ago, as a reminder to everyone around the earth that he was still in charge. He wanted to strike a chord in the minds of every peasant on the globe that they'd better remember who he was, and what the ultimate punishment would be for those who crossed him. Whenever Bahram was having an especially bad day, all he had to do was glance at his jumbo screen, and a smile would creep across his face, at the visage of the two corpses in the middle of the street.

However, on the morning which fell three and a half days after Bahram had violently taken their lives, those two prophets stood up. When they stood, everyone on the earth who could still see the giant television screens in the intersections of their highways and byways, took a collective gasp. As they watched, the breath of God filled their once dead lungs and the men were taken up into heaven in a blaze of glory. At this, Bahram stood and screamed, "Noooooooooooooooo, what is happening? This can't be true. Get someone on the satellite phone. I want to know what is going on in Jerusalem."

"Sir, communications are down. We can't reach anyone there in Jerusalem."

"I don't want to hear that. Get me someone who knows what's going on! This can't be happening. I can't believe this."

• • • • •

"Satan, Sir, I've come with news."

"Get on with it, Kakos. Can't you see I'm busy?"

"Well, Sir, I'm afraid you aren't going to like this news."

"Kakos, if you don't tell me what is going on, you won't like what is about to happen to you. Now, get on with it."

"Well, your eminence, we have a problem. I'm afraid the two prophets that Bahram killed three and a half days ago have been resurrected."

"What? Where are they now? Can we get someone out there to take care of things before too many of those damn humans see them?"

"Well, that's part of the problem, Sir. They aren't there anymore."

"What do you mean they aren't there? Then find them!"

"I don't think it will be that easy, Sir. They kind of stood up, started to breathe and then rose up."

"Rose up? What do you mean rose up?"

"Exactly what I said, your un-holiness. They rose up into the sky, like maybe God took them to heaven."

"Then it has finally begun. Start assembling your demons, Kakos. I refuse to let Him win again! I don't care who He thinks He is. He will not beat me this time! He's been planning this whole thing since before the foundation of the world, but He isn't going to get away with it..."

Satan had been holding a grudge for a very long time. Longer than humans have lived on the planet. So, his feud with earthlings was more about his hatred of God, and jealousy of the place Jesus held in the Father's heart, than any other reasons. Of course there was the extremely annoying fact that humans were created with the ability to choose heaven if they would. And that even if they made mistakes, they could still be redeemed, a ridiculous notion as far as the Devil was concerned. This in itself was a pretty good reason for him to woo them, lure them over to his side, and condemn them to the pits of hell just for the fun of it, anything to thwart God's intentions.

Satan, along with heaven's other two archangels, Michael and Gabriel, were created long before humans. Michael was designed as a mighty warrior. God used him often to defeat evil, and quite regularly to frustrate the old dragon's plans, even now. Gabriel served mostly as God's messenger mouthpiece. He'd been especially blessed to announce the coming birth of John the Baptist to Elizabeth, and then the birth of Christ to Mary. However, Satan, in all his glory, was created as the most beautiful of all the angels. Made of music and light, he was beyond stunning to behold.

As he walked the streets of heaven other angelic residents admired him and pretty soon he was beginning to think of himself as quite something. Perhaps even most worthy of all. The attitude grew, along with his ego.

Now, pride is a terrible thing. And thinking oneself more worthy than the God of the universe who created you is an especially horrific obsession. But, Satan had become bitter about the adulation offered up to the Lord and was more and more jealous as time went by. He truly believed that the adoration and worship should belong to him and him alone. He conferred with his heavenly community, and convinced many of those simple minded inhabitants to follow him.

Of course, none of this was a surprise to God. He'd created Satan, the waster to destroy, and He knew the murderous, deceitful ways of His creation. There had to be evil, after all, in order to distinguish it from good, and the darkness was necessary to separate it from light. God created everything: *"All things were made through Him, and without Him was not anything made that was made."* *John1:3* God's plan from the beginning, from before the foundation of the earth, was to create man, a being who would love Him by making a choice to do so. This, however, would mean there would also be those who chose not to love Him. By giving man this choice, He also had to make a way for His errant children, those who eventually figured out the Truth, to come back to Him when they'd made that decision, so the Savior was conceived within Him during this, His greatest plan.

The plan wouldn't have worked as He intended, if He'd told Satan the details, so He allowed the Devil, in his anger, to contrive his murderous mutiny.

Satan won over many angels in heaven, and in the day that he stood before the Lord to demand what he considered his rightful place, a third of the host sided with him. A battle ensued that would pit heaven against heaven. Michael, God's champion, warred with the enemy until he was defeated, and Satan, along with a third of the angels, was cast down to the earth.

In the garden he fulfilled his ultimate purpose. To lie and deceive and to lead man astray. To expose the iniquity hidden in man. After the spiritual separation, which was inevitable, God cast man from the garden, and set heavenly guardians in place who would keep humans from the tree of life. Simply because to live for eternity in sin would have been a greater burden than any human could endure. Instead, He set about to pave the way for the coming Prince of Peace, His only Son.

When Satan discovered he'd been created for this deceitful purpose alone, to be the enemy of all that was good and holy. That God knew all along what evil was present in his heart, and that he'd never been made privy to the plan that would determine his very existence, he rose up in anger so great that he swore to destroy all God had intended.

Until the death and resurrection of the Christ, he'd been allowed to come before the throne of God, even after the painful lies, to stand and accuse the brethren. But then, even that privilege was removed. Now his home was beneath. He roamed the earth as a roaring lion, seeking whom he might destroy. And he would destroy them all, every single one of them!

He would be lord of all.

"Come down and sit in the dust, O virgin daughter of Babylon; sit on the ground without a throne, O daughter of the Chaldeans! For you shall no more be called tender and delicate. Take the millstones and grind flour, put off your veil, strip off your robe, uncover your legs, pass through the rivers. your nakedness shall be uncovered, and your disgrace shall be seen. I will take vengeance, and I will spare no one. Our Redeemer-the Lord of hosts is His Name-is the Holy One of Israel."

Isaiah 47:1-4

"Thus says the Lord; "Cursed is the man who trusts in man and makes flesh his strength, whose heart turns away from the Lord."

"Blessed is the man who trusts in the Lord, whose trust is the Lord."

Jeremiah17:5,7

CHAPTER 10

"I love you, Mom. Please promise me you'll take care of yourself."

"You know I usually leave that up to your dad, Alec. But, don't worry, we'll be fine."

"Give Mike and Doc our love when you find them."

"That's what I like to hear, positive expectations. And, we will, Elizabeth. I know you feel especially close to Pastor Mike since he married the two of you. Did you know he married Dad and me too?"

"Yes, I remember you telling me about that. I gather you've changed quite a bit from the person you were in those days, I mean from the stories you've told me."

"I certainly have. If I didn't already know that person was me, I doubt I would believe any of those stories. I don't even think the same way anymore. And, I too feel quite close to Pastor Mike. It's true he married Dad and me, but more than that, I got to know him very well after all the time we spent together, in the cave, when I injured him so badly on the mountain. We've all known each other for a very long time. The thought of him out there, somewhere, needing help. Well, I'm sure you can understand."

"We do, Mom. We'll take care of things here; with the help of Mark, Becca and the rest of the elder's council; so don't worry about us. We will be praying for you and for Dad too."

"I love you, Daddy."

"I love you too, baby girl. Please take care of your mom for me, and I'll see you soon, Elizabeth. You too Alec."

"Do you promise? I want you to promise me."

"I'm going to do my best, Becca. You know how much I love you, don't you?"

"Yes I do, but I want you here to tell me that, not off on some mission. I still don't understand why I can't go if Jana is going?"

"Well, we only have three suits, and she called dibs first, so it's pretty simple. Besides, I'll feel better if you are back here with the kids if something starts to go down."

"Okay, but remember how much I love you, Scott. I will be praying for you my love."

"Thank you, Becca. I will be praying for all of you too. God bless you."

"Are you about ready to go? Jeff is set to head down to the plateau. He's already gotten a plane up there from the desert base."

"We're just saying goodbye to the kids, Josh. Thank you for packing up some provisions, Alec. We appreciate your help."

"I only put in the basics, because you said you wanted to travel light, but there should be plenty of water if you don't stay out too long. Elizabeth did wrap up a batch of biscuits though. She wanted you to have something to remind you of her."

"Thank you both. We will see you soon."

"We'll hold you to that, Mom. Love you, Dad. Don't worry about us. Just take care of Mom. You know she gets a little crazy."

"I know, Alec, and I will. I'm perfectly aware of how crazy your mom can get. I love you too Son."

"Hey, hey, hey, I'm right here, and I'm not crazy. I just get a little involved sometimes."

"Yes, my love. Just a little involved. Okay, let's get a move on. We're keeping Jeff waiting. God bless you all. We will see you as soon as possible. Be ready for anything, Alec. We don't know exactly how quickly things are going to happen, but all the signs are present for the second coming of Christ, so be prepared. If it happens more quickly than we'd anticipated, we will see you on the other side."

"See you soon, Dad. One way or the other, here or there. God bless."

"God bless you too, Son."

After hugs were shared all around, the small group started out for the plateau where they would take their ancient Piper PA-30 Comanche out to the plains, in hopes of finding their lost friends. The plane was a twin engine, and would cruise at respectable speeds, but Jeff liked it for more reasons than that. It was pretty good on fuel, and that was a commodity they were short on, especially after the recent trips to the holy land, traveling in the big girls; and with space for four they wouldn't be sitting on each other's laps. He didn't like the idea of his passengers jumping into a situation where none of them knew what they might run up against, but he was just taking orders, and he understood not wanting to contaminate the aircraft or its pilot. He was also aware that he might not ever see his friends again, at least in this life.

"Are you okay, Alec?"

"Yeah Babe, I'm fine. I just have an uneasy feeling."

"Now, what do you always tell me, husband? Depend on the Lord. You know He has always taken care of your parents, and my dad too. We will see them again, I'm sure of it. Whether it is here or in the hereafter makes no difference, does it?"

"No, I guess not. God is good, and He will take care of them."

"He will take care of all of us. As long as we're together, Alec, we can do anything through Christ. He is our strength."

• • • • •

"How long do you think he's got?"

"I don't know, but probably not very long."

"He asked me to say goodbye to Cathy and the kids for him."

"What did you tell him?"

"Well, of course I told him I would. I just wonder if I was telling the truth? You and I aren't doing so great either."

"If it gives him peace, then it's okay. We'll figure it out."

"When I met you, I never thought I would be fortunate enough to be your husband. But I have to say, Bella, none of this ever crossed my mind either."

"Well, it has been a heck of a ride, hasn't it?"

"All I ever wanted was to make a difference. When I was a kid I didn't know what my purpose was, and I grew up wanting a true reason for why I'd been put on this earth. I feel like God has shown me my purpose, and brought the most beautiful woman in the world into my life. It certainly has been a heck of a ride, Bella. Not a long one, but a good one. I'm sure glad we took that ride together."

"I can't think of anyone I've ever known that I would rather have been on this ride with either, Mike. You haven't been my husband for long, but you have been a good husband, and I am grateful to God that He brought us together. Whatever His plan entails, we will face it together."

Doc died at four in the afternoon. Mike and Bella weren't sure what to do. The idea of throwing his body on the mass graves outside was against every instinct they had, but that's what they'd done with all the other precious people they'd served and lost since they'd been here in this never ending series of tunnels. His was just a body after all, just like the others. Doc was the fortunate one. He, his actual person, was in the arms of the Savior, while they were still hunkered down in this white tiled tomb. No new patients had entered the subway in days. They could only assume that meant more bodies in the streets outside. That was fine. It isn't as if they could have assured them health and wholeness down here in this hole. Most of the patients, lying on cots in the tunnels, had lost their battle already. Now the couple was simply surrounded by slowly decaying corpses. The few poor individuals, who were still holding on with tenterhooks, would soon move on, and then they would follow.

• • • • •

"Hey, what's that over there?"

"What are you seeing, Jana?"

"I'm not sure what it is, Josh. I see a single column of smoke coming out of the ground right there in the middle of the city. It looks like all the fires have burned themselves out but that one. What do you suppose it is?"

"I don't know. Can you get us any closer, Jeff?"

"Let me try, Sir. Most of the tall buildings have either burned down, or were blown down during the blast, so I might actually be able to get pretty close."

"Good. Let's see who's down there."

Josh, Jana, Scott and Jeff circled the city in their Comanche, trying to see what they could see, and searching for a place to jump from the small craft, or perhaps even a place to land. Jeff had already made up his mind he probably wasn't going to get home, since the search had used up more than half the fuel in the tanks. He just hadn't told the chief yet.

They were aghast at the devastation they saw on the trip out from the mountain, but the destruction in the city was even worse. Most of the journey had occurred in total silence, as tears dampened wind burned cheeks. Their once beautiful land now looked like the surface of a different planet, a dead planet at that. Was there even a chance that Mike and Doc had found a place to survive all of this? And now they'd left the safety of their mountain home, probably for nothing.

As the plane circled, and drew closer to the source of the smoke they'd seen from a distance, Jana noticed the mass graves filled with the dead. From afar, it seemed there might still be some alive in the heaps of bodies, until they got closer and she realized the movement she'd seen was simply from scavengers feeding on the dead. Shivers danced up and down her spine as the plane got low enough to see the sheer numbers of rats, dogs and buzzards crawling in and out of the heaps. So many dead. They'd noticed bodies all along the way, once they reached the towns and villages of the plains, but nothing like this. All she could do is shake her head and cry for the great loss.

"I'm going to set down on the road over here, or what's left of it. I'll try to get as close to the smoke as possible."

"I thought we were going to jump, Jeff."

"Sir, the fuel levels are too low. I'll never get out of here anyway, so I might as well try to be some help."

"Why didn't you tell us, Jeff? You aren't even wearing a suit. You won't have any protection."

"It wouldn't have mattered, Jana. By the time we got to the city I was well past the half way mark on my fuel. Don't worry about it, I'm not. Let me try to be of assistance if I can."

"You're a good man, Jeff. Let's try to get as close as we can to the source of the smoke. Maybe there are others who've found a safe shelter there. We might at least be able to get you under some kind of cover."

From inside the subway tunnel Mike and Bella heard the sound of an aircraft, and they began to make their way, slowly, to the tunnel entrance. When they arrived they saw a small plane circling the tunnel entrance and appearing to get closer with each pass, then the craft veered off in the direction of the road. There was no way to know that the occupants of the aircraft were friends, so Mike went about arming himself, and grabbing a revolver for Bella too. They made their way deeper into the tunnel and wrapped scarves around their faces to block out as much of the smell of rotting corpses as possible.

"Who do you think they are, Mike?"

"I don't know, Bella. We haven't run into many visitors out here. I don't think they're prospective patients anyway. Not if they're flying in. With that kind of transportation they could get to a facility with much more in the way of doctors and supplies. If it was Bahram's men, I'd think there would be more of them than a four passenger piper could carry, so maybe whoever is headed this way is actually looking for us. Let's be careful until we can figure out their motives, okay?"

"Hey, I'm just following you."

"Okay, I hear voices out there. Stay behind me."

Josh, Jana, Scott and Jeff made their way from the road, to the tunnel entrance, and began to descend slowly into the subway. The only light coming from within, was that which came from a burning barrel reflecting off of rows and rows of dirty white tile. "Hello? Is there anyone here?"

"Jana? Is that you?"

"Mike? Where are you? I can't believe it."

Mike and Bella emerged from the darkness, and when they did their group of rescuers took in a collective gasp. Mike was barely recognizable, so ravaged by their circumstances; and beside him, a beautiful woman, just as thin and bald and covered with sores from radiation poisoning as he.

"Oh, Mike, we wanted to come look for you sooner, but the radiation levels were so high we didn't dare risk anyone else's lives."

"Don't worry about it, Jana. I didn't even know you folks were home from Jerusalem."

"Hi Mike, yeah, we left Israel shortly after the meteor shower. The battle was over for all accounts, because so many of the enemy were killed by flaming rocks. When we determined there was really nothing else we could do there, we loaded into troop carriers and Jeff brought us home. It was a long trip, but Jeff and his crew did a great job duct tapping the planes together and we made it. We got close to the coast just as the blast happened. We were still far enough from land that we weren't effected by any of it, and we landed on the plateau. None of the poison has made it up the mountain, at least not yet."

"Praise God for that, Josh. I'm glad you all made it back safely. I brought troops out on a humanitarian mission, you know, supplies and such. We got hit by that meteor shower you were talking about. One of the men was taken out, but the rest of us made it into the subway tunnels. We were taking shelter down here and suddenly all sorts of people, sick and wounded, began finding their way into the tunnels. Doc showed up a few days later with more supplies, and we were all here when the bombs hit."

"How is Doc? I don't see him."

"We lost him, Jana. He passed away at four p.m. yesterday. The radiation has taken just about everyone from here now."

"Doc is gone? Cathy and the kids will be devastated."

"You can tell them he saved many people, at least long enough to lead them to the Lord before they died. He fought hard against the radiation poisoning that has been eating away at us all, but it became more than he could bear. We'll all miss him, he was a good friend."

"How many here are still alive, Mike?"

"Only a few, Josh. All the troops I came with have died. Bella and I, and a couple of the patients are all that's left; but I don't expect they will last much longer. By the way, I'd like you to meet my wife, Bella."

"Your wife? I didn't know. Pleased to meet you, Bella. Congratulations! How did the two of you meet?"

"She came seeking shelter and since she's a nurse, I put her to work right away. I guess I grew on her, and since I thought she was the most beautiful woman I'd ever met, I took a chance and asked her to marry me. I lucked out. She said yes."

"So happy to meet you, Bella. I wish it could have been under better circumstances. Mike is a fine man, and I'm glad he finally found someone to love."

"Thank you very much, Jana. Mike has spoken so much about you and Josh that I feel as if I already know you. He also talks a lot about Scott, and Mark, and everyone back on the base."

"Hey, that's me, Scott I mean. Happy to meet you, Bella."

"And I you, Scott."

"Thank you, everyone. I'm glad you all got a chance to meet Bella before, you know."

"Don't talk like that, Mike. We're going to get you out of here and back up to the mountain. Maybe we can get this turned around."

"Now, Jana, we all know that isn't going to happen. I really wish the four of you hadn't trekked clear out here, just to try and save us. And, I hope you have enough gas in that thing to get yourselves back home before you fall victim to the high radiation levels."

"No, Sir, we don't have enough gas to get back home, but we can try to hike out."

"Jeff, as I said, the radiation levels are still so high, you'll never make it home."

"Well then, I guess we'll go out trying. Now, I've gotta say, I'm really glad I didn't let Becca come with us."

"I should invite you in. The tunnels keep some of the fallout to a minimum, and we do have some uncontaminated supplies left. You'll have to excuse the smell. Once my help passed away, I didn't have a way to get the bodies out to the mass graves, so in the end, this will be their final resting place."

"I'm going to stand guard, Josh."

"Thank you, Jeff. Holler if you need anything."

"Sure thing."

The smell was indeed overwhelming, so Jana buried her mouth and nose in her sleeve. As they descended into the tunnel she heard the distinct sounds of scurrying vermin as she waited for her eyes to adjust to semi darkness.

"Wow, you weren't kidding about the smell."

"It does take some getting used to, Jana. I'm sorry."

"Okay, Don't think I'm ever gettin' used to this, Mike."

"Sorry, Scott. I wish there was something I could do about it, but it is what it is."

"That's okay, Buddy. I'll deal with it."

"Hey, General, I see movement out past the edge of the city. Looks like troops coming this way."

"You all stay here. Let me go check out what's happening. I don't know what Jeff is seeing yet. I'll yell if I need you........ What do you see, Jeff?"

"There, Sir. They're still a far sight off from our present position, but they'll be here within say, two hours or so, even maneuvering around rubble, at the rate they're marching."

"Good job, soldier. Keep your eyes open. I'm going to let the others know what's going on. I'll check in with you in a few minutes."

Josh, thinking all the way, found the others hunkered down in a nearby tunnel.

"Jeff was right, it's definitely soldiers. They will be here in about two hours. Someone must have reported your clinic, and once they got into the area it didn't take much to pinpoint your location from the fire just like we did. They just followed that column of smoke from your burning barrels."

"What are we going to do, Josh?"

"Well, the way I see it, Jana, we can't stay here. Six of us against a battalion of men. They would finish us off in no time. I'm not ready to give up so easily, are you?"

"Of course not. You know me better than that."

"Okay, I say we pack up and load into the Comanche."

"Jeff said we didn't have enough fuel to get home. Isn't that a suicide mission?"

"Everything we've done so far has been a suicide mission, Scott. I'm not suggesting we try to take the Comanche home, but we can sure go as far as the remaining fuel will take us. That should put some distance between us and Bahram's men, and maybe we can figure out another plan before they get close. Hey, Jeff, could you come here?"

"Yes, Sir. What can I do for you, Sir?"

"I know you told us we don't have the fuel to get home, but if we wanted to leave, how far would it get us?"

"Well, we could probably get a hundred and fifty, maybe two hundred, miles out of her if we push it."

"Can she hold six passengers?"

"Yes Sir, we could pack everyone in, but that will cut down on the distance we'll be able to go."

"Good, then that's what we're going to do. Let's pack up the essentials, and we'll leave before they even get here."

"Hey, hey, Josh. Bella and I aren't going anywhere. The radiation poisoning is so advanced in us that there's no way to save us, even if we could make it clear back to the mountain. We're tired and weak. We'd never be able to handle that kind of a hike once the plane ran out of fuel. Besides, Jeff said you could get more miles out of her if there were only the four of you to haul. I have a better idea. We have some explosive ordinances with us, and I'm sure you folks brought some too. What do you say we rig up a nice surprise for our visitors? We'll lure them down into the tunnel and take the whole battalion out at once. What do you think, Bella? Are you up for one more adventure with me, before we go home?"

"I would follow you anywhere husband. Let's get started."

"Mike, we can't let you do this."

"Jana, we don't really have another choice. These are Bahram's men. They'll never stop until they kill us, or someone kills them. They'd be terrified to go back to their base if their mission isn't completed. No, this is the perfect plan. It will give you a fighting chance to get back to home base, before he sends more troops. And, I can tell you, nothing would give me more pleasure than to see his plans disrupted."

"Mike is right, Jana. This is the only way. Okay everyone, we don't have much time, so let's get started."

For the next half hour the six arranged an especially large surprise for their coming guests. Ordinances set into the walls of the main tunnel every ten feet, that would be set off by a huge explosion at the main entrance. This was all set to go off remotely once all the enemy troops were in the tunnel. Mike and Bella would be deep in the underground, luring the soldiers in further, and would set off the main blast point with a preset device.

Jana thought Mike looked happier than she'd ever seen him. Neither Mike, nor Bella, looked the least bit frightened. They knew where they were going, and it was a fair sight better than where they'd spent the first part of their married life. The group spent some time saying their good-byes. They knew their paths would not cross again, at least on this side of eternity. Jana gave Bella a hug, and then stood for a moment with tears in her eyes looking at Mike.

"I love you, Mike. You've taught me so much. Thank you for watching out for me until I found Josh again."

"I love you too, Jana. I always have. But, I think you're misremembering. At least about who took care of who. It has been a pleasure, and I would do it all over again."

"Mike, you have been an example to everyone who knows you. We look forward to seeing you again when we're home with the Lord. I love you buddy."

"I love you too Josh. These years together have been good ones, and I wouldn't trade them for anything. You kids get home safe, and we will see you again. Probably sooner that any of us realizes."

"Love you, Pastor Mike."

"Love you too, Scott. Go on now, all of you. They'll be here before you know it."

"Go with God my friend."

"And you also."

The four ran to the nearby road and loaded their gear in the small plane. They should be able to get far enough away to at least stretch their lead. Who knew when Bahram was expecting to hear back from his generals, or when he might send out another battalion? Jeff started the engines, taxied down the road, and took off low. The soldiers were still far enough away, that a low flying takeoff might not be noticed.

Mike and Bella made their way down into the subway tunnels, but they left evidence of life all along the way, to lure their unsuspecting enemy in. Then they settled down to wait.

Being exhausted by the afternoon's goings on, they dozed off in each other's arms. Pretty soon they heard voices. The intruders tried to make as little noise as possible, but boots on concrete floors are a dead giveaway. Mike looked at Bella and smiled. "I love you, Bella. I'm going to talk normally, as if we don't hear the troops in the tunnels."

"I understand, husband. If they hear us talking, they will think we don't know of their presence, but they still won't be able to tell what we are talking about."

"You have been the best thing that's ever happened to me, Bella. I am married to the most beautiful woman on earth, and I wouldn't change these past days for anything in the world."

"I feel the same way, Mike. You are the man of my dreams. I would rather have spent these few short days with you, here in these tunnels; than to have another hundred years anywhere else without you. You have been my best friend and the completeness of my heart."

They could hear soldiers getting closer to their location in the tunnel. Once they were sure that at least the bulk of the enemy troops were within the walls of the subway system, Mike wrapped his arms around his wife, they kissed, and he pressed the button that would bury them all beneath the city.

The blast caught their enemy off guard. The majority of the battalion was caught inside the subway, and killed instantly. Some farther down the tunnel were buried with Mike and Bella. A few, who were still outside the walls of the subway escaped, but some of those were badly injured, and now their radiation suits were also torn. The radio man survived, and within minutes he was sending out a distress signal to the base from which they'd been deployed.

"Sir, I have news from the front."

"Go ahead sergeant. What have you heard? Did they find the rebels?"

"Sir, they found the clinic in the city, and we can only assume some of the rebels were inside, but there was an explosion and most of the battalion has been lost."

"I don't care about that! Did they get Conyers?"

"Sir, we just don't know."

"I want more men out there right now, do you hear me? I want to know if Conyers is dead. I want to know how many of the rebels were taken out in the blast. And, if we didn't get that damnable Conyers and his wife, I want to know where they are, do you understand me?"

"Yes Sir. I'll get right on it, Sir."

The Lord of hosts has sworn: "As I have planned, so shall it be, and as I have purposed, so shall it stand, that I will break the Assyrian in my hand, and on my mountains trample him underfoot; and his yoke shall depart from them, and his burden from their shoulder." This is the purpose that is purposed concerning the whole earth, and this is the hand that is stretched out over all nations. For the Lord of hosts has purposed, and who will annul it? His hand is stretched out, and who will turn it back?

Isaiah 14:24-27

After this I heard what seemed to be the loud voice of a great multitude in heaven, crying out, "Hallelujah! Salvation and glory and power belong to our God, for His judgments are true and just; for He has judged the great prostitute who corrupted the earth with her immorality, and has avenged on her the blood of His servants."

Revelation 19:1-2

"O Lord, You are my God; I will exalt You; I will praise Your name, for You have done wonderful things, plans formed of old, faithful and sure. For You have made the city a heap, the fortified city a ruin; the foreigners' palace is a city no more; it will never be rebuilt."

Isaiah25:1-2

CHAPTER 11

"Satan, you sent for me?"

"How are things coming together? Will we be ready to fight the enemy soon?"

"Yes your eminence. I have been equipping the demons, and I think we will be ready to go by the morning."

"Good! I've waited a very long time for this and I don't want any hold ups, or any mistakes, do you hear me?"

"Yes Sir, I promise I am doing everything in my power to make this the invasion you've always dreamed of, Sir."

"Keep me posted. I want to make a grand entrance. He's not the only one who can put on a show."

"Get me Graham!"

"Yes Sir. I believe he's at the church getting ready for services tomorrow, so it may take me a few moments to retrieve him."

"Make it quick. We have some plans to discuss."

Bahram planned to make one final use of Graham, and his ability to fool the nations with his tricks. Amir already had the adoration of most of the surviving humans on earth, in part due to Graham's magic and deception; but he needed one final push to get those few holdouts to cross the line. The two of them would conclude their ultimate takeover with one last series of 'miracles', all conveniently caught on satellite screens around the world, which would insure the loyalty of every remaining human on the planet, well, besides those ever annoying Christian rebels.

After this, he would quietly dispose of Graham, begin discretely dismantling the 'World Church', and slowly begin the final steps in building his caliphate, in anticipation of the coming Twelfth Imam. Once the Mahdi arrived they would dispose of the remnants of the fabricated government church institution together. It had, after all, simply been a sham religion, by which to facilitate the demise of

Christianity. He'd learned well, in his years of perpetuating lies to further the cause of Islam. First destroy the base, and then a replacement base will be needed. Once the need for a new base was established, he would have the only answers that made sense. When the world saw the wisdom and practicality of Islam, and the importance of rule by Sharia Law, they would fall at his feet, or, well, at the feet of the Mahdi.

"Yes, Amir? You sent for me?"

"Yes I did, Nathan. We need to plan our next steps. I want you to dig into your bag of tricks and come up with something really big. We've got to put on a show, one last time, before we wrap things up."

"I wonder, Amir. Is it even necessary anymore? With all the disasters, the nuclear weapons, and disease, how many are there even left alive, out of eight billion souls, to win over? Aren't they all just waiting for the word? Don't they simply need someone to lead them to the next step?"

"Well, Nathan, that is where you and I differ. You are content to sit back and let the chips fall where they may. I, on the other hand, know that humans need direction, and will go where led, like a flock of sheep. There are still millions of confused humans out there, wandering around waiting for some kind of a sign. We will be that sign for them. We will lead them to the next phase of the plan. And, because they secretly want to be relieved of any responsibility; of the outcome of the decisions that need to be made; they will follow."

"You know, you've never even told me what the final plan is, Amir. What is our end game? Will I have a place in this ultimate design?"

"Oh, yes, Nathan. This plan would be impossible without you. Are you kidding? You will be amazed at the arrangements I've made for you in all of this."

"Fine, I will come up with a show to end all shows. We will make you look like the god most of them already believe you are, and then I want to know exactly what you intend to do with my part in all of this."

"Good, let me know when things are ready. And, you, soldier, get me my generals. I need to know if everything is still on track for our entrance into Israel. This time no one will be able to stop us, and I will wipe out the filthy dogs once and for all. I'm going to make many in the Middle East very happy."

"Okay, everyone strap in, this is bound to be a bumpy landing."

Fuel expended, the small aircraft glided to the ground. When landing gear connected with earth, the Comanche jumped and came down, hard, several times, shaking up its passengers. All in all, not nearly as bad as they'd thought it might be. Once they'd checked that all their parts were still attached, and breathing back to normal, all four gathered gear and collected necessities. It would be a long trip back to home base, but at least they had a jump on the next group of soldiers Bahram had likely deployed by now.

Their mood was somber. Mike's and Bella's sacrifice to ensure their successful escape, weighed heavily on their collective minds. Mike had been a good friend in life, and was now a hero in death, to all of them. Jana was happy he'd had an opportunity to experience the love of a good woman, even if for only a short time, before he went home to be with Jesus. A piece of her would always care about him, and be grateful for all the mentoring he had done with her in the mountain cave. There would certainly be an empty hole in the camp community without Pastor Mike.

Wasteland abounded in every direction, where their plane landed for the final time. Jana was sure, if they had a Geiger counter with them, it would be clicking away like mad by now. They were all grateful there was fresh water in their packs and canteens, but there was a lot of ground to cover between here and home, and they'd have to do some serious conserving.

The region they currently walked should have been thick with grasses, wildflowers, trees, and millions of acres of various farm crops, which from above would appear as a patchwork quilt. Past trips through the area; to deliver supplies, and visit sister bases; had left them commenting on beautiful, bucolic scenery: small towns and villages, reminiscent of Norman Rockwell paintings; ancient farm houses with antique red barns; fields of beef cattle and horses; and old schoolhouses filled with billions of memories and the smells of floor wax and chalk. Every cross and bell tower had long since been removed from churches scattered across the plains, due to the ban on practicing Christianity, but they knew of fellow rebels who still met in secret places, and they still connected with them when they could. From the looks of their surroundings, those meetings were at an end.

Now, the green and growing things had been burned away from large swaths of the country. In towns and villages close to the blast, buildings were leveled. But those further away had suffered a slower death. All that remained of them were pieces of ash covered wooden skeletons, with evidence of an occasional brick chimney rising up from the rubble.

As they walked, they encountered very few signs of life, but the ones they did stumble upon were frightening. A large dog; fur missing; covered with angry sores; foam dripping from its muzzle; and eyes red with confusion and disease, leapt from a large rock, when they rounded the bend in a devastated village. Lunging for Jeff's throat, he missed and made ready to pounce again. They managed to shoot him in the head before he did any real damage. Rats had taken over the land, and were still scurrying around ruins and decomposing bodies. Occasionally they were surprised by a lone person, or two, trying to survive in the devastation. But to look at them, it was easy to see they didn't have much time left in this life. When they did encounter these frightened people, they gave what they could of the little they had, and they shared the Word of God; sometimes accepted willingly and sometimes cast aside.

On the first evening of their journey, which they spent in a burned out building, they were attacked by a band of five men. Destruction often breeds violence in those who don't truly know the Lord. The men were covered in sores, with missing teeth, and heads almost completely devoid of hair. They were clearly deranged, trying to survive at the expense of others, and willing to kill to do that. The four travelers were forced to defend themselves, and the five men were killed for their trouble.

"Why? I don't understand what causes some people to become animals in times of tragedy?"

"Fear, Jana. Simple plain fear. When someone doesn't know the Truth, they have no hope and feel that they have to make a way for themselves. You see, we know the Father will care for us, no matter what, so we don't feel the need to steal from others to take care of ourselves. I think that has always been one of the easiest ways to tell if someone is a Christian. By how easy, or hard, it is for them to let go of the things of this earth."

"I know you're right of course, but I was terrified when they attacked. It was far worse than fighting enemy soldiers. Those who feel they have something to live for, or someone to go home to, seem to fight with a purpose, but also with the knowledge that we have someone to go home to as well. The only other time I've fought an enemy, who seemed to have no desire to see us as human beings, is fighting in Jerusalem against the Muslim hordes. These men fought as though killing us was the only way they could survive, just like those who follow Islam."

"To them it was the only way they could survive. They had to take from us in order to have for themselves. Many people look at the love of Christ the same way. You know, like perhaps He doesn't have enough love to go around, so they have to put on a front and pretend that they are good enough to deserve all of His love more than the next guy does."

"So sad. Do you think we should bury them?"

"I don't want to disturb the ground any more than we have to. Not with the high levels of radiation out here. The scavengers will take care of things."

Jana remembered reading once that if there was ever a nuclear event, the survivors, when all was said and done, would be cockroaches and Twinkies. And, though they still saw a thriving insect population every where they went, including plenty of cockroaches, she'd have to argue that rats seemed to have won the day. They multiplied abundantly under the current circumstances. Or, maybe they just weren't frightened to come out of the shadows now. The moment the four walked away from the five dead men, the rats swarmed, and Jana's arms were covered in goose flesh as she backed warily away. They would have the bones stripped of every bit of flesh within minutes.

"Is anyone else hungry?"

"Oh, Scott, leave it to you to remind us that we still need to eat. Sure, should we stop everyone?"

"I'm fine with that. I'm not particularly hungry, but I could use a little water and a chance to rest. I want to get a little further away from the rats though."

"I agree. Moving away from the rats would be a good idea. I don't want them to get into such a feeding frenzy that they mistake us for dessert. But Jana, I'm going to insist that you eat a little something. You have to keep up your strength, or you'll never make it home."

"Are we still playing that game, Josh? I know I'm probably a little jumpy after the dog almost took my throat out, but even the radiation alone is going to take its toll. I know the three of you have suits, but they're old, and they don't cover everything. Do you really think we have a chance of making it clear home alive?"

"Here's what I figure, Jeff. If God needs us alive for the rest of this journey, He will keep us alive. In that case it is our duty to at least attempt to go the distance. If Jesus decides to come back before we get to the mountain, the rest of our trip will be made much easier, and I'm good with that too."

"I guess you're right. Thanks for the reminder. I guess I'll Just keep putting one foot in front of the other."

"Good man, Jeff. But, first let's get somewhere a little safer and have something to eat."

• • • • •

"Do you remember when we were kids, and we used to climb the trees in the orchard?"

"Sure, so what made you think of that?"

"I guess I miss my dad, and I know you miss your parents too, don't you?"

"Of course I do, but I still don't know what that has to do with the apple trees. You're a strange woman, Elizabeth."

"I just remember how upset my dad got when he caught us up in those trees. He was worried that we'd fall out and break our necks, and he didn't want us to get hurt. I know my mom is worried sick, even though she won't admit it.

They should have been back by now, if they'd found Doc and Pastor Mike alive that is. What if we never see them again? I want to have the kind of faith that you have, Alec, the kind that your parents have, but just like my dad worried when we climbed trees, I know that people can get hurt and die, and I'm just scared that we won't ever see them again."

Alec held his wife as she cried, and assured her that all would be well. "I don't know why you think I'm never scared, Elizabeth. I have to say that not much rattles my parents, but God is still working on me. One thing I do know though, is that when we leave this place, we will be with Jesus, and I'm really looking forward to that day. The reason that doesn't scare me is because I know my whole family will be there too. You know your family will be right beside us as well, and there will be no more sadness or pain. Doesn't that sound amazing?"

"Yes it does. I hope He comes soon."

"I think He will be coming sooner than we ever believed."

Elizabeth fell asleep in her husband's arms, and dreamed of simpler times.

Graham was getting things lined up for the big magic show that would solidify Bahram's deity in the eyes of the people of the land once and for all. He had some pretty good tricks up his sleeve. However, he was becoming suspicious of Amir's intentions toward him. He'd thought about leaving. Though much of the U.S. was destroyed after the meteor showers, and subsequent atomic blasts with their poisonous after effects, there were still a few patches of semi safety around the world. Parts of the Northern regions of the country going into what used to be Canada; and sections of Europe, along with pieces of the African and Asian continents were still intact. Though on a worldwide scale there had been abundant natural disasters even before the meteors hit, there might still be a safe place or two out there.

Nuclear winter was presently taking its toll around the globe. Nathan wished someone had consulted him before trying to destroy all of mankind. He would have voted a big fat no on the whole blow up the world thing. Perhaps he could line up something comfortable for himself in another part of the world. He certainly had enough wealth to survive, and could probably keep himself hidden from

Bahram and his cronies if push came to shove. Nothing had prepared him for the absolute lunacy of Bahram and his plans, since he'd been kept so completely out of the loop. All he could think of now was how to escape before that lunacy was directed at him.

He wasn't nearly as stupid as Bahram thought he was. He'd seen the appointments of prominent Muslims to posts all over the world, and concluded that Amir planned to eventually do away with the Church. He knew what Islam stood for, and he had as little faith in that religion as any other. So, he assumed his usefulness would come to a screeching halt as soon as this last magic show was over. He'd figured out long ago that the 'World Church' was just a means to an end. A way to keep the people believing they had a right to religion. A religion that offered no real hope, but was palatable to all who participated in it, and effective for no one. He'd also seen the comings and goings of many important people from Amir's chain of command in the Middle East, and he knew there was something brewing. But he just never thought that something was atomic weapons, and complete obliteration.

As he prepared for the upcoming circus performance, he also began making preparations for a quick getaway.

Little did he know, after all this time, that even his own servants answered to the evil Bahram.

• • • • •

"How are things coming, Kakos?"

"Very good, Sir. The demons will be ready soon. We are preparing the mounts as we speak, and I think you will be very pleased with the resulting effects of our choices."

"Good, keep me posted. I can't wait to get out there. I want to be sure we time our arrival with that of Bahram's attack on Israel."

"Yes, Sir."

"Did you just come back from speaking with Satan?"

"Yes, I did. What made you ask, Keres?"

"Usually when you go talk to him he yells so loud that the very gates of hell shake. I just didn't hear anything this time, that's all."

"Yeah, that does seem strange, doesn't it?"

"Perhaps he's finally beginning to see my real worth."

"Yeah, no, I doubt that."

"I wish I hadn't been blind for so long. Look at all the wonderful years we missed together, just because I was content to sit around and feel sorry for myself."

"At least we have today. I'm just happy that you finally came to your senses, Mark."

"I am too, Dad. You really do have a rather thick skull."

"Thanks, Eva. No more comments from the peanut gallery. Shall we go for a walk?"

"Why don't you two go? I'd rather stay home and rest. I had a hard day over in the kitchens. Enjoy yourselves."

As they walked hand in hand, "I'm pretty sure she just wanted to give us some time alone together."

"Really, Dad? Can't get very much past you these days."

"Oh stop. Don't laugh at me, Rachel. Maybe I do have a thick skull, but I know I love you to pieces. Here you were right under my nose the whole time, and I didn't see how perfect we were for each other."

"But that's okay, Mark. We're together now, and that's all that matters. How do the fields look?"

"Surprisingly good. Way better than anything that's happening outside of our cavern. I don't know how long it will take before people on the outside can plant crops again, with the radiation poisoning, and now this nuclear winter keeping the sun from shining as brightly as crops require. But, people have to eat, and I'm hoping we can help provide food to other communities that don't have as much as we do. I'm just not sure where those populations might be. I also went over and helped Alec with training this afternoon, when I was done in the fields."

"I didn't know you were over there. How is he?"

"He's doing fine. He misses his folks of course, but he's a level headed guy and he won't let that get in the way of his duty."

"Are the troops doing well?"

"They looked really good. I'm proud of the job he's doing with them, and I think they will be ready for just about anything."

"So what do you think is going to happen?"

"I don't exactly know, Rachel. I think that's why Josh told us to be ready for anything. He is pretty sure that the end is more near than we've ever believed. And even though my faith has never been quite as bold as his, I think I'm getting closer to accepting that than I've ever been before."

"I know Jana feels the same way. I've been really nervous, because I hope I instilled enough knowledge of the gift of Grace into the kids, that they are prepared when the time comes."

" Well, I think you did a great job, Babe. The kids know exactly where they would be going, and they are anxious to meet their Savior. I thank you for taking care of Junior, and Eva, while I was off fighting my own demons. If it hadn't been for you in their lives, it would have been a pretty sad childhood. I'm confident that Junior is waiting for us with the Lord, and that Eva is prepared, come what may."

"Thank you. That means a lot to me. I love you, Mark."

"I love you too, Rachel. I'm so glad you waited for me."

• • • • •

Jana sat with the men and watched. Jeff had already started coughing, the deep down cough that means the lungs are beginning to deteriorate and fill with liquid. A part of her wanted to regret coming on this fool's errand, to try and save Doc and Mike, but she would never have seen how happy Mike was with Bella before he died, so she couldn't get behind that feeling. None of them would live in their present state forever, and she wasn't afraid to see what would come next. She hadn't said anything to Josh yet, but when she tried to fix her pony tail before they sat down to eat, a handful of hair came away in her hand. Even with the minor protection that the ancient radiation suits might be providing, the poison was still having its way with her. When she laid down to rest in Josh's arms, after their meager meal, she was no longer concerned about where to lay her head. If the radiation was already taking its toll, there was no reason to try and avoid it. Scott took first shift and sat guard while his friends slept.

He'd noticed a sore on his arm, and then realized his gums were bleeding. He knew they wouldn't make it all the way home, and was pretty sure Josh had figured it out by now too, mainly because he saw him brushing away hair earlier in the day. None of them would have wanted to contaminate the mountain base with the radioactive dust covering their bodies, so he was pretty sure they were just keeping up appearances for now.

He was saddened by the fact that he wouldn't see his beloved Becca, C.J., Angel, or Elizabeth again in this life; but he knew without doubt they would be reunited in the next. He'd had a great time here on planet earth, and he couldn't complain. A life that could never have been predicted if he'd gauged it by the events of his childhood. Even after the abuse by his father and mother during his formative years, his own stupid decisions, prison time, and his first marriage to Virginia; God had still decided to bless him with the best wife a man could ask for and really great kids. He had friends he could count on, who loved him. And, best of all, the love of a Savior who died and rose again for him. He knew what his future held, and that was the most important thing.

He looked over at the sleeping couple on the ground near him, and a single tear trailed through the dirt and dust on his face. Not a tear of sadness, as much as a tear of gratitude. Josh had been like a brother to him, and Jana like a sister. No one in his life had ever really loved him until those two came into his life. He wouldn't have known how to love his wife and kids properly without their mentorship. Yes, life had been good. Better than he deserved. And, if it was time to move on, time to meet his Lord, then he was ready. He only hoped he would be up for the challenges that were coming next.

Jana slept, and in her sleep she happened upon the same valley of flowers she'd seen in a dream, when she was in the small mountain cave so long ago. The cave where she'd leapt into the Savior's arms as He revealed Himself to her. The air was crisp and clear, no traces of dust and ash, flowers of every type and vibrant color filled the field. She was free of anxiety and felt at peace with the universe. Suddenly, she was aware of a presence. The same presence she'd felt in the haziness when she'd been shot on the mountain plateau. And a voice called out. "Jana."

"Yes Lord."

"I am with you."

"Yes Lord, I feel your presence."

"I want you all to be prepared. I am coming back for you very soon."

"When, Lord? Can you tell me when?"

"Only the Father knows the exact moment, daughter, but soon, very soon."

Jana woke excited, and as she lifted her head, she saw a look of excitement on her husband's face as he woke from his slumber.

"Jana, Jesus came to me in my dream. He told me to be ready. He said He will be coming very soon."

"I know, Josh, He came to me too."

"Then it doesn't matter that the radiation is killing us here, and making our hair fall out, because we will soon be with him."

"Oh, you too? I thought I was the only one."

"No, I started showing signs this morning, and I'm pretty sure Scott is too. I think Jeff is the worst off. His cough sounds terrible."

"I heard you two talking, and yes, I've been showing symptoms too. I know the Lord is returning soon, but what do we do until then?

"We continue to walk. God will tell us what to do. Until then we just walk, perhaps there will be people to minister to along the way, or another purpose. I want to be agreeing with Him until the moment we meet Him in the air, Scott."

"Me too. Who ever knew that this would happen in our lifetime? I've never been so excited about anything. And, we will see our families again too!"

"And I saw a beast rising out of the sea, with ten horns and seven heads, with ten diadems on its horns and blasphemous names on its heads. And the beast that I saw was like a leopard; its feet were like a bear's, and its mouth was like a lion's mouth. And to it the dragon gave his power and his throne and great authority. One of its heads seemed to have a mortal wound, but its mortal wound was healed, and the whole earth marveled as they followed the beast, and they worshipped the beast, saying, "who is like the beast, and who can fight against it?"

Revelation 13:1-4

"Then I saw another angel flying directly overhead, with an eternal gospel to proclaim to those who dwell on earth, to every nation and tribe and language and people. And he said with a loud voice, "Fear God and give Him glory, because the hour of His judgment has come, and worship Him who made heaven and earth, the sea and the springs of water."

Revelation 14:6-7

"And another angel, a third, followed them, saying with a loud voice, "If anyone worships the beast and its image and receives a mark on his forehead or on his hand, he will also drink the wine of God's wrath, poured full strength into the cup of His anger, and he will be tormented with fire and sulfur in the presence of the holy angels and in the presence of the Lamb. And the smoke of their torment goes up forever and ever, and they have no rest, day or night, these worshippers of the beast and its image, and whoever receives the mark of its name." Here is a call for the endurance of the saints, those who keep the commandments of God and their faith in Jesus. And I heard a voice from heaven saying, "Write this: Blessed are the dead who die in the Lord from now on." "Blessed indeed", says the Spirit, that they may rest from their labors, for their deeds follow them."

Revelation 14:9-13

"Then I looked, and behold, a white cloud, and seated on the cloud one like a son of man, with a golden crown on His head and a sharp sickle in His hand, and another angel came out of the temple, calling with a

CHAPTER 12

The magic was astounding, and the people stood in awe of their ruler. Graham's tricks duped all of those foolish who did not follow the living Christ. Every man, woman and child on the earth, who did not subscribe to Christianity, bowed to General Bahram and the evil that he represented. In the spiritual world, things were coming together, and Satan planned the timing of his arrival to the battle Amir already arranged with the kings and leaders of every Middle Eastern and Asian country who sought the destruction of God's chosen people.

Bahram proved to be very easy to manipulate, from beginning to end. He was so sure his mythical Twelfth Imam was coming to rule the universe, that Satan just had to laugh at the gullibility of all those who bowed to other religions. He would never stand in their way, no, no, no, because it made his job so much easier in the long run, when leaders from false religions caused humankind to turn from Jesus. This time he had twice ten thousand times ten thousand mounted troops, plus all those loose cannons who follow Amir, to make a stand. He would not lose again, and when he won, he would spit in the face of the God who'd cast him out of heaven.

Commander Bahram sent again for his generals, as he prepared himself for battle. It was clear that the people loved him. He would ride into Israel, but this time his army would be unstoppable. Surely, after the damages Israel had incurred from the meteors, and then the nuclear bomb he had sent their way, they wouldn't have the manpower, or strength to stand up to his vast army. And his army was not only immense, it was also made up of those who hated the Jews as much as he did. This time he would wipe them from the face of the earth, those dogs and pigs, then surely the way would be paved for the arrival of the Mahdi. Nothing could stop him now.

"I had a dream last night. It felt so real that it seemed as though God was actually speaking to me."

"Tell me about it, Alec, and then I'll tell you about mine."

"You had one too, Elizabeth?"

"Yes, but you go first."

"Well, I was walking outside and I came across a valley so filled with flowers that the intense beauty was unlike anything I'd ever seen before. Flowers of every variety, and every color. The fragrance was amazing, and I started to sit down to enjoy the place. Then I heard a voice say, "Come here, my son." I got back up and began to walk toward the voice and suddenly there was a figure in the midst of the flowers. His back was to me, but as He started to turn, I knew immediately it was Jesus. I ran, but He didn't just stand there, He was running too, and He ran right to me. I hugged Him and wept. He told me He had special plans for us, and that great things would be happening very soon."

"Then I don't even need to tell you about mine, because you might as well have been in my dream with me. Oh, Alec, I'm just shaking with excitement! This means we will be seeing Grampa and Gramma soon, doesn't it?"

"Well, we have to remember we don't know exactly when it will be, Elizabeth. No one knows but the Father, but Jesus did say it would be very soon. And, yes, I'm excited too."

• • • • •

"Scott, come here, I need you."

"What is it, Josh?"

"I can't wake Jeff. Help me get him turned over onto his back."

"Sure thing. I'll grab his legs if you get his torso."

"I'm not getting a heartbeat. I'm going to try CPR."

"What's going on, Josh?"

"It's Jeff, Jana. I can't get him to respond. No heartbeat. I'm going to start CPR."

"Well, you do the compressions, and I'll breathe for him. Okay, go ahead, I'm ready."

After fifteen minutes of intense Cardio Pulmonary Resuscitation they finally, exhausted, stopped their attempts. Jana sat back on her heels, and Josh stood up. Scott rested nearby shaking his head. "So, what are we going to do with him? He's a friend. We've lost too many friends already.

And I don't want to just leave him out here for the rats. Can't we at least try to keep him away from the rats?"

"Yeah, we can try to bury him, Scott. Since we don't have to be concerned with radiation levels anymore, let's try to give him a decent service."

"What the heck! What happened? We went to sleep and he was fine, and then he was gone. What the heck!"

"Oh, Scott, he's been going downhill so quickly. Josh and I were just talking last evening about how terrible his cough sounded. I'm actually surprised he lasted this long."

"I know we're all contaminated with this radiation, and I know Jesus is coming to get us soon, but I don't want to lose either one of you. I just don't want to be left alone. I know that sounds selfish, but I don't want to be left alone. Which one of us do you think will be next?"

"I don't think any of us will be going anywhere until the Lord comes back for us, but if I'm wrong, and Jana and I go before you, you'll do just fine, Scott. You know how to take care of yourself."

"It's not the taking care of myself part that I'm worried about. It's the being all alone part. I was always alone as a kid, and since I came to be with you, Josh, you've always included me in everything. You're my family. You two have been with me every step of the way, until I married Becca, and then you invited both of us in. I'm just not used to being alone anymore."

"I know what you mean, Scott, but you're never really alone. Jesus will walk with you, even if we can't be there. Come on, let's get Jeff buried before the rats get wind of him."

The ground was hard, and they didn't have a shovel, so they were making slow progress digging with rocks. They managed to get a depression dug and laid their friend in the shallow grave. After a prayer, they covered the grave with rocks, hoping to deter those who might try to dig him up, and they walked away. None of them really thought the rats and other scavengers wouldn't find him, but at least they'd tried. They'd already gone to half rations on their food and water, but even with Jeff gone, they were going to have to cut back yet again.

Josh thought he'd seen signs, earlier, of a new scouting team on the horizon. He hadn't shared the information with the others, because as sick as they all were from the poisons which surrounded them, he didn't know if they could rally more speed for an escape anyway. He was sure these were more of Bahram's troops. And, out here in the open they would all be sitting ducks, but what could they do? All Josh could think at this point was, "Come Lord Jesus, come."

· · · · ·

Graham had set up an escape plan, and was going to sneak off early in the morning, but Bahram's lackeys had already blown the preacher's cover, and guards were en route to arrest him.

Once apprehended, Nathan fought against his guards, knowing full well that no plans Amir concocted could possibly be good for his long term health. He was dragged unceremoniously to Bahram's office. "And where, my friend, were you headed?"

"I just thought I would take a little time off, Amir. I haven't seen my sister in a long while, so I figured I'd spend a little time with her."

"I didn't know you had a sister, Nathan. Where does she live?"

"I, well, I was going to do a little resting first, and then, well, I....."

"Exactly as I thought, my old friend. I happen to know that there is no sister, so I think you will be spending your time by my side. We are in this together, whether you like it or not. You will ride in front with me, as we go into battle, and whatever happens, we will stand for all of humanity to see. Now, go and be fitted for your gear."

"But, I don't know anything about battle, Amir. I'm sure you have more qualified personnel than I. Why would you place me in such a position of honor?"

"Why indeed, Nathan. I have grown very close to you, and would like your counsel throughout the upcoming battle. I also want you to be right up where the action is, just like I'm sure you would prefer. Now, we will be leaving soon, so, as I said before, go with my men and get fitted for your gear."

"Yes, Amir." Nathan knew this trip would be his last, and that Amir would be placing him in the most dangerous positions of the battle in order to be rid of him, but there was no way he could escape the guards at this point, so he would do what he had to do. Perhaps an opportunity to flee would present itself later."

• • • • •

"Is everything ready to go?"

"Yes Satan. We are ready to ride at your command."

"Elizabeth, gather all the ladies, and have them meet us at our place of worship. I will go and get the men. I feel a need to give praises to God."

"Okay, Alec. Is there something I should know? What do I tell them?"

"Just tell them that the Lord has need of them. We are going to lift His Name on high, and He will do whatever He needs to do with the praise and worship we send His way."

"Okay, just give me a few minutes."

Alec and Elizabeth gathered the entire mountain community for a special service.

"Alright, Alec, is there something going on that we should know about? Have you heard from your folks?"

"No, Mark, we haven't heard anything, but I have a very distinct feeling that we need to be lifting up the Lord in praise and prayer. Something is happening in the spirit world that is pressing upon me, and we need to be in prayer for those who aren't here with us. And, also for the next steps in God's ultimate plan to go as He wills. I believe there are things at play that we cannot comprehend. Spiritual things. But, we do know how to pray and praise, so we will do what we know to do."

The praise and worship band began to play and the entire congregation sang. As they worshipped the Lord, everyone present could feel the power building in their midst. Alec knew God was in command, and still firmly on the throne. He knew his own ministrations wouldn't change the designs God had for the universe; but if they could all help in some small way, they wanted to show their support for His plans, whatever they might be.

"Oh, Alec, can't you just feel the power in the air? I can sense the Holy Spirit, and His authority among us."

"Yes, Elizabeth. The Lord's presence is very strong here."

Becca, C.J. and Angel were all at the front of the group, and as they praised the Lord, Becca prayed for her husband and friends. "Lord, please take care of them, and send my husband home safely to me."

• • • • •

"I need to rest, Josh. I'm sorry, but you might have to go on without me."

"We're not going anywhere without you, Scott."

"I don't want the rest of you to be sitting ducks, just because of me. Don't you think I've noticed the way you keep looking back over your shoulder? I know we're being tracked again, and I don't want the rest of you to be compromised just because I can't go any faster."

"I'm not worried about that, my friend. Let's just all sit down and take a breather. It will all be fine. Jesus has our backs."

"Here, guys, come over here. We'll sit and have some water, then I'm sure we'll be able to go on."

"I wish I could see Becca and the kids again. I'd like to hold her one more time and tell her how much I love her."

"She knows how much you love her, Scott. And you will see her again, very soon now, I'm sure."

Scott began to cough and was suddenly having a hard time catching his breath. As he coughed and choked even harder, he leaned forward and spit up huge amounts of blood. He was hemorrhaging from his lungs, and there was nothing they could do about it. His two best friends held his hands, and he looked frantically back and forth into their faces as he struggled for air. Jana felt his grip grow stronger for a moment as he tried valiantly to hold on to life, and then she felt his hold grow weaker, until his hand finally went limp.

"Oh, Josh, we've lost him."

"No Jana, he's not really lost, you know that."

"I know, Josh. I know he's with the Lord. I'm just so tired of losing the people we love from among us. Goodbye my friend."

"Rest in peace, Scott. I have a feeling we will be seeing you very soon. Until then, enjoy this time with the Lord."

"Should we try to bury him, Josh? I don't want to just leave him laying here in the dirt."

"I don't either, Jana, but if you remember what he was saying about me looking over my shoulder, then you know we are being tracked by Bahram's men again. Scott would understand. We need to get out of here now, and try to find some cover. I think we've already lost much of our distance advantage, and they're probably getting pretty close by now."

"Then I want to let Scott help us one more time."

"What do you mean?"

"Help me roll him over onto his stomach, and I'll explain."

"Okay, Jana, but let's hurry."

Josh could see a small farmstead in the distance. So, after they'd prepared a surprise for those who followed, they made their way in that direction.

"Do you think they'll fall for it?"

"I'm betting they will. I think you should have been a military strategist, Jana. You sure do come up with some great ideas."

"Why, thank you husband. I believe all good ideas come from the Lord. And, like you always tell me, Jesus is taking care of us, so that is that."

When they arrived at the small farmstead, they looked around for cover. The buildings were destroyed, burned to the ground like most everything else in this forsaken wasteland. There was a chimney, though that would certainly not afford much protection, even if they hid inside. But then Jana saw a door. The horizontally positioned door was on a slightly raised piece of ground, like the one she remembered seeing in 'The Wizard of Oz'. She thought it might be a root cellar, or a storm shelter, so she ran in that direction. When she swung the door open her olfactory senses were assailed by the foul smell emanating from within. Josh pulled out his flashlight and stuck his head into the hole. There was the source of the offensive odor.

The family who lived on this farm had used their root cellar as a bomb shelter. It seems they'd stayed in the underground space until their food ran out, and starvation, or radiation poisoning, or plague, or one of a hundred other things took their lives. Josh dragged the bodies out and laid them closer to the burned out farmhouse. Then he found a few odds and ends pieces of wood, and other rubbish. He and Jana entered the cellar and prepared to close the door. However, first they would wait.

Not long after, they heard a loud explosion coming from the place where they'd left Scott's body. They'd cleverly rigged explosives, to their friend's corpse, to react to anyone moving him. As they'd figured it would, by mere human curiosity, it worked. There was no way to know how many enemy combatants their smart move had eliminated, or how many were still alive and seeking them, but now they could close the door and hope for the best. Josh pulled the cellar door mostly closed, and then pulled the trash they'd collected on top of the door, once that was done he pulled his arm in and secured the door from the inside. Now, all they could do is wait.

The couple moved to the far end of the cellar, and settled into each other's arms. As soon as they closed their eyes, exhaustion, radiation sickness, and lack of food overtook them as they drifted off to sleep.

• • • • •

"Commander Bahram, all is ready. The troops are assembled and the kings and leaders are waiting for your word."

"Then you have it. We ride."

Amir's forces, which included all the kings and leaders of the Middle East and Asia with all their millions of men, united to present a combined army of such magnitude as to have never been witnessed before. Amir's intent was to extinguish Judaism and pave the way for the Mahdi.

A star falls from heaven to unlock the bottomless pit. From the pit a great dragon emerges, blowing smoke and fire from his nostrils; and with him, thousands upon thousands times tens of thousands of various demonic spirits. Some of the demons look like locusts: with faces like humans, women's hair, and lion's teeth, they have tails like scorpion stings and wings. Their wings, multiplied by the millions, sound like the roar of jet engines in the air. Other demons ride horses with heads like lion's heads, and tails like serpents. Satan's armies walk the earth, and they've come to war with humanity, to take men's souls to the pits of hell.

"And you will be hated by all for My name's sake. But the one who endures to the end will be saved." Mark 13:13

The clash of weapons resounds around the globe, and the land runs red with blood.

• • • • •

A sound outside the door wakes Josh, and he gently shakes Jana to wake her. The troops have found their hiding place, and they must be ready to fight.

Suddenly, the blast of a trumpet fills the air all around the earth. Josh and Jana look at each other, and smile. They know what the sound is, though they've never actually heard it before. They rush to the cellar door to open it, no longer hiding from Bahram's soldiers.

Outside, they see troops, dressed in combat gear and radiation suits, gazing into the sky; and they witness a sight they've waited most of their lives to see. Instinctively, they know that anyone in the world, who is currently looking skyward, is seeing the same awesome sight. The air is filled with electricity, as the trumpet continues to sound.

Alec, in the fields, and Elizabeth, in the kitchens, hears the sound of the trumpet at the same moment and run to meet in the worship space. The entire community has gathered there and they rush, as one, to go out the passageway to the cold air outside. Once there they see the vision that the whole world is witnessing as one.

"Then I saw heaven opened, and behold, a white horse! The one sitting on it is called Faithful and True, and in righteousness He judges and makes war. His eyes are like a flame of fire, and on His head are many diadems, and He has a name written that no one knows but Himself. He is clothed in a robe dipped in blood, and the name by which He is called is 'The Word of God'. And the armies, arrayed in fine linen, white and pure, were following Him on white horses. From His mouth comes a sharp sword with which to strike down the nations, and He will rule them with a rod of iron. He will tread the winepress of the fury of the wrath of God the Almighty. On His robe and on His thigh He has a name written, King of kings and Lord of lords."

Revelation 19:11-16

"Then I heard what seemed to be the voice of a great multitude, like the roar of many waters and like the sound of mighty peals of thunder, crying out, "Hallelujah! For the Lord our God the Almighty reigns. Let us rejoice and exult and give Him the glory, for the marriage of the Lamb has come, and His Bride has

made herself ready; it was granted her to cloth herself with fine linen, bright and pure"-for the fine linen is the righteous deeds of the saints."

Revelation 19:6-8

"Then we who are alive, who are left, will be caught up together with them in the clouds to meet the Lord in the air, and so we will always be with the Lord."

1 Thessalonians 4:17

CHAPTER 13

The trumpet sounds for the whole world to hear. The picture Josh and Jana see is visible to every creature on earth. The eastern sky splits. It is the Lord Jesus Christ in the clouds, and He is riding a white horse. His hair and white robes flow in the wind and His eyes are filled with the fire of His mighty justice. His armies, by the millions, also on white horses, follow directly behind in robes of pure white linen. Angels hang in the air, great winged warriors who will carry out His bidding to fulfill prophesies uttered hundreds, or thousands, of years before.

Suddenly, the graves of those people who were, and are, His followers open and the bodies of His saints, old and new, rise to meet Him in the air clothed with new transfigured bodies. Then those who are still alive, who carry the mark of the Lord in their foreheads, and are His followers, join those already risen, and their bodies change miraculously in mid air.

Jana and Josh are no longer in a root cellar, but are risen, no longer sick, tired, or hungry. They look around to see all those they've loved, who went before them, right here within the vast numbers who ride the clouds. They come also, on white horses, and are headed to earth to do battle with the enemy of the Lord their God.

As Christ's army lights upon the earth, they go forth to exact God's justice. Striking down kings, leaders, and peasants alike. All those who worship the beast and his prophet, who are marked with his mark, or who have bowed down to him.

"And I saw the beast and the kings of the earth with their armies gathering to make war against Him who was sitting on the horse and against His army." Revelation 19:19

The battle is fearsome. Satan's forces are there to do double duty. They want to take human souls, but they also desire to thwart God's plan. So, with all his might Satan will try to take down the Son of God and His armies.

He allows Amir's soldiers to do his dirty work for as long as it is convenient for him, and as long as their work is beneficial to his cause. He too wishes for the destruction of Israel and her people. So, as long as Bahram's troops are killing those who have turned their backs on the gift of salvation, sending more unsaved into his ranks; or effectively killing off Jews to destroy the people of Israel, before they can acknowledge Jesus as Lord, he will allow them to murder and destroy those who stand in his way, and those who are easy pickings for the pits of hell. He is so sure of his imminent victory that he never even realizes when his forces arc becoming overwhelmed by the armies of the Lord.

Swords fly as good meets evil in a war as old as time. Satan's flying demons fill the air, while others ride in on horses sporting heads of lions, and serpents tails. Many meet their end by the sting, or the poisoned fangs. Bahram's forces employ fighter jets, tanks, choppers, and anti aircraft missiles, which they deploy to their fullest extent, but none of it is a match for the forces of God's saints and angels, led by the King of kings and Lord of lords.

From a distance, Josh watches his dad fighting alongside Jesus, and smiles when he sees that he is young and strong again. All those who'd passed away, are renewed and healthy now. He turns to Jana, and sees his beautiful wife, now even more so, surrounded by the light of God. They fight without growing tired, and move as one to defeat those who oppose the Son of man. One by one they see those that they love on the field of battle. Chuck and Emma, Alec and Elizabeth, Scott and Becca, Mike and Bella, Doc and Cathy, Mark and Rachel, all filled with the Holy Spirit and covered by God's glory. The Savior has come, and the battle is on.

"Satan, what do you want us to do?"

"We will not, we cannot lose. You will continue to fight until I tell you otherwise, do you understand me?"

"Yes Sir. Where do you want us to concentrate our efforts? They are coming from everywhere."

"For now, I would have you concentrate on those riding with the Christ. We must defeat Him."

"Commander! Their forces are too strong. We aren't making a difference in their numbers. What should we do?"

"You will fight, until death if necessary. We must clear the way for the Mahdi."

"But, Commander, their army is simply mowing us down."

"You will keep at it, until I tell you otherwise. They must not win."

The Lord's army was fighting on two fronts. Against Bahram's forces, which consisted of the kings and leaders of the earth, led by their commander, Amir Bahram; and the army of demons led by Satan; and yet, despite all, they were winning. Demons, wounded by sword and might, fell from their mounts screaming. And Bahram's armies marched onward, even though their numbers dwindled by the thousands every moment.

Suddenly a battle within the battle emerged. Satan ordered his demons to begin killing Bahram's army; for he knew these were men not saved by the Grace of God, so their deaths would add to the numbers of lost souls inhabiting the pit. If he was going to go down, he would at least have numbers to add to his tally when all was said and done.

The battle was immense and lasted through the night. Jana and Josh found that the harder they fought, the more alive they felt, as they followed the Savior.

"Then I saw an angel standing in the sun, and with a loud voice he called to all the birds that fly directly overhead, "Come, gather for the great supper of God, to eat the flesh of kings, the flesh of captains, the flesh of mighty men, the flesh of horses and their riders, and the flesh of all men, both free and slave, both small and great."

Revelation 19:17-18

As the bodies of wayward kings and wicked men fell; and demons were added to their numbers, the birds feasted on their flesh. The King of kings and Lord of lords had won the battle for mankind once again.

"And the beast was captured, and with it the false prophet who in its presence had done the signs by

which he deceived those who had received the mark of the beast and those who worshiped its image. These two were thrown alive into the lake of fire that burns with sulfur."

Revelation 19:20

Bahram, screaming and cursing, and Graham, sniveling and whining, are captured. And with all of the saints and angels watching, giving praise to the Lord, they are thrown into the lake of fire.

"Then I saw an angel coming down from heaven, holding in his hand the key to the bottomless pit and a great chain. And he seized the dragon, that ancient serpent, who is the devil and Satan, and bound him for a thousand years and threw him into the pit, and shut it and sealed it over him , so that he might not deceive the nations any longer, until the thousand years were ended. After that he must be released for a little while."

Revelation 20:1-3

Then, an angel seized Satan and bound him with a great chain. As he fought with all his might, he cursed God, and promised to rise again to destroy all of mankind, then he was thrown into the bottomless pit for a thousand years.

"Then I saw thrones, and seated on them were those to whom the authority to judge was committed. Also I saw the souls of those who had been beheaded for the testimony of Jesus and for the Word of God, and those who had not worshiped the beast for its image and had not received its mark on their foreheads on their hands. They came to life and reigned with Christ for a thousand years. The rest of the dead did not come to life until the thousand years were ended. This is the first resurrection! Over such the second death has no power, but they will be priests of God and of Christ, and they will reign with Him for a thousand years."

Revelation 20:7-10

Josh and Jana marveled at their new bodies. Transformed bodies. Bodies like that of Christ when He came back from the dead after His death on the cross, and resurrection. They could touch one another, but could also walk through walls. There was no more pain, no sorrow, nor death for those who trusted in Jesus. Then among the ranks of the armies of God, they saw an old friend, Paul. He smiled as he approached and the three embraced. "Old friends! How good it is to see you again. Isn't this a joyous day?"

"It's marvelous. I always knew it would be wonderful, but this is beyond my wildest dreams."

"I agree, Jana. And to see all those we love, who had gone before. I'm just so blessed."

Then from among the throng of saints and angels came the Lord. He walked toward them, but this time it was no dream, as in visits past. Tears streamed down their faces, at the mere sight of the Prince of Peace, but they weren't tears of sorrow, or fear, or heavy burdens, they were tears of joy. He was mighty, yet gentle; His eyes were the kindest eyes they had ever seen; His voice was like a gentle caress, yet strong as the ocean's crashing waves. He was everything they could have hoped for, and everything that made life worth living. He came to commune with them, to offer them peace and a hope for the future.

"My beautiful children. It's so good to see you again Josh and Jana."

"Oh, Lord, it's wonderful to see you too. Things have happened so quickly."

"Yes, but it needed to be this way. Now Satan will have no place here for a thousand years, and it will give us a chance to reach those out there who will be born next. We will have this thousand years, without his presence, to speak truth to those who would hear it, and I want your help in this."

"Anything Lord. Here we are, use us!"

"Thank you my children, I will."

"And now, for a thousand years, all those who believed and trusted Me will also reign with Me. Come, let us feast, and let us praise God together."

· · · · ·

A thousand years passed so quickly. For all this time Jana and Josh were in fellowship with the Lord, and by His love and mercy, went about the world ministering to those who'd been left behind.

None of those who were left behind possessed transfig-ured bodies, only the saints who met Jesus in the air on that fateful day. That was a gift given to those who had believed and trusted the Lord before His return. But, because God is merciful, He was allowing those saints who were willing, to share the gift of the Gospel with any who were born after His second coming; and in almost every scenario where they met those lost and broken people, they were mistaken for angels. Over and over they had to remind people never to worship them, but to worship God only.

Sharing was their preferred pastime, well, besides spending time with Jesus. And it seemed there was so much opportunity to do both. They wondered how the Lord had so much time for all His people, but each of those who belonged to Him felt the same way; loved and special. The missionaries: Josh and Janna, Chuck and Emma, Alec and Elizabeth, Scott and Becca, Mike and Bella, Mark and Rachel, Jim (Doc) and Cathy, along with many others, covered the globe with the message of Grace and Love. Getting around was simple. In transformed bodies they could be anywhere they needed to be with just a thought. Funny then, how sitting around a campfire, singing, worshiping, and praising God, was one of their favorite things to do.

In their sharing, they encountered those who were willing to listen, and those who were not. Strange, how even without the presence of Satan during these thousand years, there were still those who chose evil over good. Throughout their visits around the planet, they offered warnings of dire consequences for those who did not choose Jesus, but still there were always those who preferred an eternity in hell, to a life of glory with the Lord.

Jana knew her perfect, eternal life was all due to the love of the Lord. She was forever grateful for the ways He'd moved in her life to bring those who would make a difference toward salvation for her. Her parents and grandmother, Pastor Mike, and of course, Josh. They'd been through some difficult times, and she'd made many foolish decisions along the way, in her anger and self loathing, but He'd always been there encouraging her and nudging her in the right direction. To spend eternity with Jesus, and all those she loved, was a gift of proportions so large, she could never say thank you enough.

"And when the thousand years are ended, Satan will be released from his prison and will come out to deceive the nations that are at the four corners of the earth, Gog and Magog, to gather them for battle; their number is like the sand of the sea. And they marched up over the broad plain of the earth and surrounded the camp of the saints and the beloved city, but fire came down from heaven and consumed them, and the devil who had deceived them was thrown into the lake of fire and sulfur where the beast and the false prophet were, and they will be tormented day and night forever and ever.

Revelation 20:7-10

"Then I saw a great white throne and Him who was seated on it. From His presence earth and sky fled away, and no place was found for them. And I saw the dead, great and small, standing before the throne, and books were opened. Then another book was opened, which is the book of life. And the dead were judged by what was written in the books, according to what they had done. And the sea gave up the dead who were in it, Death and Hades gave up the dead who were in them, and

they were judged, each one of them, according to what they had done. Then Death and Hades were thrown into the lake of fire. This is the second death, the lake of fire. And if anyone's name was not found written in the book of life, he was thrown into the lake of fire."

Revelation 20:11-15

Then I saw a new heaven and a new earth, for the first heaven and the first earth had passed away, and the sea was no more. And I saw the holy city, new Jerusalem, coming down out of heaven from God, prepared as a bride adorned for her husband. And I heard a loud voice from the throne saying, "Behold, the dwelling place of God is with man. He will dwell with them, and they will be His people, and God Himself will be with them as their God. He will wipe away every tear from their eyes, and death shall be no more, neither shall there be mourning, nor crying, nor pain anymore, for the former things have passed away."

And He who was seated on the throne said, "Behold, I am making all things new." Also He said, "Write this down, for these words are trustworthy and true." And He said to me, "It is done! I am the Alpha and the Omega, the beginning and the end. To the thirsty I will give from the spring of the water of life without payment. The one who conquers will have this heritage, and I will be his God and he will be my son. Gut as for the cowardly, the faithless, the detestable, as for murderers, the sexually immoral, sorcerers, idolaters, and all liars, their portion will be in the lake that burns with fire and sulfur, which is the second death."

Revelation 21:1-8

CHAPTER 14

After a thousand years of ministering to the children of the lost, and bringing many into God's kingdom, Josh and Jana were thrilled to see the city they'd been told about in scripture, coming down from heaven.

Satan's release from the bottomless pit had been foretold, and yet, even with millennia of warning, many were duped by that old serpent when he returned to roam the earth again. Jana was amazed he still managed to fool so many with the same old tricks. He amassed armies upon armies of those hardened, hate filled unbelievers, and they marched on the camp of the saints, where those who witnessed for Christ resided. Once they reached the camp and the beloved city, and they surrounded all those saints; absolutely sure and certain in their upcoming victory; fire came down from heaven and consumed them all. Then, while all those he'd fooled, and the entire world, watched, the devil was thrown into the lake of fire and sulfur, where the beast and the false prophet were, to be tormented day and night, forever and ever.

• • • • •

The city, new Jerusalem, was beautiful. A river of water, bright as crystal, flowed out from the throne of God and of the Lamb, through the middle of the street of the city. There was no temple there, because the Lord almighty is the temple, and there is no need of sun or moon, because the Lamb of God is the light. The gates are never shut, but nothing unclean, detestable or false is able to enter; only those whose names are written in the Lamb's book of life.

The tree of life yields its twelve kinds of fruit each month, and the leaves of the tree are for the healing of the nations.

Jana looked deep into the face of the Savior and knew that nothing in the universe could ever be more right than being here at this time, and in this place. To be loved by Jesus, and to spend eternity with the Lord was something that only He could have designed. God is good!

"And he said to me, "These words are trustworthy and true. And the Lord, the God of the spirits of the prophets, has sent His angel to show His servants what must soon take place."

"And behold, I am coming soon. Blessed is the one who keeps the words of the prophecy of this book."

"I, John, am the one who heard and saw these things. And when I heard and saw them, I fell down to worship at the feet of the angel who showed them to me, but he said to me, "You must not do that! I am a fellow servant with you and your brothers the prophets, and with those who keep the words of this book. Worship God."

And he said to me, "Do not seal up the words of the prophecy of this book, for the time is near. Let the evil-

doer still do evil, and the filthy still be filthy, and the righteous still do right, and the holy still be holy,"

"Behold, I am coming soon, bringing my recompense with me, to repay everyone for what he has done. I am the Alpha and the Omega, the first and the last, the beginning and the end."

Blessed are those who wash their robes, so that they may have the right to the tree of life and that they may enter the city by the gates. Outside are the dogs and sorcerers and the sexually immoral and murderers and idolaters, and everyone who loves and practices falsehood.

"I, Jesus, have sent my angel to testify to you about these things for the churches. I am the root and the descendant of David, the bright morning star."

The Spirit and the Bride say, "Come." And let the one who hears say, "Come." And let the one who is thirsty come; let the one who desires take the water of life without price.

I warn everyone who hears the words of the prophecy of this book: if anyone adds to them, God will add to him the plagues described in this book, and if anyone takes away from the words of the book of this prophecy, God will take away his share in the tree of life and in the holy city, which are described in this book.

He who testifies to these things says, "Surely, I am coming soon." Amen. Come Lord Jesus.

The Grace of the Lord Jesus be with all. Amen.

Revelation 22:6-21

A FEW WORDS, AND THOUGHTS, FROM THE AUTHOR

Well, dear friend, the 'Redeemed' trilogy is at an end. But, don't worry, I still have plenty of stories up my sleeve. I thank you for buying my books and for reading. I'm addressing you, because after a few questions from others, I feel the need to speak to my readers about the contents of the books I write.

I've been told by many that my tales are very engaging, and this makes them hard to put down. Due to that, I've had certain readers upset with me, because they don't seem to get much work done while they are occupied with one of my novels. While I'm flattered that my writing entertains you, I don't want to upset your schedule, so I guess that means, read at your own peril.

On the other hand, I've had a couple of readers who've contacted me, upset about my supposed references to certain living ex-presidents or distressing historical events, as

I attempt to weave a tale. Rest assured. I am merely endeavoring to set up background for future events in a storyline. And, though I certainly want my stories to seem as realistic as possible; and I do hope they draw you in; please remember I am writing fiction. No characters are based on any particular, real person, past or present, living or dead, unless I have specifically named that person for historical reference.

I would also like to remind readers that I'm not attempting to rewrite the Bible, or change your interpretation of it. I use numerous scripture references as chapter headers, and then sporadically throughout my tales. But I am not, in any way, altering those scriptures from their original wording, as they appear in the English Standard Version of the Holy Bible. I comment especially in regard to this latest installment of the 'Redeemed' trilogy, 'Revelation'. I personally believe every word of the Bible to be inspired by God; absolutely true and without flaw. I also believe that no one has the right to take away from, or add to the text of the Bible, without answering to God for their actions.

All of my novels are stories of redemption, in one way or another. Stories that transition from darkness to light. They usually start off a bit gritty, but if we face facts, life is a bit gritty. I feel compelled to share my journey from lost to saved, by His Grace, in the undertones of every written creation from His inspiration, through my fingertips. I have discovered that Jesus is the single most important thing in my life, so why would I not want to share Him with everyone I meet, and everyone who reads my books?

• • • • •

Over the years, my husband has served as pastor for a number of church congregations, and filled in as pulpit supply in many others. I've served as co-pastor, and as youth director, for some of those same congregations. Throughout this journey we have met many people, with different opinions, and differing thoughts on 'End Time' events, or 'Eschatology'. In some cases those opinions have been very strong and unwavering. I promise that I am not necessarily out to change your opinion of coming end time events. Though, as far as I'm concerned, this particular subject would rate as more of a rib issue, than a backbone issue, in the importance of our faith as it concerns salvation and eternity.

I do believe, after extensive study in the book of Revelation, along with numerous pieces of scripture in prophetic books such as: Isaiah, Jeremiah, Ezekiel, Daniel, and Joel; and the Gospels, that end time events are definitely a little hard to make sense of in practical terms. I actually used to be terrified, trying to understand the book of Revelation. But through much investigation, I have come to think of this text as an interesting and insightful old friend.

I have conferred with Eschatology experts, and in all cases of discussion we come to the conclusion that there is no way to tell for sure if events, such as the opening of the seals, the pouring out of the bowls of God's wrath, or the blowing of the trumpets, are happening consecutively, or simultaneously. I also run into differing opinions on whether the book of Revelation is a book entirely to be spiritually discerned, a book to be taken literally, or even perhaps a bit of both. I'm not here to dispute that, as we can all agree to disagree agreeably if need be. We will, after all, be able to see for ourselves how that pans out as it happens.

The other subject that quite often gets people riled up, is the topic of a tribulation rapture. Some folks call themselves pre tribulation believers; some claim that mid tribulation is the answer; and others, swear by belief in a post tribulation scenario. My husband says, "I'm pan mill. I figure it will all pan out in the millennium." And, I would have to say I agree with him. If you've finished reading 'Revelation', the book that this letter follows, you will note that it slants heavily toward a post tribulation stance. But, that was stressed more to create an exciting story line than any other particular factor. Though, I do have to admit, after much study, that I believe the Holy Spirit has been present in my discoveries regarding Biblical truth, and I am leaning in the direction of believing a post tribulation rapture. So, if you're not sure how things will go down, be ready to endure to the end.

• • • • •

Now, though, I would like to move on to more substantive discussion. I began writing the 'Redeemed' trilogy during a time in my life when I was looking for answers to some very real problems. I had been diagnosed with stage four breast cancer, and told I had three to six months to live. My faith was by no means where it needed to be. I was the pastor's wife, but I didn't feel I had any real assurance of God's love for me, and I embraced that diagnosis of death with all the fear and grief one would expect of a non-believer.

Throughout my life I'd had numerous trials which caused me to believe there just might not be a God at all, and if there was, perhaps He didn't care about me. Physical, emotional and sexual abuse, from the time I was four years old, caused me to have a very low opinion of myself; and also made me wary of involvement with any and all outside sources; even hesitant to accept help from anyone, including my own husband. I speak at length on the subject of abuse and coming to faith in my book, 'When All Else Fails'.

Due to this, when my husband began to speak of miraculous healing from the Lord, I pretended to listen, more as a way of getting him 'off my back' than anything else. I didn't believe for a second that I was 'worthy' of God's healing.

Ironically, just a few months before my diagnosis we'd both begun reading books about the radical Grace of God. Now, this was a Grace neither of us ever imagined before, and we certainly didn't fully understand the concept, as we were both brought up believing in a harsh God of laws and punishment. To his credit, my husband was the first to crack, and begin to believe this 'Grace' message. Initially I thought it sounded a bit blasphemous, and fought against the idea with everything I had. But then came proof, by way of scripture backing up every piece of this new way of thinking. Scripture such as:

"There is therefore now no condemnation for those who are in Christ Jesus." Romans 8:1.

I refer to many more instances of scripture to back up the suggestion of radical Grace, in my aforementioned book.

After spending a certain amount of time feeling thoroughly sorry for myself, I initiated a period of intensive Bible study, and lo and behold, I began to see the beautiful heart of our Lord Jesus Christ in my reading and studying. Grace became a main theme in all my reading and studying, and, therefore, a huge source of hope.

"For I know the plans I have for you, declares the Lord, plans for welfare and not evil, to give you a future and a hope." Jeremiah 29:11

And pretty soon seeing law and judgment, beating me down, in the Word of God, didn't make sense anymore.

Due to the amount of time I was spending at the cancer center for treatments, and the fact that this scenario would likely continue for some time, I lost my job. And, because I'm not a person who can just sit around doing nothing, I started to do something I'd always dreamed of doing, I began to write the books you've been reading.

The more I read and studied God's Word, the more a simple message of Grace made total sense; and the more the Grace message made sense to me, the more I began to believe in the power of God's healing Word for my life. Throughout this time, as faith manifested in my heart and continued to grow stronger, God was doing a work in me. Eventually, miraculously, I was totally healed, (again, the entire story of my healing journey is laid out in my book, 'When All Else Fails').

I now know, without doubt, that I am a beloved child of the Most High God; that Jesus the Christ died and rose to save me from my sins; that I don't have to do anything to deserve this heavenly blessing, but simply believe; that He took all my sickness, disease, and wounds upon Himself on the cross and overcame it all; that through His blood and sacrifice, He has made me worthy and righteous; and that "By His stripes I am healed."

I am thoroughly convinced that the Lord has saved me for a reason, and as corny as that might sound, I believe He has saved me to write about His magnificence and Grace. I have now, through the popularity of my published books, an opportunity to speak in many different venues. And I still spend quite a bit of time at the cancer center, where I make new friends during every visit. As I speak with, and listen to these new friends, the topic which always seems to emerge first is, "If God is so good, why would He let this terrible thing happen to me, my child, my parent, my spouse, my sibling, my friend?" I am blessed, at that time, to be able to share the Love of God with those who sometimes question His motives. Sharing the Gospel has become my absolute favorite thing to do.

• • • • •

On the subject of end times, many ask me when I believe Jesus is coming back for His church. Obviously I don't have an exact answer for that. Matthew 24:36 is as specific an answer as you will find, and reads: *"But concerning that day and hour no one knows, not even the angels of heaven, nor the Son, but the Father only."* However, I do believe that each day brings us closer to that imminent moment of His return. And, I wonder how many reading this are ready to meet Him in the sky on that beautiful day?

I truly believe we haven't much time. Many wonder why He hasn't yet returned. And I would answer that He is waiting for us to reach every creature on earth with the message of His Grace and Truth, because He really doesn't want anyone to perish.

"The Lord is not slow to fulfill His promise as some count slowness, but is patient toward you, not wishing that any should perish, but that all should reach repentance." 2 Peter 3:9.

It's up to us to be sure our fellow human beings know about God's love and His soon return. Remember, as Jesus was returning to the Father, He gave us a command. Now it's very important to note that this wasn't a suggestion, it was a decree from our Lord.

"And Jesus came and said to them, "All authority in heaven and on earth has been given to me. Go therefore and make disciples of all nations, baptizing them in the name of the Father and of the Son and of the Holy Spirit, teaching them to observe all that I have commanded you. And behold, I am with you always, to the end of the age." Matthew 28:18-20.

I take that specific scripture passage; being a serious follower of Jesus; as not just an order, but a blessing in my life. After all, to be able to introduce others to the Lord is a miraculous thing.

• • • • •

How do we know there will even be an actual 'End Time' scenario? The Bible is rife with scripture speaking of end times. And though I don't have the space in this letter to refer to all of those pieces of scripture, many study Bibles will list them out. There are also online sites which can lead you through the books of prophesy, the Gospels, and the book of Revelation, to give you a feel of what an important topic this is, and how significant it is to the Lord. An example is:

"This is now the second letter that I am writing to you, beloved. In both of them I am stirring up your sincere mind by way of reminder, that you should remember the predictions of the holy prophets and the commandment of the Lord and Savior through your apostles, knowing this first of all, that scoffers will come in the last days with scoffing, following their own sinful desires. They will say, "Where is the promise of His coming? For ever since the fathers fell asleep, all things are continuing as they were from the beginning of creation. For they deliberately overlook this fact, that the heavens existed long ago, and the earth was formed out of water and through water by

the Word of God, and that by means of these the world that then existed was deluged with water and perished. But by the same Word the heavens and earth that now exist are stored up for fire, being kept until the day of judgment and destruction of the ungodly.

'But do not overlook this one fact, beloved, that with the Lord one day is as a thousand years, and a thousand years as one day. The Lord is not slow to fulfill His promise as some count slowness, but is patient toward you, not wishing that any should perish, but that all should reach repentance. But the day of the Lord will come like a thief, and then the heavens will pass away with a roar, and the heavenly bodies will be burned up and dissolved, and the earth and the works that are done on it will be exposed.

'Since all these things are thus to be dissolved, what sort of people ought you to be in lives of holiness and godliness, waiting for and hastening the coming of the day of God, because of which the heavens will be set on fire and dissolved, and the heavenly bodies will melt as they burn! But according to His promise we are waiting for new heavens and a new earth in which righteousness dwells.

"Therefore, beloved, since you are waiting for these, be

diligent to be found by Him without spot or blemish, and at peace And count the patience of our Lord as salvation, just as our beloved brother Paul also wrote to you according to the wisdom given him, as he does in all his letters when he speaks in them of these matters. There are some things in them that are hard to understand, which the ignorant and unstable twist to their own destruction, as they do the other Scriptures. You therefore, beloved, knowing this beforehand, take care that you are not carried away with the error of lawless people and lose your own stability. But grow in the grace and knowledge of our Lord and Savior Jesus Christ. To Him be the glory both now and to the day of eternity. Amen."

2 Peter 3:1-18

Or this excellent Scripture passage from Matthew:

"Jesus left the temple and was going away, when His disciples came to point to Him the buildings of the temple. But He answered them, "You see all these, do you not? Truly, I say to you, there will not be left here one stone upon another that will not be thrown down."

"As He sat on the Mount of Olives, the disciple came to Him privately, saying, "Tell us, when will these things be, and what will be the sign of your coming and of the close of the age? And Jesus answered them, "See that no one leads you astray. For many will come in My name, saying, "I am the Christ, and they will lead many astray. And you will hear of wars and rumors of wars. See that you are not alarmed, for this must take place, but the end is not yet. For nation will rise against nation, and kingdom against kingdom, and there will be famines and earthquakes in various places. All these are but the beginning of the birth pains.

"Then they will deliver you up to tribulation and put you to death, and you will be hated by all nations for My name's sake. And then many will fall away and betray one another and hate one another. And many false prophets will arise and lead many astray. And because lawlessness will be increased, the love of many will grow cold. But the one who endured to the end will be saved. And this Gospel of the kingdom will be proclaimed throughout the whole world as a testimony to all nations, and then the end will come.

"So when you see the abomination of desolation spoken

of by the prophet Daniel, standing in the holy place (let the reader understand), then let those who are in Judea flee to the mountains. Let the one who is on the housetop not go down to take what is in his house, and let the one who is in the field not turn back to take his cloak. And alas for women who are pregnant and for those who are nursing infants in those days! Pray that your flight may not be in winter or on a Sabbath. For then there will be great tribulation, such as has not been from the beginning of the world until now, no and never will be. And if those days had not been cut short, no human being would be saved. But for the sake of the elect those days will be cut short. Then if anyone says to you, "Look, here is the Christ!" or "There He is!" do not believe it. For false christs and false prophets will arise and perform great signs and wonders, so as to lead astray, if possible, even the elect. See, I have told you beforehand. So, if they say to you, "Look, He is in the wilderness", do not go out. If they say, "Look, He is in the inner rooms", do not believe it. For as the lightning comes from the east and shines as far as the west, so will be the coming of the Son of Man. Wherever the corpse is, there the vultures will gather.

"Immediately after the tribulation of those days the sun will be darkened, and the moon will not give its light, and the stars will fall from heaven, and the powers of the heavens will be shaken. Then will appear in heaven the sign of the Son of Man coming on the clouds of heaven with power and great glory. And He will send out His angels with a loud trumpet call, and they will gather His elect from the four winds, from one end of heaven to the other."

Matthew 24:1-31

I tend to believe that when a topic is spoken of, in the Bible, as extensively as this one, it has enormous importance. God is giving us plenty of advance warning about Jesus' return and lots of ways to check, to be sure it's the real deal; because He wants to give us ample opportunity to come to Him with open hearts to receive His free gift of salvation, and to share the message with others who may not yet know Him.

So, now, as responsible human beings, and hopefully at this point, Christians, what do we do with all this information? Well, I would posit that if we are Christians; and if we believe the Bible to be true, as we rightly should if we claim to be believers; then, we share this very important information with every living being on the planet. For how do we watch these signs of Christ's imminent return being fulfilled one by one, knowing the truth of His coming as we do, and not desire above all things to see every human being on earth saved?

• • • • •

You might ask, what difference does it make if someone is a Christian, or not? And, if they aren't a Christian, won't they go to the paradise of their selection, as pertains to the religion of their choosing? And, hey, on the subject of choices, why does anyone have to make that choice before Jesus comes back? Because, if He really cares about us, He certainly wouldn't want anyone to go to hell, would He? So, why would we have to do anything in particular to be with Him in heaven?

Well, I will try to answer each of these questions in a way that will make sense for our Christian view of the hope of eternity:

1. What difference does it make if someone is a Christian, or not?

Many people don't see how having faith in Jesus or being a Christian makes someone different in a positive way. People involved in Christian activities and those who don't get involved at all seem to be about the same, don't they? So Christianity must not make that much of a difference in people's lives, right? People experience this as true when they see Christians around them gossiping, partying, sleeping around, not exercising compassion or caring about others or the environment, etc.

When we see this behavior we assume:

Having Christian belief or faith doesn't matter in everyday life.

Christian belief is a weak person's crutch and doesn't do anything.

People's lives have not been transformed by their Christian beliefs, so faith isn't important. I need to see transformed lives in order to believe that faith does matter.

What does a transformed life look like? How should Christians look?

To me, a transformed life is when someone changes their actions and attitudes as they learn about Jesus. They grow in compassion as they learn about God's compassion; they care more about others, rather than just themselves.

A transformed life is when someone's view of themselves changes as they learn about God. For example, they have more confidence because they know they are loved and have worth, they realize their selfishness, and they desire to be more like Christ.

I'm afraid there are way too many so called Christians out there, giving Christianity a bad rap. That's something we, as true Christian believers, need to change. So that everyone who sees us, also sees the unending love and Grace of Jesus Christ, and seeing this, want to be a part of the kingdom of God.

2. If a person isn't a Christian, but they practice a different religion, won't they simply go to a paradise of their selection, as pertains to the religion of their choosing?

This can be a very confusing subject for some individuals, especially if that individual in question is coming from a different religion. Since every religion on the planet, except Christianity, is merit based, you, as an adherent of that religion, are expected to earn your way to their idea of paradise. What a comfort to know, as a Christian, that it isn't up to me to be good enough, but just to have a Savior who loves me enough. The Bible makes it very clear that the only way to the Father, heaven, paradise, is through the Son.

"Jesus said to him, "I am the way, and the truth, and the life. No one comes to the Father except through Me." John 14:6

"And there is salvation in no one else, for there is no other name under heaven given among men by which we must be saved." Acts 4:12

Many people take offense at the exclusivity of Christ. To tell people their choice to reject Jesus will have eternal consequences smacks in the face of a relativistic worldview. This, however, separates true Christianity from universalism. It's important to know that following Jesus is not one of many paths to God, it is the one and only way into relationship with God Almighty.

For those who take issue with Christians proclaiming the exclusivity of Christ there is often an underlying assumption that it's based out of intolerance towards other religions. The negative images of sandwich board preachers yelling at people that they're going to hell is what many folks assume all Christians are like, and what they believe. That simply isn't true. If we are true Christians, we simply don't want to see anyone lost. In truth, there isn't a single practiced religion in the world that is 'tolerant' of other religions in that way. All religions believe that only those of their faith will be in whatever idea of 'paradise' their religion offers as a reward for faithfulness and good behavior.

We, as Christians, have reasons for believing what we believe. We don't wake up one morning and pick a faith that we think will anger others. We are convinced that God has revealed himself uniquely in history through Jesus. We seek to respectfully share our views and thoughtfully engage with others who have differing beliefs.

Everyone, every religion, is excluding someone so there is no "inclusive position." To say that all religions are basically the same is in essence imposing a "super-religion" on the beliefs of others. This is disrespectful to people of diverse faith backgrounds and is intolerant of the distinct differences in those faiths.

3. Why does anyone have to make a choice to follow Jesus 'before' He returns?

I believe the parable of the ten virgins lays this all out perfectly.

"Then the kingdom of heaven will be like ten virgins who took their lamps and went to meet the bridegroom.

Five of them were foolish, and five were wise. For when the foolish took their lamps, they took no oil with them, but the wise took flasks of oil with their lamps. As the bridegroom was delayed, they all became drowsy and slept. But at midnight there was a cry, "Here is the bridegroom! Come out to meet Him." Then all those virgins rose and trimmed their lamps. And the foolish said to the wise, "Give us some of your oil, for our lamps are going out." But the wise answered, saying, "Since there will not be enough for us and for you, go rather to the dealers and buy for yourselves." And while they were going to buy, the bridegroom came, and those who were ready went in with him to the marriage feast, and the door was shut. Afterward the other virgins came also, saying, "Lord, Lord, open to us." But He answered, "Truly, I say to you, I do not know you." Watch therefore, for you know neither the day nor the hour.

4. If He cares about us, He wouldn't want anyone to go to hell, would He?

The answer to that is, of course He cares about us, and doesn't want anyone to go to hell. I refer you to the passage above, in 2 Peter 3:9, but this verse from Matthew, in the New Testament says it all:

"See that you do not despise one of these little ones. For I tell you that in heaven their angels always see the face of My Father who is in heaven. What do you think? If a man has a hundred sheep, and one of them has gone astray, does he not leave the ninety-nine on the mountains and go in search of the one that went astray? And if he finds it, truly, I say to you, he rejoices over it more than over the ninety-nine that never went astray. So it is not the will of My Father who is in heaven that one of these little ones should perish."

Matthew 18:10-14

So, you might ask, how exactly do we prepare to meet the Lord on His return?

First of all we need to understand that being a Christian, isn't about anything we have done, or have not done, as long as we trust in Jesus, He's already done it all. Being saved isn't about us, it's all about Him. It's not something we earn. It's a free gift. Jesus already paid the price for us, and because of that great sacrifice, all we must do is believe. Believe that He is the Son of God; believe that He came to die on a cross to pay for all of our sin and sickness; and then that He rose from the dead to live again all to overcome death, so that we might have eternal life through Him. You see, it isn't about a religion at all, it's just about Jesus. I am not good enough. You are not good enough. None of us is good enough on our own. But because He loves us, His righteousness makes us righteous in the eyes of the Father, it makes us good enough, just because we believe.

The New Testament is filled to the brim with scripture telling us how Jesus has saved us, and all we must do to receive the gift of salvation. Here are a few of those scriptures:

"But to all who did receive Him, who believed in His name, He gave the right to become children of God."

John 1:12

"For God so loved the world, that He gave His only Son, that whoever believes in Him should not perish but have eternal life. For God did not send His Son into the world to condemn the world, but in order that the world might be saved through Him."

John3:16-17

"Because, if you confess with your mouth that Jesus is Lord and believe in your heart that God raised Him from the dead, you will be saved. For with the heart one believes and is justified, and with the mouth one confesses and is saved."

Romans 10:9-10

"If we confess our sins, He is faithful and just to forgive us our sins and to cleanse us from all unrighteousness."

1 John 1:9

"But God shows His love for us in that while we were still sinners, Christ died for us. Since therefore, we have now been justified by His blood, much more shall we be saved by Him from the wrath of God."

Romans 5:8-9

"For the wages of sin is death, but the free gift of God is eternal life in Christ Jesus our Lord."

Romans 6:23

"For everyone who calls on the name of the Lord will be saved."

Romans 10:13

"Yet we know that a person is not justified by works of the law but through faith in Jesus Christ, so we also have believed in Christ Jesus, in order to be justified by faith in Christ and not by works of the law because by works of the law no one will be justified."

Galatians 2:16

"He saved us, not because of works done by us in righteousness, but according to His own mercy, by the washing of regeneration and renewal of the Holy Spirit."

Titus 3:5

"For by grace you have been saved through faith. And this is not your own doing; it is the gift of God, not a result of works, so that no one may boast."

Ephesians 2:8

"Therefore, if anyone is in Christ, he is a new creation."

2 Corinthians 5:17

"For our sake He made Him to be sin who knew no sin, so that in Him we might become the righteousness of God."

2 Corinthians 5:21

"In Him we have redemption through His blood, the forgiveness of our trespasses, according to the riches of His Grace."

Ephesians 1:7

"Jesus said to her, "I am the resurrection and the life. Whoever believes in me, though he die, yet shall he live, and everyone who lives and believes in me shall never die. Do you believe this?"

John 11:25-26

"Truly, truly, I say to you, whoever hears my word and believes Him who sent Me has eternal life. He does not come into judgment, but has passed from death to life."

John 5:24

"I am the door, if anyone enters by Me, he will be saved and will go in and out and find pasture. The thief comes only to steal and kill and destroy. I came that they may have life and have it abundantly."

John 10:9-10

There is also a flip side to this scenario. If we do not believe on the Son, the Father will judge us according to our works. And, I don't know about you, but if I had to try to get to heaven on my own merits, it would be a very scary thing.

"Whoever believes in Him is not condemned, but whoever does not believe is condemned already, because he has not believed in the name of the only Son of God." John 3:18

From here it's pretty easy. If you are one who already trusts Jesus for salvation, share. Share with everyone you meet, at work, at school, in the marketplace, everywhere you go! If you haven't opened your heart to the risen Son of God, and you would like the Christ to be your Lord and Savior, then all you must do is believe in your heart and confess with your mouth that Jesus Christ is Lord. Believe He died and rose again to save you from your sins, and know that He loves you, unconditionally! And then, share the good news with every creature!